The gaze that lifted to hers was not the same gaze she had seen just moments before. His eyes were no longer like warm honey—they were as bright and brilliant as newly minted gold, drawing her into their molten depths until she thought she might be lost within them.

"Treasure," he replied. "Is that not what you want as well?"

She was saved from answering when her father's voice called Chapel to his side. Pru watched him go, not entirely certain of what had just happened. Her hands were no longer cold and she looked down to make sure they weren't clenched or trembling.

There was a mark on her right hand that hadn't been there before. Her brows drew close as she raised it toward her face. A thin red mark about half an inch long dipped between her second and third knuckles.

Her head snapped up and her shocked gaze flew across the room to where the golden stranger stood.

Good lord, he hadn't actually bit *her, had he?*

Other **AVON ROMANCES**

Coming Soon

And Don't Miss These
ROMANTIC TREASURES
from Avon Books

Kathryn Smith

Be Mine Tonight

AVON BOOKS
An Imprint of HarperCollinsPublishers

This is a work of fiction. Names, characters, places, and incidents are products of the author's imagination or are used fictitiously and are not to be construed as real. Any resemblance to actual events, locales, organizations, or persons, living or dead, is entirely coincidental.

AVON BOOKS
An Imprint of Harper Collins*Publishers*
10 East 53rd Street
New York, New York 10022-5299

Copyright © 2006 by Kathryn Smith
ISBN-13: 978-0-06-084836-1
ISBN-10: 0-06-084836-7
www.avonromance.com

First Avon Books paperback printing: July 2006

Avon Trademark Reg. U.S. Pat. Off. and in Other Countries, Marca Registrada, Hecho en U.S.A.
HarperCollins® is a registered trademark of HarperCollins Publishers Inc.

Printed in the U.S.A.

10 9 8 7 6 5 4 3 2 1

For Luisa,
who loves vampires
and all those things
that go bump in the night.
They love you too.

Acknowledgments

As usual, this book would not have been possible without the following people, to whom I need to give thanks:

To Kara, not only for answering my questions concerning cancer, but for all the good she does every day for those suffering from the disease. You're pretty amazing, chickie.

To Nancy and Kelly, for urging and allowing me to take this opportunity

To Erika, for taking me on and helping me make this book a reality.

And to Steve, for all the support, brainstorming sessions, massages and takeout it took to get this book written. Sweetie, you're my partner in the truest sense of the word.

My adoration and gratitude go out to you all. Thank you.

Kathryn

Prologue

Friday, the 13th of October, 1307

It was obvious that the door was not meant to be opened.

Severian de Foncé ran a dirty, sword-nicked hand over the heavy wood in a loving fashion, pausing at the thick iron lock. "There must be treasure inside, to garner such protection."

The idea filled him with a multitude of emotions—great and terrible. What did the Templars hide behind this door? A treasure of the church, as King Philip claimed, or some instrument of evil? There were so many rumors about the Templars, describing them as either holy men or the worst of blasphemers. Which was it?

Adrian du Lac, one of his five companions,

clapped an equally dirty and scarred hand on his shoulder. In his other he held the torch that lit their way. "Stand aside, my friend."

Severian took the torch from his friend and stepped back toward the others—each as battle-worn and dirty as he and Adrian—so that his friend could crouch before the door and examine the lock for himself.

They had been sent by King Philip to uncover the secrets of the Knights Templar and "relieve" them of their treasures. If there was treasure behind the door, the king would want it. And the six of them wanted their share. But if evil lurked behind this thick wood, then they would have their share of it as well. They all knew it, and so did the man who hired them.

That was why they were there, risking life and limb at the whim of the king. Philip handpicked the six of them because each had a certain reputation among mercenaries and soldiers as being a man who would never back down from a fight and would honor any obligation—for a price. Their price was a share of whatever Templar riches they procured for the king.

It was not an easy way to make a living, but fighting was all any of them knew, and honor came not from their tasks, but from the completion of them. They were warriors above all else, but they could not deny their king. To do so would be to deny their own country, the very home for which they consistently risked their lives.

Once they retrieved this treasure for Philip, Severian would be wealthy enough to settle down and take over his father's estate. He would marry Marie and he would put away his sword. He would have the life he'd always wanted, the woman he'd always wanted.

Low in the stone walls of this Templar keep, beneath the ground, down a narrow set of ancient stairs, they found this door alone in the darkness. The discovery had happened by accident—a secret passage revealed by Dreux's curiosity over a cache of manuscripts.

"Well?" Severian demanded, his mind once again focusing on the task at hand. "Can you breach it?"

Severian and the others watched as Adrian pulled a small roll of leather from his boot. From it, he withdrew a tool—indistinguishable in the flickering torchlight—that he then inserted into the hole of the heavy lock with a roguish grin. "No lock has been forged that I cannot bend to my will."

His words were proven true by a clunk as the lock sprang open. His expression now one of extreme self-satisfaction, Adrian rose to his feet as he removed the lock. A low groaning creak led the way into darkness as the door swung open. It seemed almost anticlimatic after the guards they'd fought and the labrinyth of stairs, secret chambers and corridors they'd navigated to get here. They never would have found this room without the plans Philip's interrogators had tortured out of a Templar informant.

It was obvious that someone wanted whatever waited beyond this door to remain hidden.

"Such pains as these," Severian remarked to his friends, "are normally taken to protect items that are either very valuable or very dangerous. In the case of the Templars, either could be a likely assumption. Be on your guard." In unison, the six of them drew their swords.

Severian entered first, the torch in his hand illuminating the small chamber in a flickering glow. Turning slowly, he surveyed their surroundings: a rough cell, empty save for a wooden table in the center.

The table was not empty.

Frowning, he moved closer, his friends behind him. He resheathed his weapon as he neared the table. The flame of the torch reflected dully off a tarnished, crudely fashioned silver chalice.

"Mon Dieu," came a whisper from behind Severian. "Is that what I think it is?"

Severian didn't answer. His fingers trembled as he rubbed a rough palm over the stubble on his jaw. They all knew the stories, tales of the vast wealth possessed by the Templars. It was said that the knights had in their possession various holy relics, including items believed to have belonged to Christ Himself.

The mere thought of what they might have discovered made him want to make the sign of the cross over his breastplate and fall to his knees on the dirt floor. And yet, he did not.

"The *San Graal*," Dreux whispered as he stared at it with awe and wonder.

The Holy Grail.

Severian studied the roughly hewn cup, the silver heavily tarnished with age and neglect. If it truly was the Grail of Christ, why leave it here in this dark, damp chamber? If this cup was the one Jesus drank from at the Last Supper, why was it so dark and uncherished? It made no sense, and yet his heart told him that they had indeed found something special.

The cup beckoned, its discolored surface calling to Severian. He reached for it, his hand still trembling and hesitant.

"Have a care," Dreux urged. "It might be the Blood Grail."

One of their companions made a scoffing noise low in his throat, but Dreux's tone was enough to give Severian pause. Just as they all knew the legend of the Holy Grail, so had they heard of the *Un*holy Grail. It was rumored to be forged from the silver paid to Judas Iscariot, silver that long before that had been infused with the essence of Lilith, first wife of Adam and demon queen.

But it was just a story. Was it not? There hadn't been a written account of the cup for at least three centuries. In fact, it had all but faded into myth.

Perhaps that was exactly what the Templars hoped would happen.

Like a siren, the blackened chalice called. Severian's fingers brushed the silver, expecting it to be cold. But it was warm to the touch—like flesh. The trembling in his hand eased as his fingers closed around the bowl. Now that he had it in his hand, it seemed impossible that it could be evil in any sense.

A terrible swishing sound was his only warning before blades shot up through the tabletop. One pierced his flesh, the blooded blade protruding through the back of his wrist.

His howl of anguish filled the chamber, followed by a growl of anger. His friends took a step backward. Snarling, Severian pulled his injured arm straight up, hissing and cursing as the pain in his palm intensified for a split second while he freed himself. Sweat beaded his brow, but he fought the weakness. He had been pierced by swords before, subjected to worse injuries. This was a trifling wound compared to those.

He tore a strip from his dirty shirt and wrapped the fabric around his wrist, tying it tight to stanch the flow of blood.

Sweet Mary, he should have known better! His wits were usually keener than this. Had he not thought just moments before that this seemed too easy after all they'd gone through to get there? He should have known that the Templars would not leave such treasure unprotected.

Blood ran from his hand as he reached between the series of blades. He would not suffer injury for no reward. His fingers were slick as he grabbed at the goblet, but his fingers were useless. The blade that had pierced his wrist had cut something inside. He had to drop his sword and reach in with his other hand, seizing the goblet by the bowl. He pulled it back quickly, prepared now for the presence of traps.

His friends surrounded him once more, backs partially to him, their gazes keenly roving about the cell, waiting for another attack.

But nothing happened. At least, nothing his companions could fight.

A sudden wave of dizziness struck him like the broad side of a sword, weakening his knees and rolling in his stomach. What the devil? It couldn't be from loss of blood. He hadn't lost that much.

Nausea gripped him as fresh sweat formed on his brow and upper lip. His head swam as a chill settled over his flesh.

Yes, he should have known better. He could recover from a knife wound, but there would be no coming back from this.

"Dreux, tell Marie I love her."

His friends turned at the rough rasp of his voice, just in time to see him sink to his knees, the cup in his weakening fingers.

Dreux dropped to his knees. "*Mon ami*, what is it?"

"Poison." He clenched his teeth against the shivering. His muscles were tightening, causing him to curl into himself.

He was dying. Dying for a king who would be all too happy to have one less man to pay. Dying for a treasure he would never partake of. Dying without one last look at the woman he loved.

Severian looked down at the strangely warm cup that had yet to fall out of his lax fingers. It seemed that the cup held to him as tightly as he to it. His vision blurred as he stared into the dark bowl. Surely the silver wasn't brightening? It was the poison playing with his mind that made him imagine it. The poison that made it look as though rich red wine filled the cup from the bottom up. It was astounding. A miracle—were it real.

Above the humming in his ears he could hear the excited voices of his companions. Was it possible that he wasn't imagining the cup's amazing transformation? Was it possible that he held in his hand the Cup of Christ? A cup that would heal the wound in his hand and grant immortality?

The cup was halfway to his mouth before he realized what was happening—before Dreux Beauvrai's voice rose above the others. "Sev, drink."

Grasping what resolve, what courage he had left, Severian clung to the hand that raised the cup to his lips and drank. Rich sweetness rushed over his tongue. It was not wine, but what? Warm, earthy. Salt in the back of his throat. He gulped greedily.

Blood. He gagged on the realization. He was drinking blood.

He fell backward, spilling the remaining contents on himself and the floor. Warm wetness dripped from his chin onto his injured arm.

God in heaven, what had he done?

And yet, even as he sent up a silent prayer for his soul, he felt the noose of the poison loosen. His mind cleared somewhat, the pain in his body eased.

Dumbly, he removed the dirty wrapping from his arm and wiped the blood away from the wound. Raising his injured arm to the light of the torch, Severian—and his companions—watched in mystified silence as the wound began to close. It wasn't his mind playing tricks. He could feel the tissue inside knitting back together. The incision was closing where blood from the cup had touched it.

No. It couldn't be. It had to be a trick.

"My friend." Dreux clasped him on the shoulder, his boyish face a mask of worry. "Are you all right?"

"Blood," he managed to reply, his voice hoarse and distant to his own ears.

"The Grail." Dreux crossed himself, his eyes wide. "The blood of Christ."

It was Dreux who retrieved the cup from the floor. Severian watched through glassy eyes as his friend lifted the goblet to his mouth. He wanted to tell him no, but the words would not form. Blackness filled his mind, robbing him of speech and sight.

He fell to his side on the dirt floor, dimly aware that his arm no longer pained. And then he passed to darkness.

Chapter 1

Tintagel, Cornwall
1899

"**Y**ou talked Papa into buying a parcel of land because you believe the Holy Grail is hidden there?"

Prudence Ryland knew her sister would not understand. "Yes."

Caroline's pretty face was marred with concern beneath the brim of her riding hat. "Darling, isn't this clutching at straws?"

Perhaps Caroline understood better than Pru had first thought.

Squinting against the sun—her foolish little cap did nothing to shield her eyes—Pru set her jaw. "Perhaps."

They were riding back from the village, Caroline on a gray mare, Pru on a chestnut gelding. With the men out hunting and their sisters busy at needlework, Caroline and Pru had desperately needed something to pass the day—something that required air and exercise. Anything else would have left Pru alone in her head—something she tried to avoid these days.

The afternoon was warm—too warm for a velvet riding habit, as pretty as her dark green one was. But Caro had wanted one last ride before her pregnancy denied her the exercise. Sweat trickled beneath the boning of Pru's corset, making her itch. She would try to scratch if she thought it would do any good. Instead, she clenched her jaw and urged her mount into a trot.

Her sister remained silent, blast her. Caroline knew she couldn't stand awkward pauses. She always had to fill them. "Will it not be worthwhile if the Grail is there?" Pru didn't mean just for her own benefit either, but for the benefit of the entire world.

"Only if it does what the legend claims." Caroline shook her head, the sun catching fire in the copper of her hair. "Really, Pru. The Grail is as elusive as Noah's ark! Don't you think that if it really existed, someone would have found it by now?"

Yes. *No.* "Perhaps no one has thought to look in the right spot." Perhaps she truly was grasping at straws, but what else could she do?

Caroline's green eyes were bright with worry. "I am worried about you."

She wasn't referring just to this hunt for the Grail. Pru glanced away. Of course her sister worried. Everyone in her family worried. They would continue to worry until . . . until she wasn't there to worry them any longer.

She turned a bright smile on her sister. "I am fine, Caro."

Her sister recoiled as if spat on. "You are not fine! You are—" She stopped, choking on her words. Oh, no, she wasn't going to cry, was she? Poor Caroline, she was the most emotional of all of them—the one with the kindest countenance and sweetest temper. Her hair and eyes were as bright as her spirit, while Pru's own auburn and hazel pairing was darker, more shadowed. Caro cried at the drop of a hat, and it broke Pru's heart every blasted time.

Smile gone, Pru leaned over—at the risk of toppling herself to the ground between the two horses—and touched her sister's arm. "I *am* fine, Caro. No matter what happens, I will be fine." She honestly believed that, but it didn't make the truth any easier to accept.

Caroline nodded, sniffing back her tears. Prudence righted herself as they turned down the lane to their father's estate. She and Caroline talked of trifling things for the rest of the ride— mostly books they had both read and the new typewriting machine that Caroline's husband Walter had brought her. Their earlier conversation hung over them, however.

A small group of gentlemen were gathered in the horseshoe-shaped drive. It wasn't an entirely surprising scene. Thomas Ryland was a very sociable man and was often off visiting friends, or being visited; and with his family in residence for a month's visit or longer, other gentlemen from the area often joined the various outings. It was obvious, from the size of the group—and the object they were clustered around—that this was more than mere sociability.

Their father was about to go touring in his automobile—a "racing car" manufactured by the Daimler Company. Obviously the other gentlemen were there for a demonstration of the motorized carriage's capabilities. Even Prudence was aware that Daimler's racing car was capable of reaching speeds in the vicinity of fifty miles per hour. She knew because her father had told her, not because she had experienced such exhilaration firsthand. He never drove that fast with her in the vehicle.

Ever since attending the automobile show in Richmond earlier that summer, Thomas Ryland had become obsessed with the new mode of transport and was one of the few people in the area to own such a contraption. Pru's sister Georgia thought it dangerous, and that a man their father's age shouldn't indulge in such a pastime, but Pru loved the snappy little conveyance, with its red exterior and black leather seat. Her father refused to allow her to drive it—claiming that he feared for her safety.

Hmpf. She saw how her father careened about like a madman. She could not be any worse at it than he. It was something she would have to discuss with him, because she didn't want to waste the remainder of her life being treated as though she were made of glass.

There was a time when he would have indulged his youngest daughter's desire to take the Daimler for a jaunt. A time when his biggest worry would have been for the car, not for Prudence.

The grooms had seen them approaching the house and were there waiting for them. Pru and Caroline dismounted and greeted their father and his guests. Their father shot Pru a look that covered her from head to toe, lingering on her face as though searching for some sign of fatigue or pain. Dear Papa, he was so very protective. She smiled at him, and bade he and his companions a good day.

Pru stripped off her gloves as they entered the cool interior of the house. She loved this house. It was bright, but not overly so, and at night was filled with the most intriguing shadows. As a child she had loved the dark nooks and crannies that her sisters avoided. It drove her mother to distraction looking for her. No one ever seemed to understand that she didn't want to be found.

Odd, then, that she should be so afraid of going into the dark now, when she had so loved it as a child. Perhaps that was because a child never worried that the darkness would be everlasting.

Pulling on the pin, she removed the little boat-shaped hat from her head, glad to have it gone. "Tea, Caro?"

Her sister made a soft snorting sound that never failed to bring a smile to Pru's lips. "Of course. Why do you always ask me that foolish question?"

Pru grinned as they crossed the Italian marble floor, the heels of their boots clicking smartly on the polished peach and cream tiles. "Because someday you may say no."

"To tea? Never."

As they walked, Pru breathed the scents of Rosecourt deep into her lungs. Fresh flowers, beeswax, lemon and cloves. These were the smells that had surrounded her all her life, the smells that comforted her when all else failed.

As a member of one of England's wealthiest families, Pru's father had been guaranteed a fortune, but Rosecourt Manor had come into their family via a friend of Thomas's grandfather. Apparently the late Earl of Carnover had a soft spot for the youngest of Devlin Ryland's grandsons and gave him the estate as a marriage present. As Pru's parents had produced four girls, the house would eventually go to the eldest son of one of those daughters. It was not a legacy Pru had to worry about.

She and Caroline entered the parlor together. The heavy rose-colored drapes were pulled back to reveal creamy sheers that allowed the full light of day into the room but saved the furniture from the sun's fading rays. The walls and carpet were matching cream, a soft contrast to the Lodden print on the chairs and sofas. William Morris's delicate print lent bold color to the room with its swirls of of blue, gold, red, green and rose.

"What about that Grey fellow?" Caroline asked as she perched daintily on one of the chairs.

"Marcus?" Pru frowned as she pulled the bell

for tea. Had she missed part of the conversation? "What of him?"

Caroline shrugged her narrow shoulders as she removed her kid gloves and toyed with the empty fingers. "He seems a nice enough gentleman."

"He is." She had met him at a lecture he'd given in London one evening about a year ago when, tired of parties and craving something familiar to distract her, she had stumbled upon a leaflet advertising Marcus's talk on Grail lore. Having grown up in the legendary birthplace of King Arthur, Pru considered herself well acquainted with Grail legend. At one time she had entertained the notion of becoming something of a historian, or perhaps an archaeologist, but those dreams had fallen by the wayside with so many others.

Marcus brought back the excitement she always felt when the Grail was involved. He offered facts and documented cases, not just ideas and theories. He gave everyone in the lecture hall reason to believe the Grail truly existed, and he gave Pru something even more. He gave her hope. It was then that what had once been a historic fascination became a personal obsession.

Prudence approached him after the lecture. They talked about Arthur, the Grail and Tintagel, and when Pru mentioned the ruins not far from her father's estate where she and her sisters had played as children Marcus Grey became very interested, especially when she told him that before an underground passage collapsed, she had found what appeared to be artifacts from centuries before. Over the course of the next few days, when

Pru wasn't in the company of the esteemed gentlemen hired by her father, she spent her time
with Marcus, and by the end of the week, both of
them were convinced that the ruins might be
worth investigating further.

So, like everything she did, Pru threw herself
into the project with all the determination and
strength she could muster. Her father bought the
land without much pleading. He always indulged
her and perhaps some part of him shared her enthusiasm.

She had also thrown herself at Marcus, mistaking their friendship for something more. He had
been too much of a gentleman to take advantage
of her after a passionate kiss. For a long time Pru
wondered if her "condition" was to blame for his
refusal, but now she saw what he had seen. They
were incredibly well suited as friends, but not as
lovers. Marcus was like the brother she'd never
had. Thank God he had known how to behave
better than she.

Marcus also handled the "Catholic situation"
better than Pru would have. Marcus didn't want
strangers poking around their project any more
than Pru did, but he thought it better to cooperate and be charitable. All the church wanted—
apparently—was access to whatever they found in
the ruins, and of course something as important
and powerful as the Holy Grail was better in the
hands of people who would respect and protect it.

They were welcome to the Grail once Pru had a
chance to use it. One sip, that was all she asked,
then they could take it and lock it away.

However, she was curious about how the Vatican had found out about her little project. It wasn't as though she'd advertised the fact that she was on a hunt to find a cup that could cure the ill and grant eternal life.

"Well?"

Pru's gaze jerked back to her sister. "What?"

Caroline rotated her wrist, making a wheel-like motion with her hand. "Do you like him or not?" She let Pru fill in the rest for herself.

Holding up her hands, Pru seated herself on the sofa. "Not in the way you mean, no." She could claim it without guilt, as it was completely true.

Caroline opened her mouth to continue, but was prevented from saying any more by a knock on the door. It was a maid with their tea, and hot on her heels was the man himself, Marcus Grey.

At twenty-eight Marcus was a charming mixture of poet, scholar and adventurer. He was tall and trim, his shoulders broad, his hips narrow and his legs long. His thick dark hair was usually wind-blown, his cheeks rosy from spending much of his time outside. Despite all its efforts to age him, the sun had succeeded in nothing more than giving his complexion a healthy glow. His wide gem-blue gaze was bright as it settled on Pru. "I hope I'm not interrupting."

"Of course not," Caroline replied with a charming smile. "Sit, Mr. Grey. Join us for tea."

Needing no further invitation, Marcus sat on the other end of the sofa from Pru and angled himself toward her with all the comfort of a man not the least bit interested in her as a woman. Her vanity could take offense at the slight, but why bother?

"What have you been into today, Marcus?" Pru asked as she poured him a cup of tea. He liked it with very little cream and several lumps of sugar.

"Your father showed me the ruins of the tiny chapel that used to exist on the estate. He told me to explore and dig to my heart's content." A wide grin brightened his face. "So I did."

Pru returned his smile. It was very difficult not to be happy when Marcus was. Caroline looked positively enraptured. "I thought we agreed you would not go digging without me." Her chastising tone was weak at best. "Did you find anything?"

He shrugged. "An old pair of spectacles and a boot, but that isn't why I came looking for you."

"Has something happened?" Anticipation fluttered in her stomach. "Something to do with the Grail?"

He held up an opened letter. "I have heard from our friend in France again."

Friend? Was that how he viewed LaFavre, the arrogant little priest who had first contacted them? Pru set her spoon on her saucer as the turmoil inside her quieted. "What does he want this time?"

Marcus took a swallow of tea. "He wrote to tell us that two representatives of his church should be here within the next two or three days."

"So soon?" Now, this was interesting. "The church must be very anxious to see what we uncover." She kept her tone light, but that anxious feeling surfaced once more. If the Catholics were this interested in her little expedition, then they must have reason to believe she was actually on to something! As concerned as she was about the church's involvement, she couldn't help but view their interest as a good sign.

Clearing her throat, Pru forced her expression into one of polite restraint. "Who are they sending?"

Setting down his now empty cup, Marcus opened the letter. His gaze moved over the paper until it found the information he sought. "A Father Francis Molyneux and a man named Mr. Chapel."

"Chapel?" Pru's mouth tucked to one side. "I wonder if he ever gets teased about that—a man named Mr. Chapel working for the church."

Marcus chuckled. "Perhaps he considered his name a sign of his true calling. Regardless, I have much to do to prepare for their arrival. They will no doubt want to see all of our notes and research."

Pru regarded him from beneath arched brows as she fixed him another cup of tea. "Will they see *all* of our notes and research?"

Again came the grin. "No."

She grinned back, caught up in their conspiracy.

Finishing his tea in one long gulp, Marcus excused himself, as he wanted to start going through his papers to select what the Catholic representatives would see.

"I do not know why you do not take advantage of him," Caroline mused boldly once they were alone again. "He is a lovely man."

Lovely was a perfect word to describe Marcus.

"I do not want to take advantage of him," Pru explained, sipping her tea. "And even if I did, you know very well it would be wrong of me to do so."

"Why?" Caroline's countenance grew fierce. "Why can you not indulge in an affair? What is wrong with seeking a little happiness for yourself?"

Pru's own brow puckered. She swallowed against the lump in her throat. "You know why, Caro." Normally her sister would never dream of making such a scandalous suggestion. Then again, it wasn't as though Pru had to worry about her reputation. And she would be lying if she said she didn't wonder the same thoughts on occasion.

For one moment, Pru saw the pain in her heart reflected in her sister's eyes before Caroline's expression twisted with frustration. Caroline's cup and saucer rattled as she set them on the tray. She rose to her feet, her posture stiff and restrained.

"We all go through life knowing we will someday die, Pru."

"Yes." Pru sought to keep her tone gentle, even though the urge to scream seized her. She wanted to rail and rant about the unfairness of it all. "But most assume they will live to be old and gray. I may not even see the new year."

Her sister's gaze sliced through her. Caroline was about to make a dramatic exit—a talent she excelled at. "All the more reason for you to stop acting like you are already dead."

There were tears in Caroline's eyes as she swept from the room like a diva. The sight of them broke Pru's heart.

She slumped against the sofa and covered her face with her hands. Caro didn't understand. And Pru had no way of making her see that she intended to live—just not the way Caro wanted her to. She was chasing a miracle, and it was so close she could taste it.

How could she expect anyone to understand that she was almost as afraid to "live" as she was to die?

Chapter 2

On the evening that "those Catholic fellows," as her father liked to call them, were to arrive, Pru decided that red would be a good color for the gown she would wear to dinner. Red was strong and bold, and with any luck she would feel strong and bold in it. God knows she needed that strength almost as much as she needed the Grail itself.

At first the doctors hadn't told her much about the cancer that was slowly but deliberately killing her—she was a delicate female, after all. They told her father what they would not tell her, afraid that the truth would be too much for her to comprehend.

Perhaps she should have left it at that. Thanks to the medical books in her father's library, she knew more about her affliction than what the doctors would ever tell her. Sometimes she could feel it inside her, gnawing, whittling away at her strength.

It had started in her ovaries, which the doctors had removed, but it hadn't been enough. They could not operate now, nor could they tell her how much time she had left. On her last examination—not much more than a month ago—they had told her that if she was lucky she would live to see the turn of the century.

There were so many things she wanted to do before she met her end. She wanted to drive the Daimler as fast as it would go. She wanted to see the great pyramids of Egypt. She wanted to experience real passion. Unfortunately, it seemed unlikely that she would achieve any of those things.

Her maid, Fanny, arrived just as she was exiting the bath, her thoughts a mixture of bitter melancholy and resigned practicality. A towel hid the scars on her abdomen from the maid's pitying gaze. Pru's dinner gown was cradled in the girl's arms, rich and opulent as a perfect crimson rose. Darker red lace lay over the bright, accordion-pleated chiffon, adding rich depth to the sumptuous garment.

Once dry and dressed in stockings, chemise and corset, Pru sat to have her hair dressed. A simple loose bun high on her crown left a full halo of hair around her face. Fanny wove fresh dark roses around the bun and arranged a few auburn strands artfully around her ears.

Her only other adornment was a sheer gold ribbon around her neck that fastened with a pearl button in the back. Anything else with such a gown would be garish.

Pru stepped into the dress, her heart hammering as Fanny pulled it over her shoulders. It seemed a shame to waste such a gown on men who probably wouldn't notice how nicely it clung to her torso or pushed up her bosom, but Pru wanted to wear it. It was maudlin, but God only knows if she'd ever have the chance to wear it again.

"You look real lovely, miss," Fanny confided bashfully.

Pru smiled in pleasure. She did look lovely. She also looked healthy, her cheeks rosy and bright. She appeared confident and not about to be intimidated by men who might—or might not—try to take her miracle cure away.

Leaving the warm blue and burgundy haven of her room, Pru made her way down the corridor toward the winding staircase that led to the ground floor. Perhaps the dress hadn't been such a good idea. She didn't want the priests to think she was mocking them. But it was such a beautiful gown. . . .

Oh, perdition! She was in it now, and life was too short to fuss over the color of a dress no one but her family and a couple of priests were going to see.

All heads turned as she entered the drawing room. Was that her father who gasped? Matilda was staring at her as though she believed Pru had taken complete leave of her senses. Of course,

Matilda was the very picture of English delicacy in a lacy gown of rose chiffon. Caroline was demure also, in creamy ivory. Only Georgia had opted for a stronger color—Pru could always count on Georgia—and stood there smiling in a gown the color of tiger lilies.

It wasn't just the color of her gown—a color Pru had never worn before—it was the gown itself. It was very feminine and daring and provocative, and it had been a long, long time since Pru had taken the time to make herself look like a woman of her station should in a social setting. Even Marcus looked impressed.

But Pru was more concerned with the reaction of people who didn't know her. Her gaze searched the group as her father called her forward. There was only one unfamiliar face—an older man with graying hair and kind eyes. His collar gave away his profession.

"Father Molyneux, this is my youngest daughter, Prudence. She is the one who started this whole business."

Pru glanced at her father with an expression that was part smile, part frown. Was that praise or censure she heard in Papa's tone?

"It is a pleasure to meet you, mam'selle." The priest's voice was low and soothing, his accent heavy but not too thick.

Smiling, she offered him her hand. "I am looking forward to working with you, Father." Strangely enough, she was. Perhaps she was simply naive, but this man wasn't the least bit intimidating.

"And where is your companion? I understood we were to have two guests." Pru glanced around, searching for another unfamiliar face.

"Yes," Molyneux answered. "My friend needed to step outside to indulge in his nasty habit of smoking." His gaze lit over Pru's shoulder. "Ah, Chapel, there you are!"

Eager to catch a glimpse of their second guest, Pru turned.

Perdition.

Mr. Chapel was tall—wonderfully so—and dressed in black jacket and trousers with white waistcoat, shirt and tie. Tawny hair streaked with gold was brushed back from a tanned face. His brows were thick and high, his nose long and straight. His lips were neither thin nor full, but a pleasant balance of the two, wide and sensual. His cheeks and jaw were chiseled, as though carved by a master sculptor. But it was his eyes that drew her attention the most. Even from this distance, his eyes looked as bright and clear as honey.

Good God, she was staring at the poor man! And he was staring back, adding to the uncomfortable heat that crept through her blood.

"Mr. Chapel," her father began the introduction. "May I present my daughter Prudence."

Dimly, Prudence remembered to offer her hand. Mr. Chapel took it in his much larger one. His fingers were strong and warm, with a heat that seemed unnatural—or perhaps it was just because her own fingers were like icicles that his felt so deliciously heated.

"It is an honor, my lady." His voice was low in

pitch, smooth as honey, with an accent that didn't sound like any French she had ever heard before.

"I hope you enjoy your stay in Cornwall, Mr. Chapel." It was a trite comment, but the best she could manage, given the fact that her mind seemed to have shut down.

"No mister," he said, running his thumb along her knuckles as he lifted her hand to his mouth. His gaze remained fixed on her face. "Just Chapel."

Pru watched his languid motions in a daze. His breath warmed her chilled flesh, sending a thrill throughout her blood so acute that her spine tingled at it.

"Chapel," she repeated, shamefully hoarse, as his lips brushed her skin.

The sound of his name on her lips seemed to startle him, for he jerked just the tiniest bit. There was a stinging on the back of her hand, but as soon as he lifted his gaze to hers, the fleeting sensation was gone, replaced by a disjointed confusion that Pru was certain everyone noticed.

Fortunately, they were all too busy talking among themselves to witness the flush in Pru's cheeks, or the predatory interest in Chapel's eyes. This was not how a priest was supposed to look at a woman.

But he wasn't a priest.

He released her hand—more's the pity. "Have you been with the church long, Mr.—Chapel?"

He smiled, as though they shared a private joke. "It seems like centuries."

That meant he must have been in service for quite some time, but he couldn't be any more than thirty. Perplexed, Pru raised her gaze to his, only to find it unnervingly locked upon her face. "Are you studying to be a priest?"

His expression might have been comical if it weren't so horrified. "No."

That revelation—abrupt as it was—should not have sent her heart pounding as it did. "Oh. Forgive me. I thought—"

He held up a hand. "There is no need to apologize. Your conclusion was a logical one."

Pru's gaze narrowed as she studied him. She couldn't help it—she had never seen a man like him before in her life. "Then why are you here?"

He blinked at her bluntness, but didn't hesitate to answer. "I'm here in a purely historical capacity."

She tilted her head in interest. "Historical?"

He nodded, seemingly unbothered by her curiosity. "Yes. I am a historian."

So he was like Marcus, then, except that Marcus loved talking about his work, and often did so with great enthusiasm to anyone who would listen. Mr. Chapel was slightly more subdued. He also exuded a quiet strength that Pru found intriguing.

Pru took a step toward him. "You should talk to Mr. Grey, then. No doubt you will be interested in what he has uncovered."

Chapel moved backward, increasing the distance between them once more. After looking at her with such heat in his eyes, he was acting very cool all of a sudden.

Had she said something off-putting? No, she

could not think of any remark that might have
been taken as an insult, unless he thought her
mention of Marcus and his research was a slight
against his own expertise.

She took a step toward him, closing the polite
distance between them. "So, as a historian, what
do you hope to find here in Cornwall, Chapel?"

The gaze that lifted to hers was not the same
gaze she had seen just moments before. His eyes
were no longer like warm honey—they were as
bright and brilliant as newly minted gold, drawing her into their molten depths until she thought
she might be lost within them. Heat engulfed her
as his lashes lowered, his nostrils flaring ever so
slightly. He drew a deep breath into his lungs as a
sensual smile curved his lips.

Good God, he was *smelling* her.

Honey-colored eyes opened, locking with hers.
Pru's throat tightened. She lifted her hand to her
breast in an attempt to quell the pounding there.
Chapel's gaze flickered to her fingers, cooling so
suddenly that Pru scarcely knew what had happened. When his eyes met hers again, there was
none of the brightness there that had been present
before. In fact, his gaze was totally unreadable.
Had she imagined it all, then?

"Treasure," he replied in a tone as neutral as his
expression—*too* neutral. "Is that not what you
want as well?"

Pru swallowed. He knew this was more than
a treasure hunt to her, of that she was certain.
No one outside her family knew why she wanted
the Grail, not even Marcus, but somehow this

man knew that she had personal reasons for wanting to find the holy cup.

She was saved from answering when her father's voice called Chapel to his side. The man who was not a mister, not a priest, bowed to her and excused himself without a flicker of regret. Pru watched him go, not entirely certain of what had just happened. Her hands were no longer cold and she looked down to make certain they weren't clenched or trembling.

There was a mark on her right hand that hadn't been there before. Her brows drew together as she raised it toward her face. A thin red mark about half an inch long dipped between her second and third knuckles. It was a scratch. Gingerly, she touched it with her other hand—it was fresh and it hadn't been there before she met Chapel.

Her head snapped up and her shocked gaze flew across the room to where the golden stranger stood, engaged in conversation with her father.

Good Lord, had he actually *bit* her?

Chapter 3

He knew it was a mistake to come to Cornwall.

Chapel sat on the edge of his pristinely made bed and stared out the window at the black night spread before him. He could wait no longer, sitting in this room, listening to the slow and steady heartbeats echoing around him, pounding in his head like tribal drums.

The pint of pig's blood he had consumed earlier sustained and strengthened him, but it had been like eating turnip when what one really craved was chocolate. Earlier, he'd had to step outside to clear the scent of human from his senses. But just when he thought it safe to go back inside, he'd met Prudence Ryland, who appealed not only to his hunger, but to other base appetites as well.

Ba-dum. Ba-dum. Hearts beating in the darkness. Prudence's was one of them. His own heart struggled to beat in response, but it was no use. It had been too long since the organ in his chest had kept such rhythm.

He rose to his feet, clad in trousers and shirtsleeves. He could hardly sit there all night listening to the sounds of the house. Night was his time to thrive, the time when he felt the most vital and *alive.* He was restless and eager to burn some of the energy bubbling inside him.

Silent as a cat—yet another benefit of his curse— he crept from his room and down the stairs through the house, his keen eyes helping avoid accident. The last thing he wanted to do was wake Mr. Ryland or that daughter of his.

The thought of her gave him pause, right in the middle of the great hall, in a ray of moonlight that slipped through one of the many windows. *Prudence.* Could she have been named any less aptly? That one had the heavy scent of recklessness upon her. Even now, hours later, he could recall the scent of her as she fanned herself before him.

Of course, he had tried to distance himself. Her rich red gown hugged every inch of her from shoulder to thigh in a manner that would have been most shameful in his day. She had a beautiful figure—a little thin, but curvaceous all the same. Her skin was so fair, her eyes so bright. It hadn't helped that her thick auburn hair had looked ready to tumble out of her topknot and spill about her shoulders. Red hair. Red gown. Red lips. Her entire appearance taunted him.

The sound of her voice saying his name had shaken him so acutely that he feared he had nicked her with a fang. Need flooded him at the taste of her flesh—not just the need to feed, but the need a man feels for a woman.

One more reason why his stay in Cornwall should be a short one. For his kind, feeding and sex were closely linked and often went together as naturally as did eating and drinking for others.

Why this woman aroused him was a mystery. Something in her scent, perhaps? The challenge in her feline eyes? There was something unusual about her, a deep melancholy that matched his own, but she was so very, very full of life and hope. Yes, hope clung to her like a veil, and that was what drew him to her.

And as the thought of her filled him, so did her scent. At first he thought it might have been his imagination, but another breath proved it wasn't. She was near, and though he knew he should walk away, he found himself following the smell of her rather than avoiding it.

The trail led him to a partially closed door. A thin trickle of light seeped from the edges, as did the perfume of Prudence Ryland's flesh. Of its own accord, his hand rose and pushed the door open. It didn't even squeak, giving him several seconds to watch her in appreciation.

Prudence Ryland reclined on a dark blue velvet chaise in the center of the room, clad in a flimsy, virginal nightgown and wrapper, her wine-rich hair falling about her shoulders. Chapel's mouth went dry at the sight of her. His heart gave a little thump against his ribs, as though it simply wanted to let him know it was still there.

Everything about her wept life and hope and a sense of desperation that called to him. She looked so fragile he longed to protect her, so delicate he wanted to shelter her and so damned tempting that he wanted to sink his fangs into her just to know the bittersweet tang of life once more.

Leave. Every ounce of good sense he possessed demanded that he go. He hadn't fought temptation for more than four centuries just to surrender to it now. He turned.

"Don't let me chase you away, Mr. Chapel."

Her low, honeyed voice sent a shiver down his spine; her taunt set his teeth on edge. He faced her. "I have no wish to intrude on your privacy, Miss Ryland."

She smiled as though she found him amusing. Kittens and children were amusing. *He* was a monster—a monster little girls like this one should not toy with.

Little girl? Compared to him, perhaps, but when she stood, it was all too obvious just how much of a woman she truly was. Ivory silk hugged the curve of one breast, the length of a smooth round thigh.

"You are not intruding," she informed him. "Please do not let my presence stop you from searching out something to read."

How could her presence not stop him? How could anyone—even a mere mortal—concentrate on titles and contents when such sweet-smelling flesh was so near?

Still, she would think it odd if he did not acquiesce, so he went to one of the many shelves and started looking. She did not turn her attention away from him as he had expected. In fact, she perched herself on the arm of the chaise and watched him as though he were some kind of fascinating subject. In return, he watched her out of the corner of his eye.

Her head tilted. "Were you having trouble falling asleep?"

The question was innocent enough, if not a little nosy. "No. I've always been a bit of a night owl." That was an understatement. "You?"

She shrugged her elegant shoulders. "I tend to sleep better when it is light outside." A self-deprecating chuckle followed. "That sounds foolish, doesn't it?"

A strange tightness pinched at Chapel's chest as he turned to face her and her bashful gaze. Where was his temptress of earlier?

"No," he replied with a shake of his head. "It does not sound strange. I sleep better during the day as well."

She smiled then, a tremulous, uncertain curving of her lips. "There is something about the dark that makes me . . ."

"Restless?"

Wide hazel eyes snapped to his, bright with something that looked uncomfortably like vulnerability. "Yes."

She didn't seem eager to converse further on the subject and Chapel wasn't about to ask, lest she return with her own questions about his predilection for nocturnal wanderings.

He went back to reading book spines. Nothing appealed to him. He'd much rather talk to his delicious companion.

"Was there something in particular you were looking for?" she asked. "I know where to find almost any book in this library."

No doubt she did. "I thought it might be prudent to reacquaint myself with Arthurian legends. Tintagel is full of them, is it not?"

She grinned, revealing straight white teeth. "It is. He was supposedly born here, you know."

He nodded, following her to a shelf on the other side of the room. Despite the discreet distance he put between them, her scent teased him. "Yes, I know."

She took a slim leather-bound volume from a row of similar books and offered it to him. "That's why there are so many Grail afficinados and hunters here year-round."

Chapel eyed her curiously as he accepted the book. "But you believe you've actually found its hiding place."

She glanced away, but not before he saw the eagerness in her eyes. "Yes."

"Earlier I told you why I was here, but you've yet to tell me why you are so eager to find the Grail." He gestured at her with the book. "You do not seem the type to desire either fame or fortune."

Her gaze lifted to his, her chin defiantly angled. "The satisfaction of finding that which no one else has ever found."

No, that wasn't it. The Grail meant more to her than that. He could feel the need engulfing her so strongly it stung. For her sake, he hoped it was not the Blood Grail hidden beneath the rubble of her ruins. "I suppose a woman finding the Cup of Christ would certainly set all those stuffy scholars and priests on their ears."

Her eyes darkened. "It certainly would." A blush lit her cheeks. "Present company excluded, of course."

Was that laughter rumbling in his chest? A smile took hold of his lips, awkwardly curving them upward, as though the muscles of his face had forgotten how to form the expression. She smiled back and Chapel was suddenly very tempted to lean down—there were only a few inches between them—and press his lips, not against her neck to bite, but against her mouth to taste and kiss.

He backed away. "Thank you for the book. I will leave you to your own diversion now."

Prudence's eyes widened—the gaze of a child not wanting to be left alone at night. "You do not have to leave."

Her obvious desire for companionship weakened him, but he was not the one to grant her wish.

"With all due respect, Miss Ryland, it would not do for you and I to be caught together, given your attire." It wouldn't do if he was found with his fangs buried deep in her soft flesh either.

That vaguely mocking smile from earlier curved

her lips once more. Was she insulted that he thought to leave her? "I assure you, Mr. Chapel, your virtue is safe with me."

If that was true, why did her hazel gaze keep sneaking back to the open neck of his shirt?

"It is not my virtue that concerns me." And she truly didn't seem to realize the danger to her own.

Slender arms folded across her silk-clad chest. "Why, Mr. Chapel, are you trying to tell me that I am in danger from you?" Her tone was glib, but he heard her heartbeat speed up.

Chapel moved toward her with lazy determination. Her heart picked up its pace, bringing a smug smile to his lips. It had been a long, long time, but he remembered how to play this game. "What do you think?"

The innocently voiced question had her gaze raking over him like flames over dry tinder. Color bloomed in her cheeks as her gaze lifted to his. "You do not frighten me."

"I think I do, but not in the way I should."

Her eyes grew round as she stared at him. Hazel wasn't a fair description. Her eyes seemed a different shade of green every time he looked into them. Her lips parted, but no sound came forth. It was almost as though she were a statue, she was so still, but the blood warming her cheeks reminded him of how full of life she was, how delicate and fragile.

Her throat worked at a swallow, forcing the tendons and cords of the slender column into brief, sharp relief. The muscles in Chapel's jaws tightened as a tingle raced through his gums. One leap and he could pin her, sink his fangs into the sweet hollow between her neck and shoulder. She would shudder in his arms, soft gasps of delight slipping from those pliant lips as he fed, her fragile heart pounding against his chest.

"Do you often go roaming at night, Mr. Chapel?"

Her velvety voice kept him from acting on his desire.

"Chapel," he corrected, taking a step backward. "It's just Chapel. And yes, I do often roam at night, Miss Ryland."

"Pru." She smiled slightly. "Miss Ryland makes me feel like an old spinster."

Which was exactly what she would have been back in his day, a thought that shocked him because she seemed so young. He shrugged. "Women of your status can afford to wait before marrying."

Fine brows lifted. "Wait? Perhaps I simply do not wish to marry."

There was challenge in her words, but no truth in her eyes. "Perhaps, Pru, you have yet to meet a man who could match your expectations of a husband."

Her wide lips curved on one side. "That is entirely possible, I suppose. What of you?"

Caution rose within him. "What of me?"

She took a step toward him, those slender arms lifting her breasts against the neckline of her gown and wrapper. He stared at the tantalizing tracings of blue just below her fair skin. Pru seemed unaware of his straying gaze. Bold indeed—both of them. Far too bold to be safe. "You are unmarried as well, are you not? Why?"

He said the first thing that came to mind. "No sane woman would have me."

She blinked at his obviously unexpected honesty. "Oh. Perhaps we are more alike than I thought."

The smile he gave her was a kind one. Let her believe they were alike if it made her feel better. "Perhaps."

Her gaze drifted toward the wall of windows. Moonlight touched her cheeks through the glass, brightened her eyes so that they seemed even more feline.

"But I have never roamed the night." Her voice was so low, so wistful that at first Chapel thought he might have imagined it.

She withdrew from him quickly, with all the grace and agility of a doe. Dumbfounded, he stood there, still as a statue, and watched her flee. What, in the name of God, was she doing?

She threw open one of the windows and, grasping the frame, stepped up onto the sill. Her head turned, her eyes flashing brightly at him from over her shoulder. How wild and free she looked in her loose gown with her unbound hair and flushed cheeks.

"Coming, Chapel?"

The wise course would be to let her go. But what if Temple was in the area? What if he was half starved and Pru stumbled upon him? Even though he couldn't sense his old friend's presence, that didn't mean he wasn't out there, just out of range.

But it wasn't Temple who was the real threat tonight. It was his own thoughts and desires.

When had he last walked with a woman? He wanted to share the dark with this fragile, mysterious woman.

Pru did not wait for his reply, but jumped out the window. Cursing, Chapel followed. As he leapt the few feet to the ground, he had the sudden and awful realization that he had been right.

It had been a mistake to come to Cornwall.

Chapter 4

Pru had never done anything so impulsive or reckless as jumping out of that window. An hour later she still did not know what had made her do it.

They walked in silence, the thick grass swishing against their footwear. Her slippers were thin but dry—something that would never have occurred to her before she became obsessed with illness. To catch a cold would cost her days of exploration, and she couldn't have that.

"How did you find out about my search for the Grail?" The question had been gnawing at her since the Vatican's first letter.

Chapel shrugged his wide shoulders beneath a halo of silvery moonlight. "The Vatican has spies everywhere."

Was that actually a joke? There was no hint of amusement on his face, nor flicker of mirth in his gaze. "Are you serious?"

Another shrug, but there was the barest hint of a smile on his lips. Her shoulders sagged in relief. He was joking.

"I assume it was through your research," he replied. "I believe a priest who attended several of Mr. Grey's lectures was very interested in his work and heard of your plans. You didn't honestly believe you could keep it secret, did you?"

"No. I suppose not." Her gaze followed a rabbit diving into a bush, only its white tail discernible in the murky night. "Although I find it hard to believe the church would give so much credence to my search when they haven't involved themselves in others'."

His gaze was dark as it met hers. "Perhaps they believe your search will actually uncover something."

Oddly enough, his words gave her some comfort.

They continued their walk in silence. The breeze was warm and gentle as it lifted her hair and caused her nightgown to whisper against her legs. Next to her, Chapel's thin lawn shirt clung to his chest and arms. The white fabric was an eerie blue in the icy light, the muscles beneath defined and heavier than Pru would have first suspected for a man of his scholarly bent. Of course, Marcus was athletically built as well.

But Chapel appealed to her in a way Marcus did not.

Better not to think of that, however. "What do you know of the Holy Grail?"

The question seemed to surprise him. His steps faltered for the span of a heartbeat. "At the Crucifixion, the Roman Longinus used his lance to pierce Christ's side. Joseph of Arimathea collected the blood in a chalice—the Holy Grail."

Of course, he knew the origin of the cup—didn't everyone? "Surely your knowledge runs deeper than that?" She tried to keep her tone light, but annoyance crept in. She had agreed to share her finds with the church; could they not at least extend similar courtesy to her?

He shot her an aggrieved glance and stopped beside her. They were in the middle of the garden, in the open but totally alone. Under the garden lamps his hair was rich gold, his eyes bright and fathomless. Lucifer just before the fall, was the fanciful notion that popped into her head. Believing this man to be a docile servant of the church was a mistake. She knew that now.

"Joseph brought the Grail with him to England when he established the first Christian church in Glastonbury. It is thought that the Grail was lost after his death, only to be found by King Arthur almost five centuries later. That is, of course, the legend you and your partner are pursuing."

Pru opened her mouth to comment, but he cut her off. "There are those who believe the Grail fell into the possession of the Knights Templar, and that Pope Clement the fifth sought to claim the cup when he ordered the Templars imprisoned in 1307. King Philip of France was happy to oblige, sending soldiers to relieve the knights of their treasures. Many Templars fled to England, supposedly bringing the cup back to this country. Whichever legend you choose to believe, it seems that most scholars believe England to be the final resting place of the Grail, unless, of course, you believe that Henry Sinclair took the Grail to Nova Scotia in 1398. Shall I go on, Miss Ryland, or have I succeeded in impressing you?"

He certainly seemed to know his Grail lore, which impressed her indeed, but his caustic tone tightened her jaw. "I meant no disrespect, *Mr.* Chapel."

He had the nerve to chuckle at her pointed use of propriety where his name was concerned. "What do *you* know of the Grail?"

She frowned, hurrying to keep up with his long strides as he began walking once more. "I have done extensive research, if that is what you are asking. Marcus and I have compiled information spanning centuries." She couldn't keep the hauteur from her voice. Marcus might have spent more years seriously researching the Grail than she had, but she had made up for that with determination and single-mindedness.

Chapel stopped walking. Pru hadn't paid attention to their direction and now she found herself deep within the garden—far from the house and any sense of propriety. Every feeling she possessed was sharp and focused on the man beside her. He smelled of warmth and a sweetness she couldn't place, and in the delicate light of the moon he appeared like something out of a romantic tale of knights and damsels. Never had she felt so aware of a man, and certainly not so soon into their acquaintance.

She backed away, unable any longer to fight the urge to retreat. He did not follow, but watched her with a keen understanding that disturbed her even more than her attraction to him. Did he know that if he chose to kiss her right now she would let him, just because she had the sudden desire to discover how he would taste?

"People hunt the Grail for two reasons, Miss Ryland."

Obviously he was not aware of her attraction to him at all. Thank God.

"They think it will bring riches and power, or they believe it will grant eternal youth." He tilted his head as he regarded her. "Which is it that drives you, greed or vanity?"

There was no trace of censure or derision in his expression or tone. He was simply curious.

"Desperation," she admitted hoarsely, truthfully, holding his gaze even though it humbled her to do so. Not riches, not eternal youth, just the chance to enjoy a normal lifetime.

"A better reason than most. What about your Mr. Grey?" He slid his hands into his pockets in a deceptively casual—and unthreatening—manner. "What are his reasons for hunting the Grail?"

"First of all, I do not think hunting is the appropriate term. Second, Marcus's reasons for locating the Grail are purely those of scholarly interest." At least that's what he had told her, and what she assumed. Any other reasons he might have didn't matter—Pru honestly didn't care.

"And third, he is not *my* Mr. Grey." Fourth, why had he looked at her as though he understood her "desperation" without knowing anything about it?

He eyed her strangely. "Forgive me. I meant no disrespect."

The way he said it made her feel a fool, but his tone was not the least bit mocking. In fact, he sounded as though he felt sorry for her.

She would prefer he mocked her instead.

"However well you know Mr. Grey, I would advise you to use caution, Miss Ryland. The search for the Grail has driven men to act out of character on more than one occasion. Your desire to find the Grail and sheltered existence make you a target for those who would take advantage." He turned his back to her and began walking once more.

Again he sounded as though he spoke from experience, but she'd address that later. He also sounded like her former governess, chastising her for misbehaving. "Are you often out in society, Mr. Chapel?"

He didn't look back and she didn't follow. "No."

"I thought as much."

He stopped again, turning his head to pin her with those unreadable eyes, but there was no mistaking the rueful expression on his face. "I have offended you."

"Yes." Pru's jaw was still tight. "I believe you have."

"I'm sorry." He raked a hand through his hair. "I'm not very . . . *good* with people."

"Really?" Her tone was clipped. "I never would have guessed."

His smile was sheepish. He wasn't the least bit offended by her sarcasm or her candor. "I said I was sorry."

Yes, he had. The proper thing for her to do—the polite thing—would be to accept his apology and perhaps even offer one of her own.

"I appreciate that," she said instead. She moved past him to lead the way back to the house.

His hands went back into his pockets as he fell into step beside her. He had nice hands—long and elegant but strong. His forearms were tanned, lightly dusted with golden hair that caught the moonlight like newly minted gold. "But I do think you should be cautious in your endeavor."

Pru's teeth scraped together. "Of course. You obviously have given this excursion much more thought and consideration than I have."

Dark brows hardly rose at her caustic reply, but his earlier mirth was gone. "Not this excursion, but one very much like it, yes."

So she was right—he had been on such an expedition before. One that had failed. Hers would not be so unlucky. It couldn't.

"I assure you, sir, that I have put a great deal of work and effort into this quest."

"That I do not doubt."

At least he was willing to give her that. "Thank you." Good Lord, she sounded positively smug! How had he managed to get under her skin on such short acquaintance? He looked at her as though he understood her when there was no way he could. It was both comforting and annoying.

"But you said yourself that you are desperate, and desperation makes a mockery of caution."

Perdition, but the man did not know when to leave a subject alone! "Are you going to tell me the moral of this tale, Mr. Chapel, or are you going to extend the anticipation for as long as you can?"

Again, he didn't look the least bit offended—a fact that irked her—but his expression was strained in the moonlight. "I was once as eager as you to learn the Grail's secrets. A man died as a result of my actions."

"Oh." No wonder he had spoken as he had. What she first understood as condescension now took on an entirely different meaning. What an utter *cow* she was.

Hesitantly, she reached out to him, her fingers falling on the solid crook of his elbow, just above the roll of his cuff. "Would you care to talk about it?"

His gaze dropped to her hand, so quickly and so intently that Pru imagined she could feel it burning her flesh. She did not release him, though. Instinct told her that he was like a wild animal and if she moved too quickly he might pounce.

Slowly, his gaze traveled up her arm, tingling her flesh as it moved ever closer to her face. Sensation rocked her as his eyes locked with hers. The glow she thought she had seen earlier had returned, lighting his eyes from deep within. It had to be a trick of the moonlight, because no one had eyes that bright, that beautiful. It was as though his gaze beckoned to her, pulled her closer. She could feel her body leaning toward him, her lungs struggling for air as he completely overwhelmed her.

His firm, sensuous lips parted, revealing a glimpse of startlingly white teeth. Were those his canines she saw glistening in the dark? No, they couldn't be—it was just a trick of the night.

"You aren't going to bite me again, are you?"

He jumped, jerking his arm from her grip. He shook his head as if to clear it. "What?"

Smiling at the knowledge that he had been— even if just for a second—as captivated by her as she by him, Pru held up her hand so that he could see the scratch on the back of it. "Are you not responsible for this?"

Eyes narrowed, Chapel studied her knuckles. "Responsible for what? There is nothing there."

Now it was Pru's turn to frown. Flipping her hand around, she lifted it toward her face, stopping when the moonlight stained her flesh. He was right. There was no mark. She tilted her knuckles to the light. Still nothing. The scratch had completed disappeared.

There was no way she could have imagined it, but how was it possible that it had healed so quickly? Unless it hadn't been a scratch at all, but merely a welt. But she could have sworn . . .

"It will be dawn soon." His voice sliced through her thoughts. He was watching the waning moon with a slight furrow in his brow. "We should return to the house."

Her hand forgotten, Pru grinned at his tone. "Still worried about my safety, Mr. Chapel?"

Chapel's gaze met hers. He obviously didn't share her amusement. "My own."

It was so difficult to gauge if he was jesting or not. "Too much safety can lead to regret," she informed him with mock sageness.

He tilted his head to one side. "As can recklessness."

He took himself far too seriously for one so young. She smiled at him. "Do you have many regrets, sir?"

A dry chuckle escaped him as he glanced down at the path beneath his feet. "It seems I've built my life on them at times."

She understood that. "Well, I refuse to do so any longer," she informed him, stifling the urge to poke the solid wall of his chest with her finger. "One regret I hope to not have when I die is that of never having truly lived."

His lips thinned, his expression almost bleak, as though he took her words to heart. "I hope that for you as well, Prudence."

Slightly stunned, not only by the sound of her name on his lips, but at the gravity of his tone, Pru stared as he presented her with his back and set off in the direction of the house.

He spoke as though he believed he might play some part in her demise, which was, of course, ridiculous. Yet she couldn't shake the feeling that she was in danger from him—not physical, but emotional. The conviction was in the way she felt his loss as he walked away, in the sadness she felt at the emptiness in his gaze.

And it was in the way, that just once, if only to see him smile and to bask in his praise, she wished she could live up to her name.

"Thank you for walking with me."

Chapel glanced at her as he quietly closed the door behind them, sealing them in the dark stillness of Rosecourt Manor. "It was my pleasure, Miss Ryland."

"Was it?"

Was she being coy or simply doubtful? "Have I given you reason to believe otherwise? I apologize if I have."

Her cheeks were flushed from exercise and the night breeze. The sweet scent of her blood hung around her like an expensive and exotic perfume. He wanted to bury his face in the curve of her neck and simply breathe her in.

"I fear I might have given you little choice but to follow me."

He shrugged. "One always has a choice."

Now her eyes were bright with mirth. "Even a gentleman?"

He smiled. "I cannot speak for gentlemen."

Her laughter, soft as it was, warmed him, made him want to laugh himself.

"Then I have not offended you?"

"My dear lady, of course not."

She regarded him for a moment, her head tilted thoughtfully to one side. "You know, Mr. Chapel, I believe you would actually tell me if I had offended you."

Such a short acquaintance and she was already beginning to know him. "I am afraid I have very few of the social graces. A defect due to my being out of society for so long."

Prudence nodded. "In that we are kindred spirits, I think."

She did not honestly think they were anything alike, did she? Why, she was everything light and airy and full of life, and he was darkness personified. Yet he did feel a certain connection with her, just as he was aware that she embodied everything out of his reach.

That was not good. Not good at all. It made her all the more tempting.

"Perhaps," was all he said in reply, but he gave her a smile so as not to offend her. "I should make my way back to my room. Thank you for the walk and the lively discussion, Miss Ryland. It has been too long since I have enjoyed the company of a woman who knows her mind as well as you."

She blushed under his praise, bringing an ache to his gums as well as other parts of his anatomy— his heart being one of them.

"I often go to bed just as the sun is rising," she admitted. "Perhaps we could walk again sometime."

That would be a big mistake, of that Chapel was certain. "No doubt we will."

He wished her a pleasant slumber as they walked up the stairs together—an action that was uncomfortably intimate—and then left her to return to his own room.

The sun was climbing into the sky when Chapel slipped between the cool sheets of his bed. Inside his sanctuary, it was dark as pitch, but nothing more than a set of heavy drapes and the bedding curtains stood between him and death.

A better man might walk out into the blistering sun and meet the fate he deserved like Dreux had, but Chapel was not eager to meet the damnation waiting for him. He'd rather take his chances on redemption, even if it took forever to claim it.

The God he trusted in was not so cruel that He would ignore Chapel's efforts. The vampire race had begun with Lilith, first wife of Adam and concubine of the fallen angel Sammael. Sammael had made his lover a demon queen, and she gave birth to the first of the vampires. Surely there could be no good in such origins, but he refused to believe that his soul could be completely lost. Molyneux constantly told them that while God had cursed the vampires to walk the night, He had also spared them, and that must mean that there was a plan, even for Chapel and his comrades.

The Blood Grail, that was what they called the cup that had turned Chapel and his friends into blood-drinking fiends, had been embued with the essence of Lilith as a punishment for her betrayal of Sammael. It was through Lilith that God discovered that his trusted angels on earth plotted against His human children. For her duplicity, Sammael cursed Lilith into thirty pieces of silver so that she might be passed from man to man as she deserved. Judas Iscariot was one of the men to whom that silver was passed.

The silver was forged into a chalice shortly after Judas's betrayal of Christ. No one knew when the Templars took possession of it, only that they had sought to hide it from the world.

Until Chapel drank from it, thinking it would save his life and then, seeing how it cured him and thinking it was the Holy Grail they'd found, his friends followed. They were all infected with Lilith's curse.

At first the power had been wonderful—addictive, even. That power had made him forget about Marie for a time. But then Dreux had killed himself, unable to stand the immortality—the *immorality*—any longer. That was when everything changed—for all of them.

When the five of them parted ways hundreds of years before, Temple assigned himself the task of protecting the Blood Grail. Tintagel, Cornwall—here where this hunt for the Holy Grail was taking place—was one of Temple's hiding spots, but not even Chapel knew the exact location.

He and Molyneux were there to investigate the expedition. If the true Grail was found, he was to claim it for the Holy Roman Empire. If it was the Blood Grail, he had to keep it from falling into hands that might abuse it and protect the humans from Temple, who might very well be in a feral-like state brought on from years of seclusion and lack of blood.

It was blood that kept the demon inside in check.

Without it, the demon became as demanding as a spoiled child, progressively getting worse until the vampire host lost all control and went on a murderous rampage. He had seen it happen once— when Dreux had tried to deny the bloodlust. It had taken all of Chapel's strength to subdue his friend.

Temple would rather die than harm anyone in such a fashion, Chapel knew that for a fact, but he might keep himself hungry in order to keep his senses sharp and his instincts keen—useful advantages if he was threatened by forces trying to take the cup. Not so beneficial to those who stumbled upon him. There was no way to predict how he might react to being discovered by a group of treasure-hunting humans.

Molyneux had convinced Chapel to come by claiming that he was the only one who could stand against Temple, and he was right. But who would protect the innocent from Chapel? Someone would get hurt if his own control failed. Not to mention the fact that someone was bound to notice that he was rarely around in the daytime and that he avoided the sun like the plague.

How long had it been since he had seen the sun, felt the warmth on his face? Long enough that he no longer missed it, but wondered about it like something never before experienced.

And now here was Prudence Ryland, as bright and warm as the sun ever dreamed of being. Just standing next to her was like raising his face to a midday July sky. The waves of hope radiating from her were as soothing as they were painful. A reminder of all that he had lost.

No, that was wrong. He hadn't lost his hope. His faith, perhaps, but not his hope. He had let the church poke and prod him, study and demean him. He even let them burn their brand into his flesh—a cross on his right shoulder. The hot silver had seared him like nothing before, and the holy symbol still burned and itched, the scar tissue pink and bright. It was the only mark he had kept since becoming a vampire. Had it done anything to save his soul? Doubtful.

His hope wasn't lost, it was buried, and somehow Prudence Ryland made that old grave seem much more shallow than it once was.

He was struck by the urge to protect her. When she had reached for him and asked if he wanted to talk about Dreux's death, he had felt a pain he'd never experienced before. It had been as though his heart had cracked in two. Why should she care about a stranger's pain?

He swore then that he would not allow Lilith's curse to corrupt her.

Not everyone cursed by the Blood Grail would be like Temple and Chapel—or even Bishop, for that matter. Others would see the curse as a way to further themselves, as Reign had. Or they would fully embrace the darkness inside them, as Saint had done. After all these years, it hurt to remember how his friend had turned his back on them all and left to enjoy what he had become.

Chapel did not want to embrace the darkness, even though it seemed to call to him from deep inside, urging him to give in to his true nature.

He did not want to be responsible for that darkness overtaking Prudence.

He didn't want to be responsible for anything at all, as he had told Molyneux before leaving France. The consequences were too great if he failed.

"If I kill anyone," Chapel had warned, crossing to the ancient wardrobe in the corner, "their blood will be on your hands."

The aged man shook his head with a dark expression. "*Non, mon ami.* Their blood will be on your lips, and not even God can absolve you of that."

Rage flooded Chapel's veins. His heart pumped with it—kicked off the dust and began to pound, heating his flesh, fanning his hunger. His fangs slid from the sheath of his gums, his eyes felt hot, his skin tingled. Lightning-fast, he pulled back his fist and slammed it through the wall of the cellar. He plowed through brick, mortar and hard-packed earth until he was buried to the shoulder.

Molyneux jumped to his feet, knocking over his chair. He stared at Chapel in horror and fear so genuine and great that Chapel could smell it, sweet as roses. As the rage slowly ebbed from his body, guilt took its place. Molyneux had never looked at him that way before—never.

Chapel extracted his aching arm from the wall with deliberate slowness. He didn't want to frighten his friend any more than he already had. He brushed dirt from the sleeve of his robe.

"Forgive me," he said, avoiding the other man's gaze. "I don't know what came over me."

From the corner of his eye he watched as Molyneux righted his chair, pushing it to the table. "I do. My blood doesn't strengthen you as it once did and you are frustrated because you have fought for so long and you have seen no reward."

"Is that what you think? That I need a reward?" He hadn't even wanted to think about the fact that Molyneux's blood might not be enough anymore.

"Perhaps you will find your salvation in England," Molyneux had suggested, his tone hopeful.

Chapel's smile was bitter on his lips as the memory of that conversation dulled with the onset of sleep. Perhaps Molyneux was right, but he suspected that the only thing waiting for him here in England was a temptation too great for him to resist.

Chapter 5

"Will Mr. Chapel not be joining us?" Prudence asked, slathering a warm roll with butter and jam.

It was late the next morning and Prudence, fresh from bed, had just sat down to enjoy a leisurely breakfast with Caroline, her father and Father Molyneux. Marcus would have been up and at the ruins hours earlier. Prudence would join him as soon as her meal was over.

"I am afraid not, Miss Ryland," Father Molyneux replied in his wonderful French accent.

Pru wasn't used to people not elaborating. "Is he hunting with the other gentlemen?"

Molyneux dabbed his mouth with the corner of his napkin. "He is abed, mam'selle. My young friend tends to slumber during the daylight hours."

"Bit of a city dandy, is he?" It was her father who asked, his tone jovial rather than mocking.

The priest smiled. *"Au contraire.* He has a rare affliction, contracted in the East, that makes him sensitive to the sun."

"Is it serious, Father?" Pru poured herself a cup of coffee and then topped up the priest's as well.

Father Molyneux saluted her with his coffee cup as he raised it to his lips. *"Merci."* He took a sip. "Chapel's condition is very serious indeed. In fact, the simple light of day could be fatal were the sun's rays to light upon his flesh."

Good Lord! Pru stared at the older man with all the horror she felt. And here she felt sorry for herself! She was much more of a night person, but at least she could go outside and feel the sunlight upon her cheek if she so desired.

Of course, she'd give that up if it meant her life, as Mr. Chapel had clearly done.

It was an odd affliction, but Prudence didn't question the story, even though Chapel looked surprisingly tanned for someone who rarely or never saw the sun. Why would a priest lie about such a thing, though? And to what end? Unless it was part of some plan on the church's part to steal the Grail away from her?

Now she was just being paranoid. Father Molyneux didn't act like someone with an agenda of his own. Perhaps Mr. Chapel merely had a naturally dark countenance just as she was naturally pale.

Prudence nibbled daintily on her bread. It and coffee would be her only breakfast this morning, though she normally had a more robust appetite. Even with her corset looser than usual around the abdomen, it was uncomfortable and confining as the monster inside her made its presence known. It made her sick just thinking about it.

She forced herself to take another bite. "Surely Mr. Chapel would be fine inside the house during the day?"

Crossing his legs, Father Molyneux seemed to contemplate the question. "*Oui*, he could be, but the room would have to be very dark to be comfortable. I am sure he would not expect you to take such measures for him."

"Nonsense," she replied before her father could. "He is our guest."

She decided she would go to the library right after breakfast and take Mr. Chapel some books on Tintagel and King Arthur. Her generosity had nothing to do with wanting to see the man again. Nothing.

Despite that claim, Pru's heart fluttered nervously behind her ribs as she gathered her stack of books half an hour later. They were heavy and awkward in her arms and the burden did nothing to ease the ache in her belly. She could ring for help, but then someone would know what she was doing—and the servants would gossip. No, she would much rather do this herself, despite any discomfort.

Leaving books behind was an option, but he deserved a good selection. Honestly, she wanted to impress him with the amount of reading material she could supply. He knew so much about the

Grail, enough to rhyme off key facts and rumors with bored ease, it was important to her to prove that her knowledge was vast as well.

Only she had a feeling that her knowledge wasn't nearly as vast as Chapel's. He spoke almost like he was reciting dates from experience rather than book-learning. It was impossible, of course, but it was a little daunting speaking to him on the subject.

Fortunately for Pru's arms and back, Chapel's room wasn't that far. She only had to stop once to rest. He was in the west wing in a room with north-facing windows overlooking the courtyard and the cliffs far beyond.

At least she hadn't put him in a room with direct exposure to the sun. That would be too awful. Of course, it would have been a complete accident, as Chapel had kept his condition secret. Male pride might be to blame, but she didn't flaunt her own illness either, so she wasn't about to pass judgment.

Discomfort grew with every step, the bowing of her back pulling painfully on her abdomen. She should have left books behind, that was her mistake of pride.

Finally, a little breathless and sore, she reached Chapel's door. Balancing her books on one hip, she raised her hand to knock.

Her knuckles rapped once before pain doubled her over with a cry. Books fell to the floor, their pages fluttering like wings trying to keep them from hitting the ground. One struck her toe, but the pain was insignificant compared to the knife in her belly. Gasping, Pru stumbled to her knees, her hands striking the carpet seconds later. Sweat beaded her brow and upper lip as lights danced before her eyes.

"Not . . . now," she gasped, supporting herself on one hand as the other went to her stomach. Oh, God, it hurt!

The door beside her opened. The pain was bad, but her embarrassment threatened to overshadow it. As she lifted her head, her breath came in a sharp gasp when she saw what loomed above her.

It was Chapel—or at least it *looked* like Chapel. The golden hair was mussed but familiar, as were the wrinkled linen shirt and black trousers, but the face . . . the face wasn't familiar at all. It was feral-looking and frightening, his eyes blazing gold fire as his lips pulled back in a snarl.

And then their gazes locked and there was nothing in his eyes but concern. Good Lord, the pain was causing her to hallucinate.

"Mon Dieu." His voice was little more than a hoarse whisper as he fell to his knees beside her, his hands reaching for her. "Prudence, are you hurt?"

"I fell," she gasped with a wince as the cancer's knife twisted again. "The books . . . they were too heavy and I . . . fell."

He was frowning, golden brows knitted. Whoever would have thought that a man could be so lovely when he frowned?

Oh, God, the pain was going to her head!

"Where does it hurt, *enfant*?"

He had a lovely accent too—not quite as heavy

as Father Molyneux's, and different—as though his speech were influenced by more than one culture.

"I'm not a child," she rasped, allowing him to draw her into the warm circle of his arms. She hated being fussed over, but it felt so nice to feel so safe.

Prudence didn't answer his question and Chapel didn't bother asking again. Sweet Jesus, when he thought of how close he had come to hurting her . . .

He hadn't expected anyone to knock on his door. By this time Father Molyneux should have told everyone about his strange "affliction," and that should have been enough to guarantee him privacy. He should have known that a woman who went strolling with him in her nightgown in the middle of the night would not be opposed to showing up at his door.

No, she hadn't just shown up. A quick glance at the books spread out around her filled in the rest of the story. They were all about Tintagel and Arthur. He didn't have to be a genius to know that she had hauled them to his room so he would have something to occupy himself.

So foolish and kind was little Prudence, and the sight of her in pain sliced at his heart.

He had woken up at the sound of her knock, the demon inside him instantly aware that it was day and that he was in danger. His feral, protective nature took over, instinct blocking everything else. He had been prepared to fight for his existence tooth and claw, but when he saw Prudence on her hands and knees before him, her expression one of such suffering, the demon had fallen as quiet and soft as a frightened child.

He swept her into his arms and stood, her weight insignificant against his own strength. She was so pale, her face dewy with pain. No mere fall was responsible for this.

"Where is your room?" He would take her somewhere comfortable and then he would ring for the servants.

"The east wing," she replied, her countenance strained. "Third on the left."

The hallway was blessedly dim as Chapel strode down it; the only windows were at the far end. Thankfully Prudence seemed too distressed to realize that he was walking faster than he should, or that he carried her as though she weighed no more than a kitten.

Luckily, Rosecourt, while a large estate, was nowhere as monstrous as some aristocratic houses, and the trip to the east wing was blessedly short. Chapel kept as close to the wall as possible to avoid the daylight filtering from the hall. It wasn't a bright day, but still he felt the heat on his face and hands that the clothed parts of him were spared.

The east wing was a copy of the west, and just as blessedly dim. Almost instantly his skin began to cool, stinging ever so slightly.

Why hadn't he rung for help from his own room? Why was he playing the hero and risking discovery this way? He was asking for trouble.

"Thank you." Pru's eyes were thickly lashed

slits as she gazed up at him. "It cannot be comfortable for you to be in the light."

What? Chapel's heart seized as though in a vise. How did she . . . ? Oh, of course. Molyneux had told her their lie.

"It is nothing." One more lie surely wouldn't hurt at this point, especially when it spared her guilt.

He stopped at the third door on the left side of the corridor, balancing Pru's weight with one arm as he reached for the handle.

Her eyes flew open. "Wait!"

Chapel froze. "What?"

Instead of pointing out that he was a freak of nature, she regarded him with a gaze that was equal parts fear and pain. "You cannot go in there."

He managed a smile. "I assure you, your virtue is safe with me, Miss Ryland."

Her lips curved slightly as he repeated her words from the night before. "That was not my concern, Mr. Chapel. My curtains are open. I would not have you suffer on my account."

Him suffer? She was practically gasping with pain and she was worried about him? God save him from this woman whose goodness dug at him like a needle beneath the skin.

"Put me down," Pru commanded softly. "I can make it to my bed on my own."

He scowled at her, opening the door as he did so. "Do not be ridiculous."

She struggled against him, a sparrow against a lion. "Chapel, please!"

It was the desperate way she said his name that stopped him. This wasn't just about his safety, this was about her needing—for some reason only she knew—to go into that room by herself, to stand on her own feet and defy her pain.

Why? What was wrong with her? This was no mere fall. Something had brought this on, and whatever it was angered her.

Well, he could relate to that. Slowly, carefully, he lowered her to her feet, keeping his hands on her shoulders until he was certain she could support herself. She was hunched but steady when he let her go.

"Do you need me to send for someone?" As much as he wanted to ask what afflicted her, he couldn't. It was none of his business, and probably not something she wanted to share.

And damn it, he didn't want to know. He already was beginning to realize that this incident might be related to the search for the Grail. "Desperate"—that was how she had described her quest. He didn't want to know what made her so desperate, because whatever it was, it was undoubtedly something he could not fix.

And he knew how desperation felt.

"I will be fine from here. Thank you." Her gaze was vulnerable as it touched his.

He merely nodded, watching as she slowly, painfully turned her back on him and pushed the heavy oak door open. Heat struck him as the full blast of the day raged against his presence in its domain. He recoiled as though shoved, stumbling back into the shadows as Pru, oblivious to him now that she was in her sanctuary, closed the door.

And then he was alone. Slowly, he straightened and began the journey back to his own room, moving at lightning speed through the open hall to avoid the sun's vengeance again.

He returned to the dark of his chamber with stinging flesh and a heart heavy with concern for the strange young woman who drew him in like a moth to flame, but was as distant and untouchable to him as the sun.

The laudanum Pru took for pain helped her sleep the rest of the day. Caroline insisted that she take dinner in her room and remain abed, even though it was the last thing Pru wanted. Marcus came up for tea in the evening and to update her on the day's progress. They met in her sitting room, of course. Caroline might encourage Pru to be improper, but she still abided by all the rules of decorum.

Even though Marcus was enthusiastic about how close they were coming to getting into the ruins, the highlight of Pru's evening was the single red rose that arrived at her beside in a slender crystal vase.

"It's from Mr. Chapel," Georgiana informed her the next morning, her attention seemingly on the perfect crimson bloom. "Why would he send such an offering?"

Warmth blossomed in Pru's chest. "Because he is a nice man?" It was the best she could offer in her weakened state. How she hated being weak.

At one time she could dance all night at a London ball and be ready for a picnic by noon the next day. Now she slept more than she danced and she couldn't remember the last time she'd been to a picnic that included more than just family.

"Hmm." Georgiana's hazel gaze was shrewd. "I wonder how he knew you were under the weather."

Only Georgiana could refer to a life-threatening illness as "under the weather." "He was there yesterday when the pain came upon me. He helped me to my room."

Georgiana nodded, her expression unreadable save for a slight smile. "Then I suppose he is a nice man after all. Now, how do you feel about getting out of this bed and enjoying the sunshine?".

Georgiana helped her dress and pin her hair. They took tea in the garden and when Pru said she'd like to go to the excavation site, Georgiana sent for a little buggy and drove Prudence there herself.

The excavation was located on a low hilltop near the cliffs. Tall grass waved in the breeze, dots of wildflowers swaying among the blades. The sun shone high overhead, lulling Pru into a sense of deep contentment as gulls cried in the distance. The surf lapped gently at the rocks below, flushing the air with the scent of salt and wet sand.

If there was a heaven, this was surely it, and it wasn't nearly so frightening as Pru sometimes thought.

The men digging stopped to don their shirts as the buggy approached.

"Blast," Georgiana remarked with her usual dryness, "I was so hoping to catch a glimpse of Marcus without his shirt."

Pru laughed. Her abdomen didn't even twinge—blessedly. The pain was gone today, but the effects of the laudanum lingered, making her mouth dry and her limbs heavy.

Marcus—clad in the lamented and grimy shirt—met them. His brow and cheeks were flush, streaked with smudges of dirt. His teeth flashed white in the tan of his boyish face.

"I hoped you would come today," he greeted, stripping off his gloves to help her down from the runner.

Those words were like wings to her heart. "Oh? Have you found something?"

Setting her on the ground, he flashed her another grin as he turned to assist Georgiana. "You'll see."

"Oh, I hate it when you do that!" But she laughed anyway. After yesterday's reminder of the perilousness of her life, she needed something to get excited over. Something to cling to.

He led them to a hole on the least-sloped side of the hill. The landscape was dotted with uncovered foundations and bits of stone. The structure that had stood here once before had been a series of smaller buildings surrounding a larger one.

Marcus stood grinning at the slanted opening. "I had a suspicion that this might be some kind of cellar, set off as it was."

That would explain why he approached from the side rather than straight on.

Pru climbed to the top of the hill and looked down into the hole the men had begun to expand. The wondrous sight that met her anxious gaze was definitely a stairwell—as old and crumbling as the rock might be, there was no mistaking it.

"An entrance," she breathed. She lifted her gaze to Marcus.

Her friend was practically beaming. "Yes. This could be the secret cellar where Arthur hoarded his most valuable possessions. If my calculations are correct, I hope to reach the door by the day after tomorrow."

So soon. *Oh, God, thank you.* Limbs trembling, Pru jumped at Marcus, all her joy rushing out of her in near-hysterical laughter. He caught her in his arms and swung her around as the diggers cheered. The moment he set her down, Pru was off thanking each of the men who were helping Marcus, shaking their hands and hugging them and not caring if it was proper or not. Georgiana, she noted, was not spared Marcus's enthusiasm either. He didn't swing her sister around, but he certainly swept her into one of his exuberant embraces. Georgiana didn't seem to mind one bit.

With the promise to celebrate that night at dinner—and with thoughts of planning a larger party in the near future—Pru returned to the house.

Father Molyneux was walking through the garden as Pru and Georgiana drove up from the site, so Pru bade her sister to stop and she went to join the priest as Georgiana continued on.

"Father!"

The older man waved in greeting, flashing her a genuine smile as she approached.

"Miss Ryland, how lovely you look this morning. I trust you are recovered from your earlier illness?"

Chapel must have told him. Oddly enough, that realization wasn't annoying so much as it was warming. The poor man must have really been concerned. She would have to thank him that evening.

"I have, Father. Thank you. May I walk with you?"

He looked genuinely delighted with the suggestion. "Of course. My friend Chapel has told me of the beauty of your roses. I thought to seek them out for myself. Perhaps you would do me the honor of showing them to me yourself?"

"But of course." She took his offered arm. She wondered if Chapel's experience with their roses was limited to having a servant cut one for him, or if he had sought out that perfect bloom himself. Most likely he had someone do it for him, but she rather preferred the image of him in the garden just after sunset, painstakingly searching in the dusk until he found the flower he wanted.

Truly, what woman wouldn't prefer the latter?

"I am so pleased to have found you," Pru told him as they walked. "I was at the site this morning and Marcus has uncovered a stairwell. He hopes to find an entrance to the cellar two days hence at the very latest."

"That soon?" Father Molyneux's expression was

one of astonishment. And there was something
else. Was it fear? How odd.

"Yes. Isn't that exciting?"

"Terribly." Pru wasn't so certain he meant that
in a good way either.

"Begging your pardon, Father, but you do not
seem as joyous as I expected."

He graced her with a soothing smile—one that
only men who were totally at peace with themselves could manage. "I assure you, my dear lady,
that if the Grail is in that cellar, my joy will know
no boundaries."

Now it all made sense. "You are not convinced
that we have found the right location."

He shook his head. "It is no slight against yourself or Mr. Grey, but I have witnessed many of
these excursions and the devastation their failure
brings."

There was something too shrewd and knowing
in his warm gaze. Pru glanced away from it. She
would not think of failure, not now.

"But this one might succeed." How she hated
that whine in her voice.

He patted her hand. "*Oui.* And for you I hope it
does. But I wish you to be cautious, Miss Ryland."

"Cautious? In what respect?"

"These places that have been hidden have often
been hidden for a reason. Do not enter it alone,
and please have myself or Chapel with you. I do
not wish to sound presumptuous, but he and I
know what traps to look for."

"Traps?" Marcus hadn't said anything about
traps or such dangers!

Her dismay must have been evident, because he patted her hand once more. "I'm sure Mr. Grey has done his research into these matters as well, but it would ease my old heart if the two of you would agree to take one of us inside with you."

It seemed a small request, and it wasn't as though Marcus and his men couldn't overpower the priest, or even Chapel, for that matter, if one of them decided to try stealing the Grail from them.

"I will discuss it with Mr. Grey, but I see no reason why you should not accompany us, Father."

He smiled at her, so sweet and serene it was difficult to suspect him of anything nefarious. "Thank you, my dear. Ah! I see we have reached your roses. *Quelle beauté!*"

He released her to move to the bushes, the joy on his face undeniable as he took in the array of color and blooms. Pru watched him with a smile, but her heart was troubled by the priest's warning.

Even more troubling was the realization that if there was any danger awaiting them in the cellar, the man Pru wanted there with her was Chapel.

"How is she?"

Father Molyneux paused in the act of brushing lint from the back of Chapel's evening jacket. For some reason the old priest seemed to take pleasure in acting like a valet—or a father.

"She seemed well, *mon ami.* Her spirits were high and I saw no sign of illness other than a bit of fatigue."

Tugging on his sleeves, Chapel nodded. "Good." But there was no denying that something had truly been wrong with Pru the day she collapsed in front of his door. People didn't experience pain like that for no reason.

An illness or affliction would certainly explain her quest for the Grail. For her sake, he hoped that was indeed what she found inside the cellar.

"What if they find the Holy Grail?"

Molyneux's gaze met his in the mirror. His smile was one of patience, the kind given to a curious—but mistaken—child. "The Grail is not there."

"How do you know?"

He shrugged. "I just know. Whatever they find in that cellar, it will not be the Cup of Christ. I only hope it will not be the Blood Grail either."

The idea of Prudence believing she had found the cup of life when really it was the cup of damnation was sickening.

"She must not be allowed to drink from it until we are certain."

Molyneux gave his coat one last swipe with the brush. "That goes without saying. It will be your eyes and memory that we trust; mine are not what they once were. You will recognize it, *oui*?"

Chapel stared at himself in the mirror. His countenance no longer unsettled him as much as it once did. This was the face that he had seen for centuries, and it was his.

"I will recognize it," he vowed. "As if I could ever forget it." Every crevice, every imperfection and tarnished inch of that cup was forever ingrained in his memory. His master, his curse, his bane, it was that chalice from which he had willfully drunk.

Molyneux tugged at the shoulders of Chapel's coat. The light black wool fit snugly, contrasting sharply with his crisp white shirt and wine-colored cravat. Six centuries ago he never would have dreamed of dressing this way.

"Miss Ryland believes they will uncover the door to the cellar within the next day or two. I believe a celebration is planned. We must be ready."

Chapel turned away from the mirror. "Hopefully I will be able to get inside the night before."

"Hope can have nothing to do with it." Molyneux's brow creased. "You must get in. We cannot risk Temple being found."

"I cannot sense his presence here."

"He may be preventing you from doing that as protection."

"I suppose." He knew it could be truth—and that it probably was—but he didn't want to think that Temple could shield himself so perfectly, not from him. He couldn't help but think that if Temple were in the area, he would somehow make himself known. Even if he was shielding himself, surely he could sense Chapel's presence?

A comforting hand clapped his shoulder. "I know you do not want to fight him, *mon ami*. I pray it does not come to that. Temple has sacrificed much to protect the False Grail. I would hate to have him sacrifice his very self as well."

Chapel glanced away. "Especially to me, of all people."

The fingers on his shoulder tightened. "It was not your fault. You did not force the others to drink."

"No." But he had foolishly taken the first drink and he had known the others would follow. They never allowed one of them to do something without taking the same chance themselves.

He would fight Temple if he had to, but only if it was the Blood Grail in the cellar. Despite Molyneux's thoughts, the treasure in that hillside just might be the one Pru sought.

He would keep hoping that, because he would much rather see triumph on Prudence Ryland's face than be forced to kill his oldest friend.

Chapter 6

Dinner was a painful affair. Chapel enjoyed every morsel of food, but it was the people around him who most appealed to his hunger, a fact that shamed him, given that he'd begun to know and like many of them. Molyneux had given him a vial of his blood just before dinner to pour into his wine, but Chapel hadn't a chance to do so just yet.

"How long have you lived in Paris, Mr. Chapel?"

It was Pru who asked. Molyneux was right about her looking healthy and well, for which he was thankful. Unfortunately, her presence at the time was the most disconcerting of them all as the sweet, warm scent of her made his fangs twitch.

About six centuries, give or take a few decades here

and there. He couldn't very well tell her that. "It seems I've lived there forever, Miss Ryland."

Her sister Matilda, who was there with her husband, smiled dreamily. She was a lovely woman with ginger hair, hazel eyes and a smattering of freckles across her nose.

"Frederick and I went to Paris last summer. I simply *adore* the cafés there. I got so fat!"

Everyone at the table laughed, so Chapel chuckled with them.

"You must find our little village very rustic compared to Paris, Mr. Chapel."

His gaze fasened on Pru once more. God, but she was a lovely little thing. A few weeks of eating too much cake and she'd be soft in his hands and melt on his tongue.

He *had* to get Molyneux's vial into his wine, otherwise he was going to start slathering like a damn dog—or worse, a werewolf, disgusting creatures.

"I find this place very charming, Miss Ryland. Forgive me, I seem to have dropped my napkin."

Under the guise of retrieving the pristine linen from the carpet, he thumbed the top off the vial Molyneux had given him and swallowed the contents in one quick gulp. The vial then very quickly went back inside his jacket before he straightened in his seat.

No one was watching him, an oddity that came as a bit of a shock. Both he and Molyneux had been treated as curiosities since their arrival and it was a welcome reprieve to discover that their novelty was finally wearing off.

It also gave him a chance to do some watching of his own.

Prudence was seated across the table from him, three chairs to his right. Her vibrant hair was styled in an elegant twist, leaving the sculpted lines of her face open to his appreciative gaze. The soft light and the rich violet of her gown lent a rosy hue to her cheeks and a bright gleam to her hazel eyes. Certainly he must have seen women just as lovely in the course of his long, long existence, but he couldn't remember for the life of him.

"Mr. Chapel?"

It was Prudence's father who spoke. Damn. He probably wanted to roast him for staring at his daughter like a dog after a bone.

"Yes, sir?"

Thomas Ryland made a face. "Please, call me by my first name. 'Sir' makes me think of the headmaster at my old school and I couldn't stand the man."

Chapel smiled—he'd been doing a lot of that the past few days. "Fair enough, but only if you'll call me Chapel."

"I have been meaning to ask you about that, Mr. Chapel." Prudence raised her wine to her already delicately stained lips.

He arched a brow. "About my name?"

She dabbed at her lips with her napkin. "Yes. Forgive my impertinence, but how is it that you came to be simply 'Chapel'?"

All eyes were on him once more, as though

everyone wished to ask the same question. Everyone save Molyneux, that is.

"It would be an honor to assuage your curiosity, Miss Ryland. I was a foundling, discovered on the chapel steps, and so named by the good fathers who took over my care." It wasn't a lie; he simply chose to leave out that he was a full-grown man at the time and that centuries had passed since that day.

Both Caroline and Matilda looked sorry for him, and a little uncomfortable, no doubt because they now believed him an unwanted bastard. It was preferable to the truth, however, so he could tolerate their pity.

Prudence, on the other hand, simply smiled, turning her attention to Molyneux. "And were you one of those who raised him, Father?"

Now, there was a question that might have been cause for laughter in different company. If either of them had watched the other grow into a man, it had been Chapel watching Molyneux.

"Yes," the priest answered, a twinkle in his eye as he grinned at Chapel. "But I take credit for his virtues only, Miss Ryland."

That wicked hazel gaze came back to Chapel. "Oh-ho, that implies that you have vices, Mr. Chapel. Surely Father Molyneux would not mislead us on that account?"

Chapel sipped his wine. "The good Father would mislead you in any way that might cause me discomfort, Miss Ryland, just as any family member would to another."

All four of the Ryland sisters laughed at that, and began recounting just such stories about one another, which thankfully took attention from Chapel once more. He was not accustomed to such scrutiny. His facade of humanity might not hold up under much more intense study.

During dessert Thomas offered both Chapel and Molyneux full use of his library for their personal and professional use. Chapel didn't bother to tell him that Prudence had already given him a great many books to peruse. That an unmarried lady had gone alone to his room was not something a gentleman announced at dinner.

It wasn't something a *gentleman* announced at any time.

After dessert, just when Chapel thought he might escape the confines of the house for some fresh air, free of the rich scent of human life, Marcus Grey approached him.

The man was young, handsome, mortal and spent a lot of time in Pru's company. There was very little reason for Chapel to like him, and yet there was very little reason for him to despise the man either, save for the fact that Chapel would like to be him, if even just for one day. *Day* being the key factor.

"Mr. Chapel." The young man's voice was low and oddly respectful. "I understand from Miss Ryland that you have a fair bit of knowledge about the Grail."

"I have a bit." So Pru had been talking about him, had she?

"What would you consider your era of expertise?"

"Medieval lore." It was the first response that came to mind.

"Would you happen to know much about the Knights Templar and their expulsion from France?"

If he drew breath like a normal person, Chapel would have choked on it. Did he know anything? Did actually being there count? Of course, he couldn't tell Mr. Grey that he had been one of King Philip's soldiers.

"Uh, yes. I do know about the Templars."

Blue eyes brightened and cheeks flushed with interest. Chapel could smell the warm blood coursing through the boy as his heart picked up an excited pace. His gums ached. He was in no way sexually attracted to this man, but the demon inside him didn't have a gender preference when it came to food.

"Perhaps we could discuss the Templars sometime during your stay."

Chapel nodded. He'd have to make sure he was well fed first. "I would enjoy that." Provided he didn't reveal too much information that he couldn't explain knowing.

As he stepped forward to leave, the young man stopped him with a hand on his arm. Chapel stared at the bronzed fingers against the black of his coat. This young man didn't have the hands of a scholar, but the callused, dirty hands of a warrior. The sight made Chapel remember a time when his hands had looked the same, when his sword and his friends had been all he needed.

His gaze must have unnerved Mr. Grey, for he released his grip cautiously and edged away, as one might from a wild dog. Chapel looked up—against his better judgment—and met the young man's questioning gaze.

"Was there something else, Mr. Grey?"

It wasn't fear reflected in the blue eyes, it was intrigue and curiosity. To be honest, it was as worrisome as it was refreshing.

"Miss Ryland tells me that you are more of a night person, Mr. Chapel. Should you like to tour the dig site, I would be happy to take you there at dusk some evening so that you might view our progress."

Was Marcus Grey extremely polite or extremely stupid? Either way, Chapel had to struggle for a reply. "Thank you. I would like that very much."

He would have to take Molyneux with him—someone who would stake him if he went for Marcus's throat. The young man didn't know how naturally he offered himself.

Or perhaps he did.

Marcus's voice stopped him as he made to turn away once more. "Would you happen to know anything of a band of mercenaries sent by King Philip to find the Holy Grail during a raid on the Templars?"

Surprise and pain gutted him. Images slammed into his mind before he could guard against them—images of the six of them, so brash and full of life. So cocksure and stupid.

"Yes," he rasped, hating the sound. "I know of them." The question was, how the hell did Marcus Grey know about them?

Footsteps sounded behind him. Mr. Grey was coming closer—oh, the boy was so very foolish. Chapel did not turn around. He should have, but he knew he would not look right to Marcus Grey if he did.

"Do you know anything about a man named Dreux Beauvrai?"

Chapel closed his eyes. A familiar tightening took hold in his chest as Dreux's face swam in his mind. Did he know of him? Bitter laughter threatened to spill forth. God, yes.

This time he did turn, schooling his face as best he could. "I know something of him, yes."

Marcus's face brightened. "Then I would very much like for us to talk. Researching these mercenaries, especially Beauvrai, has become something of an obsession for me."

Was this just a coincidence, or something darker? Or was it God's way of torturing him? Molyneux would suggest that perhaps it was a way for Chapel to exorcise his demons, but Chapel knew better. There would be no release for him, not just yet.

"Of course. If I can give you any new information, it would be my pleasure to do so. Now, if you would excuse me?"

Grey looked a little abashed. "Of course. My apologies for keeping you."

Somehow, Chapel managed a smile. "None necessary. Good evening Mr. Grey."

Leaving the young man behind, Chapel slipped outside through a set of doors off the dining room and found himself alone on a small terrace that led out into the garden.

It was quiet out here, the air scented with sea and sand, animals and flowers. He lit a cigarette to cover the remaining human fragrance in his nostrils.

This was more difficult than he ever could have imagined. God must be testing him indeed.

A slight sound behind him snapped his attention. Then a sense of the known swept over him. *Molyneux.*

"*Mon ami,* are you all right?"

Chapel shrugged. No, he wasn't all right. His fangs had extended enough to prick the inside of his lower lip and he could feel the hunger gnawing at his insides.

Molyneux came up beside him. Chapel sensed rather than saw his friend open his hand. He looked down.

Molyneux offered him a small bottle. Chapel knew instantly what was in it, even though it was bigger than the normal vials he supplied.

"This is very hard on your control, *non*?"

"*Oui.*" His hand trembled slightly as Chapel reached for the bottle. As his fingers closed around it, something overtook him.

No, not something. *The* thing. Clenching the bottle, he turned on the priest with preternatural swiftness, catching Molyneux by the shoulders and forcing him into the shadows, pinning him against the warm stone of the house.

The priest's eyes widened. "Chapel, what are you doing?"

"You tempt me with vials and bottles." Chapel shook the bottle in the old man's face. "You knew how this would be for me, didn't you, old man? You brought me here. The safety of all in this house rests upon your withered shoulders. The least you could do is open a vein for me—or better yet, let me open it for you."

Saliva pooled on his tongue, anticipation tingled in his jaws.

Molyneux met his gaze, and Chapel could see the fire in his own eyes reflected back at him. "I am sorry for your suffering, Chapel, but you do not want to do this."

"Don't I?" Chapel laughed, low and dark. "Oh, but I do. You know I do."

"You are not a monster. You are not a killer."

"Killer? I don't want to kill you, Molyneux. I just want more than you've been giving me, you little tease." He was losing control, and it felt so *right*. "I want what you've denied me."

"I have never denied you anything. It was your decision to stop feeding on humans. Your choice. You made a vow. Do you want to go back on that now, when we have more important matters to attend to?"

Chapel trembled with the effort to keep himself from plunging his fangs into Molyneux's neck. He would kill him if he drank, he knew that. It had been too long and he wouldn't be able to stop. It would take a whole group to slake his thirst—like the Rylands' dinner guests.

Prudence. The thought of her should have sent him into a frenzy, but instead it sent a chilling wave through him, tamping the demon down enough for him to take hold of himself. He could not hurt anyone who meant anything to Pru. He could not hurt her. He did not want her to know what he was. He didn't want any of them to know, but especially Pru. It didn't matter why, he simply clung to that knowledge and forced himself within.

Slowly, he released Molyneux, smoothing from his friend's jacket the wrinkles he had wrought and turning away. He removed the stopper from the bottle and downed the contents in one gulp. It eased the hunger and quieted the demand for more.

"I am so sorry," he spoke over his shoulder.

"As am I. I had no idea it would be this difficult for you."

Chapel chuckled. "I did."

Silence stretched between them as Molyneux slowly approached. The old priest was nothing if not brave. "Perhaps we have gone about this all wrong, my friend."

"What do you mean?"

"Perhaps feeding off humans is the only way to keep yourself under control."

"But it's a sin. You know that."

"Not if you don't kill them. And there are so many people out there who are not innocent—killers, thieves . . ."

Chapel smirked. "Protestants?"

Father Molyneux pursed his lips. "You know what I mean."

"I do, and I appreciate the sentiment, but sin is sin, old friend."

"Perhaps it is not a sin. Perhaps it is the only way for you to retain your humanity. Perhaps your powers are divine, not evil."

"Are you drunk? What the devil are you talking about?"

"You are as He intended. Neither of us can presume to know His plan, but perhaps if human blood gives you strength, then you are meant to have it."

"You're mad." The words were spoken to Molyneux's back, as the priest had already started back toward the doors of the house.

Molyneux paused long enough to grace him with a fatherly smile. "No, I am old. I've had many years to come to this conclusion. Perhaps you would too if you would just stop nailing yourself to a cross long enough to consider it."

And Chapel was left alone to ponder those shocking words—and he was so shocked, he hadn't even noticed that his cigarette had burned down to his fingers until he smelled his flesh start to burn.

Marcus rushed up to his room immediately after leaving Chapel. His mind and heart raced as he closed the door behind him.

Inside the privacy of his private quarters at Rosecourt, he unlocked one of the portmanteaus inside his wardrobe and withdrew a packet of private papers.

Heart pounding in anticipation, he rifled through the pages until he found what he was looking for—a letter from a member of a secret and modern branch of the Knights Templar who held close ties to the occult. The letter was part of the package they had used to seduce him into working for them, into helping their cause.

They were the ones who had confirmed many of his theories concerning the excavation and the history behind it. They had given him so much information about Dreux Beauvrai—his ancestor. They had confirmed the rumors that Dreux had become—of all things—a vampire simply by drinking from a cup known as the Blood Grail, which they had stolen from the Templars.

And the Templars—or Order of the Silver Palm, as they preferred to be called—wanted the Blood Grail back.

The order suspected that it might be the Blood Grail hidden in the ruins near Rosecourt. Marcus wasn't sure what he believed, but for Pru's sake, he hoped the order was wrong. Still, the Templars had promised him information for his trouble, and they had seduced him into compliance with the letter his trembling fingers now pulled from the sheaf of papers.

There, scrawled before his eyes on a piece of well-handled vellum, was a list of the men who had been part of King Philip's mercenary group along with Dreux Beauvrai. The list also contained several aliases the men—or vampires—were said to have used.

"Good God." He found what he was looking for among the black ink. In one heart-stopping moment, what seemed at first like a foolish notion was confirmed. The suspicions he'd formed not even half an hour before were now certainty.

Still, he read it one more time just to be certain his eyes weren't deceiving him. They weren't.

Severian de Foncé.

Also known as *Chapel*.

Chapter 7

"I hope I'm not interrupting."

Chapel looked up from his book. It was later that evening; he hadn't expected to see her again. Pru stood in the doorway, her loveliness highlighted by the soft lights and the low strains of a ballad coming from the phonograph in the corner. "Not at all."

He had been lounging on the chaise but sat up as she entered the room, his book set aside and forgotten as the warm scent of her enveloped his senses. She invoked his hunger, but it was back under his tight control. What he seemed to have less control of was his body's response to her.

She was more properly dressed than she had been the first night he had encountered her in this very library, clad as she was in the same violet gown she had worn to dinner. The tight bodice thrust the perfect swells of her breasts high on her chest and accented her small waist. Breastbones and collarbones stood out sharper than they should. So delicate, so fragile.

He had seen her eat at dinner and knew that she did not starve herself. Perhaps she was just naturally thin.

Or perhaps illness had caused her to lose weight.

"I never had a chance to inquire after your health, Miss Ryland. I trust you are recovered from your ordeal?"

She blushed as she approached him, stopping a few feet away to seat herself on a nearby chair. "I thought you agreed to call me Pru. And I am quite well, thank you. I am indebted to you for your assistance that morning."

He smiled. "Well, I couldn't very well leave you there, could I?"

Pru's lips lifted lopsidedly. "You could have, especially when seeing me to my room risked your own well-being."

"It was a risk I took willingly and would again."

Her face pinkened, a sweet flush of blood to her delicate cheek. "Thank you."

He'd risk more than just a sliver of sunlight for that sweet smile of hers. What a siren she was, a tantalizing slip of seductive innocence. Molyneux had suggested that he needed to drink human blood more often, but the idea of marring Pru's flawless flesh, of puncturing her and violating the purity of her throat, was distasteful, no matter how much he longed to do just that.

A knock at the door signaled the arrival of a maid bearing a tray with a pot, two cups and an assortment of finger foods on it.

"I hope you do not mind," Pru said to him, "but I thought you might desire some refreshment."

Yes, he did, just not the kind she thought. "Thank you. That was very considerate of you."

She preened under his praise. It was somewhat sad that such a simple statement pleased her so.

They drank their tea and ate with pleasant small talk between them.

"How long have you known Mr. Grey?" he asked, trying to keep his tone disinterested as he finished the last of his tea.

"Oh, about a year?" She shrugged. "Sometimes it seems I've known him forever, he has become such a fixture in my life."

He envied Marcus Grey, the little bastard. "You must be very close."

She eyed him suspiciously—like a woman who knew jealousy when she heard it. "He's like a brother to me."

Christ, he was actually blushing. Was he that transparent? Flirtation was his only savior. "We all should be blessed with such sisters."

Pru chuckled and peered into his now-empty cup. "Would you like for me to read your tea leaves?"

That was a question he hadn't expected. "You can do that?" It wasn't exactly an aristocratic pastime, at least not in his experience.

She nodded. "My governess taught me. I find it helpful when I want to know more about a person."

"You may find there are things about me better left unknown."

She made a *tsk*ing sound as she picked up his cup. "How maudlin. You make yourself sound very dramatic, Chapel, but I've a feeling you're not nearly as dark as you like to pretend."

Chapel laughed—a bark of sound. She had certainly put him in his place! If only she were right.

"Go ahead." Even if there was something dark there, Pru wasn't likely to interpret it as truly sinister. He gestured easily toward the cup as he leaned back against the chaise, crossing an ankle over his knee. "I've never had this done before and I am eager to hear what the leaves have to say about me."

Her eyes widened. "Really, you've never had your leaves read before?"

"I've never had my fortune told in any way."

"Why not?"

"Perhaps because I'm not often in the company of hum—people."

"Were you going to say 'humans'?"

"Humanity. Forgive me, sometimes my English is not that good."

She seemed to believe that, for which he was grateful. She handed him the cup upside down on the saucer and told him to turn it three times counterclockwise while making a wish. He did as he was told. He wished for salvation, no big surprise there. Then he handed the cup back to Pru.

She lifted it and peered inside. "Well, your wish is very close to the top."

"What does that mean?"

"It means you're going to get it—relatively soon." She frowned. "There's a woman attached to it."

"A woman?"

His shock must have been audible, for Pru raised her head and smiled at him. "Yes, a woman. One of those people with whom you do not often associate."

Cheeky wench. "Can you tell who it is?"

Color burned up her cheeks as she stared into the cup. Slowly, hesitantly, her gaze lifted to his. "I may be impertinent, but I feel that it is me. Can you think of any way that I might be attached to your wish?"

Chapel's heart pinched. He could ask that same question. "Because I wished for you to find the Grail." It was a lame lie, and one he shouldn't have uttered, for he saw hope flare in her eyes.

"Thank you," she murmured.

Their gazes locked and time seemed to stop. Her guileless stare drew him in, surrounding him with the suffocating desperation of her hope and fears. Whatever drove her to find the Grail, it drove her relentlessly.

He knew her need. He understood the obsession of chasing something just out of reach. He didn't know why the Grail meant so much to her, and in truth he didn't want to know. What he wanted was to take her into his arms and kiss those rosy lips. He wanted to taste her, feel her lithe body shiver against his. He wanted to possess her in every way he could: body, blood and soul.

Their faces were just inches apart when she jumped to her feet like a frightened rabbit.

"I should go." Her voice trembled with desire. Her scent was rife with it. She wanted him too—and she would allow him to possess her. She would possess him in return.

"Yes." He looked up at her, and the uncertainty on her face. "You should. Unless, of course, you want me to kiss you."

She hesitated and the demon inside leapt. Chapel came to his feet fast—so fast, Pru started.

"Go," he growled. "Go now." If she didn't, he wouldn't be able to stop himself. He would kiss her. He would claim her. He would bite her. Molyneux might think that feeding from humans was his true nature, but that didn't mean he had to give in to it.

Not yet.

She pivoted on her heel and ran to the door, where she paused long enough to glance over her shoulder at him. And then she did the damnedest thing. Impertinent indeed, for she flashed him a shy but undeniably arousing grin before puckering those ripe lips and blowing a kiss to him. And from the way the breath was knocked out of him, Chapel knew he had caught it.

She should have let him kiss her.

She should have said to hell with her fear and allowed herself the pleasure of his lips on hers. It was what she had wanted—what he had wanted as well.

Why, when her life was going to be so painfully short, did she not seize the moment? Why had she been so terribly afraid of a simple kiss?

Because of the suspicion that nothing with Chapel was simple. He was a complicated man, and getting involved with him would only complicate her own life further.

She wanted to experience life and love. Yet at the same time she knew it would be just as painful as it would be wonderful to fall in love. It would not be so wonderful, however, for the person who fell in love with her. Selfish as she might be, she didn't want to hurt Chapel.

Chapel didn't know that she was sick. He might have suspicions, after her collapse at his door, but there was no way he could know that she was dying. It wasn't fair to him to offer any kind of relationship while he was blind to the truth.

So she had two choices: tell him she was dying and see if he still wanted anything to do with her, or keep silent and stay away.

Actually, there was a third choice. She could keep silent and take whatever he offered her, but that was a selfish choice and one she could not make in good conscience.

Why was he the one who drew her to him, who made her want to be bold? He made her wish for more time, made her desperation to find the Grail all the more oppressive. She wanted to know everything about him.

And yes, she wanted him. No man had ever

made her want to break society's rules like Chapel did. Not even when she was younger and new to the *ton* had a man turned her head like this.

It was as though he understood what drove her, even though there was no way he could.

"All right, I demand to know what it is you're thinking about."

Prudence looked up, straight into the questioning gaze of her sister Caroline. Georgiana and Matilida were watching her as well. It was just the four of them around the breakfast table, as they had decided to break their fast in the small sitting room this morning. Everyone else had already eaten and it gave the sisters some time alone together—a habit Pru relished.

"Is it Marcus Grey who has your thoughts?" Georgiana teased.

Matilda smirked. "Or the mysterious Mr. Chapel?"

Caroline rolled her eyes. "That leaves me to inquire after Father Molyneux. Why must it be a man that has her so quiet?"

"Because," Matilda muttered, "nothing ever makes *her* quiet."

The look Caroline shot their sister could only be described as annoyed. Her attention came back to Prudence. "Are you unwell this morning, dearest?"

That, of course, brought an expression of contrition to Matilda's fair countenance. Pru sighed.

"I am fine. Mattie, don't you dare feel guilty. If the three of you must know, yes, I was thinking of Mr. Chapel. Satisfied?"

Georgiana obviously wasn't. "Not Mr. Grey? You are daft, my dear, daft."

Matilda scowled at her. "Mr. Chapel is extremely handsome. And he has that air of intrigue about him."

"Just what you want in a man." Sarcasm dripped from Georgiana's tone. "Besides, he's *blond*." She made it sound like a curse.

"Dig out your pitchforks," Matilda replied with equal dryness.

"He almost kissed me last night," Pru blurted.

That brought an end to her sisters' bickering. One by one, they turned their heads to stare at her—at the one they sometimes still referred to as "the baby."

"He what?"

"You were alone with him?"

"You didn't let him?"

The questions came at her so quickly, Pru wasn't quite sure who asked what, although she was pretty sure it was Matilda who expressed shock at her denying Chapel.

She had to admit that the more she thought about it, the more she questioned her own sanity as well. To think she could have felt those lovely lips against her own. . . .

"We were in the library last night. We had tea. I read his leaves." She didn't mention seeing herself in his cup. That would give her sisters far too much to speculate on, and give herself hope where there was none.

"He tried to kiss you for reading his leaves?"

Georgiana chuckled and cast a glance at Matilda. "Must have been some reading!"

Matilda ignored her. "As much as I find Mr. Chapel . . . interesting, you know it is not good for you to be alone with him. It isn't proper."

Pru's brow creased. "Proper? The three of you have been trying to throw me at any man you can for the last six months, and *now* you want to lecture me on propriety?"

Matilda shrugged, but she didn't meet Pru's gaze. "The gentlemen we chose for you were not quite so intimidating as Mr. Chapel."

Intimidating? Yes, she supposed Chapel could be a little overwhelming. She was wary of him on occasion as well, but she was comforted by the power of his presence now too.

"When you say he tried to kiss you, do you mean he tried to force himself on you, dear?"

Pru reached across to pat Matilda's leg. The action seemed to ease the worried lines of her sister's face. "Not at all. He was a perfect gentleman." For the most part, anyway. A perfect gentleman wouldn't have tried to kiss her at all.

"How disappointing." Georgiana sighed. "Perhaps he isn't as dangerous as I thought."

Pru stared at her. "Will you make up your mind? First you are all offended thinking he tried to force himself on me, and then you seem disappointed that he didn't."

Georgiana feigned a look of indignation. "My dear Lord, I am certainly not disappointed that he didn't try to force himself on you. You are my baby sister. I'm disappointed he hasn't tried to force himself on me."

Georgie's naughty grin filled the room with laughter. The four of them were still laughing when a knock sounded on the door and Marcus stuck his head inside. He was covered in dirt and the look on his face brought a heavy weight into Pru's stomach.

"What is it, Marcus?" Her voice shook ever so slightly.

"There was a cave-in during the night. At the dig site."

Chapter 8

The moon was a bright silver ball high in the sky when Chapel approached Pru's dig site. Despite the lack of ambient light, he could see perfectly.

The night was his time to thrive and he felt the difference between darkness and day as acutely as the difference between sand and silk. As much as he sometimes wished he could feel the warmth of the sun again, he could not imagine ever giving up the joy of the night to do so.

It was like the difference between kissing Pru and being denied the pleasure. And that was one difference of which he was keenly aware.

He was also aware of the man standing beside a mound of rock on the crest of the hill. Even without his scent on the breeze, Chapel recognized him as Marcus Grey. For some reason he felt a kinship with this young man, despite his uncomfortable curiosity.

Marcus Grey was no threat to him. Few mortal men were. But Marcus might be a threat to Pru, and for that reason Chapel could not trust him completely.

If Grey betrayed Pru, it wouldn't matter that he meant something to her. Chapel would kill him.

"You have put in a long day, Mr. Grey."

The young man's head jerked up. He looked tired, and disappointed. "Mr. Chapel. Yes, it has been a long day."

Chapel climbed the hill to stand at his side. He looked into the hole and saw the rocks piled there. He frowned.

"That does not look like an accident."

Marcus glanced at him, not the least bit surprised. "It wasn't. I do not know for certain who did it, but it appears that someone decided that the entrance to this cellar should not be uncovered."

Had that person been Temple? Yes, Chapel could feel his friend there. The feeling was faint, so Temple was either masking himself or had already moved on. He prayed it was the latter.

"Yet you intend to uncover it regardless." The young man was either incredibly brave or incredibly stupid.

There was a pause, then a decisive nod. "Yes."

"There are those who would suggest you not tempt fate, Mr. Grey."

Marcus nailed him with a dark blue gaze that was almost black in the darkness. "Would you like to be the one to tell Prudence that we should give up?"

No. He wouldn't. In fact, he would prefer to face Temple rather than that. "Why is this so important to her?"

"You will have to ask her that." Marcus turned his attention back to the hole. His shoulders slumped. "She hasn't given me leave to share that information."

Fair enough. If Grey held Pru's secrets this dear, perhaps he would hold Chapel's as close as well. "Why is it so important to *you*?"

Hands in his pockets, Marcus made his way down the hill to a small buggy. "May I offer you a ride, Mr. Chapel?"

Truthfully, Chapel could make it back to the house faster on his own, but he wanted to hear Grey's story, so he accepted his offer and joined him on the padded seat. A flick of the reins and the two bay horses drew the conveyance into motion.

He didn't have to wait long for Grey to speak. "Remember I asked you if you knew about Dreux Beauvrai?"

"*Ah, oui,* one of your mercenaries."

Was it his imagination, or did Grey shoot him an amused glance? It was enough to send a shiver of apprehension down Chapel's spine. There was no way Grey could know about his link to Dreux.

"Yes. Beauvrai was one of Philip's mercenaries. He was also a direct ancestor of mine."

The information hit like a brick to the gut. Dreux's blood ran in this man's veins. Here, beside him, was a living, breathing part of his long-departed friend.

No wonder he felt a kinship with him. Dreux's scent would be faint on him, but it was there—low enough that he couldn't identify it, but strong enough that it appealed to a part of him.

Dreux never knew his son. He was born after Dreux became a vampire, and Dreux, having seen the consequences of Chapel's return to Marie, allowed his wife to believe him dead.

If Dreux hadn't killed himself, he might have been here to meet this young man. Would family not have been a reason to go on?

Not for Dreux, no.

Aware that he had been silent too long, Chapel cleared his throat. "Is that why you hunt the Grail, because your ancestor did?"

"No." Marcus spared him the slightest of glances as he focused on the buggy path ahead. "Because I think he found it. Or at least what he *thought* was the Holy Grail."

The churning in Chapel's gut worsened. "What do you mean?"

"There is some dispute among my research sources as to just what Beauvrai and his companions found during their plunder of the Templar base." Marcus shot him another glance, as though he were hoping Chapel might have something to add. Chapel remained silent. "Some believe it was the Holy Grail. Others believe it was an artifact of dark power."

Oh. God. Chapel's fingers gripped the seat, biting into the bench so hard that the polished wood groaned. "Is that what you hope to find, this dark object?"

"It doesn't matter, not to me. For Pru's sake, I hope to find the Holy Grail, but that is not the true treasure I expect to find in that cellar."

That he hadn't said he wanted the Blood Grail was the only thing keeping Grey alive at this moment. It would not be a task Chapel relished, but if he had to, he would kill to keep the Grail out of the wrong hands—it was why he was there. Even if if meant killing one of Dreux's blood, he would do it.

"And what treasure do you hope to find?" His tone was even, calm, nothing in it belying his panic.

"I believe there is something in that cellar that will tell me what really happened to Dreux Beauvrai and his companions."

"You talk as though you believe there to be some great mystery. They all died shortly after the Templar raid." It came out more hotly than he intended.

Grey shook his head. "I have reason to believe that they did not die. I have documents—written accounts that Beauvrai was spotted *alive* after he was supposed to have died. There is even a story in my family that he went to the funeral of his firstborn and was spotted by his widow. She supposedly fainted at the sight of him."

She had. Sweet Jesus, she had. How did Grey know this? "Really, Mr. Grey." He forced a chuckle. "Such tales. Are you sure you are not related to Bram Stoker?"

"You believe in something as fantastic as the Holy Grail, but not in vampires, Mr. Chapel? I'd thought you a man open to the possibilities of those things which we cannot prove."

Vampires. Grey had actually said it aloud.

"I have traveled extensively, Mr. Grey. I have seen a great many things, but I have seen no evidence that can prove the existence of Dracula or his kind." That wasn't a lie. He hadn't *seen* any evidence. He was evidence.

"What do you know of Severian de Foncé?"

Chapel's heart fell to his stomach. "He was one of Beauvrai's companions."

"There are accounts that he became a vampire as well. Supposedly he killed his own fiancée."

Closing his eyes against the pain that he knew would glow there like a beacon, Chapel drew his strength. He would not think of Marie. He would not.

"De Foncé is dead." It was a low growl, uttered from between clenched teeth. "I have seen his grave for myself."

"Yes," Grey replied. "I would imagine you have."

What the hell? Chapel stared at him.

Grey's eyes left the dark path ahead for but a

split second. "Being the historian that you are, I mean."

That wasn't it at all. Regardless, Marcus Grey was no threat to him—not physically. Perhaps it was time for this young man to realize what he was up against.

"If you believe these legends, Mr. Grey, then you must know that whatever it is you seek may very well be guarded by one of these vampires."

"One of these vampires is exactly what I'm hoping to find, Mr. Chapel."

"You have no more sense than a squirrel. No, less." He could not keep the anger from his voice. "If you do find one of these vampires of yours in that cellar, he will not be happy to see you, do you understand?"

Marcus nodded. "I know. Isn't that why the church sent you and Father Molyneux?"

Chapel's eyes closed in resignation. "How much do you know?"

The buggy stopped and Marcus turned in his seat to face him, his boyish features highlighted and shadowed by the lantern on the front of the carriage.

"I know that the church suspects there is something in that cellar as well. Which one do you think it is? Bishop, Saint?"

"You do not know enough, then. Were what you are suggesting possible, it would not be them." Then he realized his fatal error.

Marcus Grey knew the names the church had

given them, and now he knew that Chapel knew them too. He looked up.

From the fear in Grey's eyes, it was obvious that he realized he might have revealed too much. It also revealed that he *knew* too much. Dropping all pretenses, Chapel let the demon side of him rise to the surface. If Marcus Grey was so randy to see a vampire, then he would give him one. His eyes warmed and his fangs extended. He could see himself reflected in Grey's wide eyes and he saw how both terrible and beautiful he was.

"How long have you known?"

Grey's mouth opened. To his credit, the young man was nowhere near as terrified as most would be. "Yesterday. I saw your name in my papers."

"Who else knows?"

"No one. I swear."

Chapel believed him. Grey smelled of fear and awe, but not deceit.

"Dreux killed himself because he could not live with what he had become." The young man may as well know the truth. "Temple and I undertook the protection of the Blood Grail."

"Temple." Grey breathed the name like it was sacred.

A faint stirring tingled in the air, setting Chapel on guard. His old friend was nearby. "I very much fear that he is what is in that cellar, Mr. Grey. I do not have to tell you what he will do to you if you enter his domain."

"I just want to know about him—about all of you."

Chapel could throttle him. Perhaps he should kill him now and be done with it. "And what of Prudence? Were you just stringing her along?"

"Of course not! My research indicates that Temple is the keeper of the Holy Grail as well."

Now, *that* was news! Was it possible? He had always been told that the Grail was missing, but the church had a tendency to bend the truth to their will. Perhaps Temple was in charge of it as well—which made his remaining hidden all the more imperative.

"I will kill you rather than allow you the Blood Grail." There was nothing but brutal honesty in Chapel's tone. "You and Prudence can take the credit for finding the Holy Grail if it is there, but then it returns with me and Molyneux. Whichever cup is there, I cannot allow it to fall in to the wrong hands."

Grey nodded. "Fine."

Chapel wasn't finished. "You will allow me to enter the cellar before you or your men. If Temple is there, I will warn him and he will leave with the Blood Grail and anything else that needs to be protected. He will decide what will be left for you to find."

"And in return?"

He seized Grey, hauling him close. "I will let you live. Temple may not be so kind."

Grey was afraid, but not nearly scared enough. "Will you tell me about him? About all of you?"

"No."

"You want to know why the Grail is so important to Prudence, don't you?"

Chapel's lip curled. Marcus blinked, his gaze fastened on 's mouth—and no doubt the fangs that were revealed. "You would barter with her confidence?"

"If you will keep her safe. If you won't hurt her . . ." He paused. "Perhaps."

He searched Grey's gaze for any hint of duplicity and found none. Frowning, he released him. "Why is this so important to you?"

"It just is. I want to cooperate with you, Severian. Will you cooperate with me?"

"Call me by that name again and I'll drain you." The surprise was that he meant it. But more disturbing was that he wanted information about Pru badly enough to let Grey live, even though he shouldn't.

"But do we have an agreement?"

"You really don't have any sense."

Grey actually grinned. "Not much, no."

Some of the tension eased from Chapel's shoulders. "You remind me of him somewhat."

"I do?"

"Yes. There isn't enough time tonight, and I won't do it with you near, but before you enter I will investigate the cellar and make sure it is safe."

"How do I know I can trust you not to take whatever you find inside?"

"You don't."

Marcus mulled that over for a moment. "Will you tell me anything about what really happened to the six of you?"

Chapel gave him a very pointed look. "No, but

I will try to keep the same thing from happening to you."

Back at the house, Chapel made his way toward the library, as was his habit. He needed a drink—not that it would do him much good. And he needed to think about what the hell he was going to do with Marcus Grey. How was he going to explain this to Molyneux?

And more importantly, would Pru join him tonight, or would she avoid him as a rabbit avoids a fox? Perhaps it would be for the best if she avoided him. The last thing he needed to do was reveal himself to her—or form an attachment, especially to a mortal.

Even if he could make her understand what he was, even if she could accept it, their time together would be far, far too brief, and far too painful when it ended.

That was, of course, assuming that Pru would like to have a relationship with him. She had run away from him, after all.

That he was even thinking these things amazed him. After so many years, why now? Why her?

Was it the desperation she wore like a perfume? Or the life that radiated off of her like a beacon? There was comfort in her presence, a sense of belonging so acute it almost hurt.

She made him feel like a man, not a monster. And for the first time in a long time he thought of a mortal as a possible companion, not food. There had been women in his life and in his bed since he had become a vampire, but he hadn't allowed anyone to affect him as Pru did.

It was after midnight. The house was relatively quiet. Servants bustled in all corners. Some occupants were already snoring in their beds, living their lives on country hours.

Prudence was not one of them. Centering himself, Chapel weeded through the other sounds of the house, searching for her. She was with one of her sisters and they were laughing with such joy that it brought a smile to his own lips. He would not eavesdrop on their conversation. To know that she was happy was enough.

She must have been disappointed with the delay in their dig, but thank God for it. If they had broken through . . . if she had been there when Temple rose . . .

His stomach churned at the thought. Perhaps Grey wouldn't have been foolish enough to put her at risk, but how could he stop her? Prudence was nothing if not the direct opposite of her name.

The fact that he might have to destroy his old friend weighed heavy on him, but he wouldn't hesitate to destroy Temple or Marcus Grey if one of them hurt Pru. She was good and pure and sweet—everything that had been taken from him when he had been cursed. He would do anything to preserve her, even give Grey the information he sought.

When he entered the library, a maid was there, stoking the fire. It never ceased to amaze him, the dampness that could permeate an English house, even in the summer.

She bobbed a curtsy at him as he entered. "Begging your pardon, sir. I'll be but a moment."

He waved away her concern. "No matter. Take your time."

And the little peach of a girl did just that. In fact, she seemed to take much more time than he would have thought necessary to make the room a comfortable temperature. And why did she keep looking at him?

Then, as she straightened herself, he realized what was going on. Mixed in with the scent of burning coal was the soft, unmistakable fragrance of female. The heat of the embers warmed her flesh—her blood—with a gentle flush.

This peach wanted to be plucked, and from the way she was eyeing him, Chapel knew she expected him to do the plucking.

Merde. Averting his face, he turned his eyes heavenward. What was this, a test? Was this whole journey meant to test his resolve, to tempt him beyond reason?

"Is there anything else I can get you, sir?" Temptation came closer. He could feel her standing behind him.

He turned, trying to force a smile. "No, thank you."

She was obviously not prepared to take no for an answer—either that or she thought him a little slow on the uptake.

A young, strong hand slipped up his arm in a

very forward manner. "Are you sure of that? It would be my pleasure to *serve* you."

He smiled kindly. "I'm certain the pleasure would be all mine, but no."

The maid's pink lips slipped into a pout and she dipped her head so that her honeyed ringlets bobbed becomingly around her face. "Am I not pretty enough for you, sir?"

How could he do anything but chuckle at such absurdity? "My dear girl, you are as tempting as a summer peach, but I am not the man you are looking for. I will not be satiated with just one bite."

His metaphor did nothing to dissuade her. In fact, it made her try harder. She moved closer, pressing her full breasts against his chest as her eyelashes lowered coyly. "Take as many bites as you like. I don't mind being eaten."

He'd wager she didn't at that. His fangs ached to put her claim to the test, just to take a little taste. He wouldn't have to sink them in all the way, and he could always pull out if the urge became too strong.

Heat burst behind his eyes as she tilted her head back, offering her throat and breasts to him as his head lowered of its own volition. His canines slid from the sheath of his gums, extending to their full length.

Please, God. Don't let me do this. It was all the hope he had, as his own will seemed to have deserted him.

And at that second, his prayers were answered.

"Mr. Chapel? I— Oh, pardon me!"

Slumping back, Chapel drew a deep breath as

the fire in his blood cooled and his fangs receded. There was a God.

Then he looked at his savior. *Merde* again. God had an awful sense of humor. His savior was none other than Pru.

And she was looking at him as though he had just ripped her heart from her chest.

Chapter 9

~~~oOo~~~

She should turn away. She should leave, go to her room and try not to think about what she had just seen. It was none of her business what he did, or with whom he did it.

Did he make a habit of trying to kiss women in libraries? She should be angry—and she was—but she felt foolish as well. Foolish for thinking that she might mean something to him. Foolish for taking his feelings into consideration when she contemplated having a relationship with him.

Yes, she should leave, but she wasn't going to.

"You may go now." The look she bestowed upon the maid was one she rarely used on anyone, let alone household staff. She refused to feel guilty about it either, as the maid looked far too eager to take whatever Chapel had to offer. She wouldn't have the girl dismissed, that would be too cruel, but she just might have a chat with the house-keeper about her.

Bobbing in a quick curtsy, her eyes averted, the girl gathered up her things and made a hasty exit. Pru waited until she was gone to turn her attention back to Chapel.

He didn't even have the courtesy to look embarrassed or penitant.

Damn him.

"Pru, I can explain."

She laughed—a shaky, vulnerable sound that grated on her nerves. "There is no need. Thankfully I wasn't a few minutes later or I might have had to wait for the maid to dress before she could leave the room."

Now he looked affronted. "*That* never would have happened."

He didn't truly think she'd believe that? "Oh, you would have simply tossed up her skirts and removed as little as possible, is that it?"

Worse yet, he didn't seem the least bit shocked by her language. That he might expect such talk from her only added to her anger.

"I mean I wouldn't have had sex with her."

She ignored that strange—and probably false—statement. "How many other women have you tried to kiss since your arrival?" It shouldn't matter. She shouldn't care, but she did.

"Other than you? None."

Liar. "Does this maid not count as a person?"

He looked affronted. "She tried to kiss me."

As though that would make a difference even if

she did believe it. She might have laughed were the words spoken by anyone else. "You did not seem to mind."

He smirked—an expression that suited his handsome face far more than contrition would have. "And you seem jealous."

She would have stomped her foot if she were not so sure it would make him even more smug. "I most certainly am not!" Now who was the liar?

"No?" Folding his arms across his broad chest, he took a lazy step toward her. "Then why so concerned with who I kiss?"

"I'm not." She would not retreat. She would not. "I'm merely looking out for my servants."

He stopped no more than a foot away from her. "Of course you are. You obviously had nothing but that maid's best interests in mind when you asked if I was going to screw her."

Heat rushed to her cheeks. She had practically given him permission to talk so bluntly. "You are very presumptuous." He was also very right, but she was not going to admit that, not when he was coming toward her like a cat stalking a bird.

"I am many things." He took another step and stopped mere inches from her. Pru knew she should retreat—every instinct demanded that she do just that, but to move would be to show fear, and she couldn't do that.

Not because she was afraid he would kiss her, but because she was afraid he wouldn't.

He hadn't kissed her the other night when she had wanted him to. Would he leave her wanting tonight as well?

And was it wrong of her to want a kiss from a man who seemed to give them freely to everyone but her?

"I am many things," he repeated, his fingers brushing her cheek, bringing a shiver to her flesh. "But a liar is not one of them. I did not kiss that maid."

"Because I stopped you before you could."

"True."

Well, he had said that he wasn't a liar.

"But I haven't kissed a woman in a very long time, Pru. And if I had kissed that maid, it would have been because you would not allow me to kiss you."

She met his gaze with as much hauteur as her trembling self would allow. "Oh? Is that my punishment for not kissing you?" He thought she didn't want to kiss him? How could any woman not want to kiss a man who looked like him? How could she not want to kiss him when he made her feel like she was the only woman in the world whenever they were together?

And how could she think about kissing him when he said things that made her want to slap him at the same time?

"Not *your* punishment." His strong fingers trailed down her throat. Could he feel the pulse pounding there? "Mine."

"Yours?"

His hand was warm and gentle on the back of her neck. "Denying myself the taste of you has caused me more pain than you will ever know."

How was she to respond to that? They had

known each other but a few days and already she was melting at his words, longing for his touch. It was madness, the desperation of a dying woman.

Then she would be as brazen as only a dying woman could be.

Hesitantly, she raised her gaze to his, letting him see the emotion there, the desire. "I would not want to cause you further discomfort."

His golden eyes widened for a split second and then his head lowered. Pru closed her eyes and waited, her heart hammering.

Chapel's lips were warm and firm against hers, the pressure of them insistent yet sweetly soft. It was electric, the connection between them, like lightning striking a barn, or a match to tinder.

Pru sighed against his mouth and felt his answering smile. She smiled as well, allowing him to tease her lips apart. As his tongue slid into her mouth, she jerked in surprise. Was that a chuckle she felt rumble in his chest?

Emboldened by his mirth, Pru stroked his tongue with her own, letting instinct guide her. What did it matter that she knew very little of kissing? She was going to take advantage of this moment, not waste it by worrying whether or not she was doing it right.

Obviously she did something right, because his arms went around her, hauling her tight against him. He was warm and solid, so much man and muscle. Her hips fit against his legs, the pressure of his thigh sending little tremors of delight low within her.

Good Lord, her legs were shaking! She clung to

his shoulders as they feasted on one another. He tasted like cloves—sweet and spicy. And he held her as though he never wanted to let her go.

Every woman should be held like this once in her life.

There was a growing hardness against her belly. He was as aroused as she was, and the knowledge thrilled her. She pressed herself against him, her hips slowly undulating. Sensation rippled through her. If only she could melt her body into his so she could feel him everywhere.

Chapel broke the kiss, gasping for breath.

"No," Pru uttered. Her hands clutched at his neck and hair, trying to force his head down to hers once more.

"We have to end this." Chapel's voice was ragged and hoarse. "Pru, if we do not, this will quickly become more than just a kiss and I won't have the strength to stop."

She understood what he was saying. She didn't like it, but she understood. Slowly, she nodded, stepping back gingerly so as to be certain her limbs would support her.

He would have taken the maid there, but he wouldn't take her. Should she be flattered or insulted?

He released her and she, him. He watched her with a hunger that made her want to leap into his arms once more, and a sadness that made her want to comfort him and tell him everything was going to be all right.

"I should apologize," he said, his eyes as bright as twin doubloons.

"Don't you dare." There was more of an edge to her tone than she'd intended.

He grinned. "I didn't mean for the kiss. I meant for not taking it further."

Her face had to be as red as a holly berry. "Oh. You may apologize, then."

That edge of sorrow was back in his smile. "Do not think I don't want you, Pru. God knows I do. But I'm not going to prove you right in thinking the worst of me this evening. I'm not a libertine. I just want you to know that."

She believed him. Not just because she wanted to, but because there was such an expression of sincerity on his lovely face. Besides, a libertine wouldn't have stopped.

"Thank you," she replied, her voice low and rough.

He stared at her for a moment, his smile fading until nothing but regret remained. "Good night, Pru."

And that was her cue to leave. She smiled. "Good night, Chapel. Sleep well."

A brow rose sharply. "That's unlikely."

She should feel some remorse at that, some kind of shame, perhaps. Instead, Pru left him standing there with a smile on her face.

It was a good night indeed.

Was this punishment or reward?

Remembering Pru's kiss, her lips hungry and moist beneath his, it was difficult for Chapel to think of such pleasure as anything but a blessing, even though he had been terribly uncomfortable for some time afterward.

How long had it been since he'd wanted a woman without wanting her blood? For his kind, sex and feeding were often closely linked and went together like port and cigars. Marie had been the last. Even then, he'd been human. When he came to her after being cursed, he'd wanted her like a starving man wanted an eight-course meal.

Do not think about it.

He had come to her but two days after his change. It had been night, of course, and very late. He'd come into her room through the balcony— leaping up from the ground as though it were no more than a few inches rather than two floors. Of course, he and the others had just discovered their new abilities and used them without discretion, not caring if anyone saw them or not.

If they had been more careful, Marcus Grey probably would not have heard the rumors about his ancestor and his companions.

Marie had looked like an angel as she slept, her blond hair spread across her pillow like a fall of silk. Her skin was the color of fresh cream poured over ripe peaches and her lips were every bit as ripe and succulent. He found her even more allur-ing and beautiful than he had before becoming a vampire. She'd been weeping, a balled-up hand-kerchief in her hand. Word of his death had reached her already.

He'd smiled, thinking she'd be happy to be with

him again—that she would want to be with him forever.

He gave in to his hunger, dipping his head to the ivory swell of her breast, where a fragile trace of blue just beneath the surface beckoned. He hadn't fed since the night before and the need gnawed at him, and she smelled as good as she looked.

Fangs slid easily from his gums, filling him with a surge of power. Invincible. He was invincible, immortal and so very, very powerful. There was nothing that he couldn't do, nothing that could be denied him now.

Marie jerked awake with a cry as his teeth pierced her flesh. She was hot and sweet against his tongue, even as she screamed.

Her fear was what stopped him, slicing through the desire to feed. Fear had never been the aphrodisiac to him that it was to Saint, or even Bishop. Lifting his head, he allowed her to see that it was him. He smiled lovingly at her, heedless of the blood on his lips. The sooner she realized it was him, the sooner he could go back to feeding, and the sooner he could crawl into bed with her and claim her body as his own.

The sooner he could make her the same as him. Instinct told him how to do it. He knew how it was done just as his body had known how to make love the first time.

Blue eyes widened in horror as they stared at him. The perfect bow of her mouth fell open with a soul-splintering scream.

Chapel clamped a hand over her mouth, his fingers dark against her pale cheeks.

"Sssh, *ma petite. C'est moi.*"

Muffled sobs of panic and fear puffed against his palm. She knew who he was and she was terrified.

He tried to calm her, but the scent of her blood and the pounding of her heart were so distracting, so tempting. He would not be able to handle her properly while his hunger bated him. He lowered his head once more to her breast and fed until he was stated.

When he lifted his head again, there was madness in her eyes. The air was rank with her fear, sweat and urine.

Disgusted, his sensitive sense of smell offended, his heart horrified, Chapel backed away. What had he done?

Marie twitched as he stood, like a small animal faced with a predator. She glanced down at her exposed breast. Slowly, she drew her nightgown up to cover herself, her movements unnaturally slow.

"My love."

At his voice, she looked up, a pale shadow of the girl he loved. "Severian?"

He nodded, a sigh of relief slipping from him. She was not mad. She knew him. All would be well.

"*Oui.*"

"They told me you were dead." The pain in her soft voice cut through him like a blade.

"I have come back for you."

Her gaze slipped back to her chest. Blood seeped through the virginal white linen.

She screamed again, shrill and long. His ears rang at the sound and he pressed his palms against them, trying to shut out the terror.

Marie bolted from her bed. He blocked the path to the door, thinking she would stop, but she twirled around instead and ran to the balcony doors.

He didn't move fast enough, shock making him sluggish. Or perhaps he hadn't truly believed that she would do anything to harm herself. He had been so certain that she would be happy to see him, that she would want to be as he was.

She threw herself over the balustrade a mere second before he reached it.

He leapt over the railing as the chamber door burst open behind him. He landed on his feet beside his fiancée's prone form.

Marie lay on the ground, her nightgown bunched around her milky thighs, her eyes wide and sightless, her neck bent at an unnatural angle as a thin trickle of blood ran from the marks on her breast toward her collarbone.

Dead. She was dead, and it was all his fault.

Guilt, rage and pain flooded him, so much that he howled like a wolf at the moon with it. On the balcony, Marie's father crossed himself as Chapel fell to his knees beside the body of the woman he loved.

Emptiness claimed him then and he stared into the sightless blue eyes until he felt the thick steel of a sword pierce his back. He looked down and saw the tip protruding from his chest. Pain lanced through him as the blade was pulled back out. Rage followed.

Slowly, he rose to his feet and turned to confront his attacker. It was Marie's father, who stared at him with an expression very much like the one Marie herself had fixed upon him.

"Mon Dieu."

"Do not waste your breath," Chapel told him as he pushed the man aside. "He cannot help you. He cannot help any of us."

He left his village that night and did not return for more than two hundred years. When he went back, he went to that exact spot where he had held Marie, as though expecting there to be some kind of marker. There wasn't.

He went to her grave. It looked so old and fragile, the letters worn and the stone chipped and patched with moss. He knelt there in the crypt, where he prayed for forgiveness and for her soul, but nothing happened. If God was listening, He didn't respond.

Marcus Grey had heard incorrectly. Severian de Foncé hadn't killed his fiancée.

Chapel had.

And Pru Ryland's kiss wasn't a reward. He wasn't so certain it was a punishment either, but it was a reminder.

A reminder of everything he had wanted and destroyed. A reminder of everything he could never, ever have.

"He did what?"

Pru hauled her sister out through the terrace doors. Caroline's question was so loud, the mice in the attic probably heard her.

Once the doors were closed and the two of them were alone on the heavily foliaged terrace, Pru turned to face her older sibling. The sun was slowly sinking on the horizon. She'd waited all day for the chance to tell her sister about the previous evening.

"He kissed me."

Eyes wide and bright, Caroline pressed a hand against her mouth as a high giggle escaped. "Oh, my dear Lord! Well, don't just stand there, silly. Tell me everything!"

They didn't have much time before the others would come looking for them for dinner, so Pru would have to be quick. Still holding Caroline's arm, she guided her away from the doors, lest someone overhear them.

She told her sister how she had found Chapel in the library and how she had thought he was going to kiss the maid.

"The cad." Caroline frowned. "You let him kiss you after that?"

Of course Pru then had to explain how she now believed that Chapel hadn't pursued the maid, but that the girl had propositioned him—and was turned down. She'd asked her own maid about the girl and found out that she had a bit of a reputation among the servants for "entertaining" male guests. ·

Caroline shook her head. "You need to dismiss her before she gets herself with child."

No doubt her sister had no idea how harsh that sounded, but regardless, Pru had no intention of letting the girl go because she liked men.

But she had gone to Mrs. Dobbie, the house-keeper, for a chat. She hadn't given the older woman all the details, but she told her that she didn't want the girl punished, merely advised that she might want to effect some changes in her behavior—for her own benefit, as well as that of her position within the household.

"It was divine," she announced, after revealing the rest of the tale—minus a few details, of course. Caroline did not need to know that Pru had rubbed herself against Chapel like a cat in season.

Caroline looked pained. "Darling, I know I've often encouraged you to pursue a gentleman, but you will be careful, won't you? I would hate to see you hurt in any way."

Squeezing her sister's hand, Pru nodded. "I will." Why argue? Why worry Caroline by telling her that she had no intention of being careful? What did it matter what happened between her and Chapel? The worst that could happen was that he would break her heart. She would get over that, either by the time given to her by the Grail, or by the death that nipped at her heels.

She told herself that was what would happen, but a part of her wasn't so certain. Fear was not going to keep her from following her heart, however.

No, it would serve no purpose to say these things aloud.

"The others will be waiting for us," she said, pulling her sister toward the doors once more. "Let's go in."

The others were indeed waiting for them. Chapel was talking to Marcus, but his head snapped up the minute Pru entered the room, as though he sensed her arrival. The idea warmed her like a fire on a cold day, flooding her extremities with delicious heat. The sight of him made her chest tight, he was so lovely.

In black and white evening clothes he looked as stark and golden as an angel. The lines and planes of his face softened as their gazes locked. His honey eyes seemed unnaturally bright, as though lit from an inner fire. He smiled—just for her. Every woman should know the joy of having a man be joyful just for her presence.

He could smash her heart to bits and it would be worth every minute.

She had selected a dark green gown for dinner that hugged her torso and made her skin look like cream. Obviously it had been the right choice, because Chapel looked at her as though he'd like to lap her up.

Oh, dear. Where was a fan when she needed one?

A pang in her abdomen killed her pleasure. No. Not now. Oh, God, not now.

Another jolt sliced through her. Stricken, she raised her gaze to Chapel. His surprise and dismay was plain as he rushed to her side.

"Pru, what is it?"

That he called her by her Christian name was proof of just how shaken he was. Pru couldn't even enjoy his concern, she was in so much pain.

Wet. There was wetness between her legs.

The color rushed from Chapel's face. "You're bleeding."

Her gaze jerked to his. How could he know that? He'd said it low enough that no one else could hear, but it was as though he had realized it at the same time Pru had. How?

"Take her to her room." It was her father who spoke. "Marcus, go fetch the doctor."

The next thing Pru knew, she was in Chapel's strong arms and he was heading toward the stairs, so fast that her sisters had to run to keep up. He didn't look the least bit burdened by her, and his eyes . . . his eyes burned like coals.

The pain was making her deluded. That was the only answer for it. No one's eyes could be that bright. No one was that strong.

But she wasn't imagining the fear or the concern on his face. He was worried about her and she was touched by it—more so than she wanted to admit.

"To the right," she heard Matilda instruct when they reached the top of the stairs. Of course, she had no way of knowing that Chapel already knew where Pru's room was.

He didn't respond, he just moved with that same strange swiftness, a muscle in his jaw twitching.

"What would I—oh!" A spasm brought a sheen of perspiration to her brow and she clenched against it. "—do without you to carry me?"

He gave her the slightest of smiles. His eyes at least looked a bit more normal now. "Knowing you, you'd find a way to carry yourself."

Pru chuckled. It hurt, but she did it anyway. This familiarity they shared pleased her, gave her comfort at a time when she usually would have found only pain and fear. It wasn't usual, for so short an acquaintance, but she wasn't going to question it. She was simply thankful for it.

They entered her room. Gently—so much so that she almost didn't feel it—Chapel laid her on her bed. Before Pru could thank him for helping her, he was pushed aside by her sisters, all of whom were intent on babying her.

How frightened they looked. It broke Pru's heart to see them, so she closed her eyes and ground her teeth as another wave of pain came.

She thought about Chapel, pictured him in her mind and imagined his strength surrounding her. She imagined him holding her again, his arms tight around her, unwilling to let her go. She imagined his smile and thought about how much she enjoyed knowing she was responsible for it.

And prayed she wouldn't die without seeing him again.

Chapter 10

Chapel sat on the floor outside Pru's door. No one seemed to mind that he kept vigil there, even though it was highly improper. Molyneux sat in a chair beside him, Pru's family across the corridor. Even her brothers-in-law were there, though they looked highly uncomfortable. Marcus paced near the top of the stairs.

Chapel avoided the young man. Marcus looked at him as though he expected him to be able to do something for Pru, and that frightened him, not because he didn't know what to do for her, but because he knew exactly what Marcus had in mind.

Was Pru that sick? She was sick enough that she was bleeding inside. He'd smelled it as soon as he'd reached her. It had been fresh blood too, not monthly feminine blood.

Pain and blood. It was a combination that had followed him for centuries, and it was *never* good.

She would have to be very ill indeed for someone to think being made a vampire would be a fitting cure for her. Of course, there was the Holy Grail.

The Holy Grail. Until now he hadn't given much thought to the possibility that it was what was hidden in those ruins. Until now all his energy had been directed at protecting the Blood Grail. And now that he had an idea why Pru was so anxious to find that cup—why her interest in the legend had turned to obsession—he wanted it to be there as well.

He watched her family rather than think of all the things that might be wrong with Pru and all the miracles that might be just out of her reach. Her father stood by his daughters, the husbands of whom were a few feet farther down the hall—close enough to lend support to their wives but far enough away to give the family a little privacy. They talked quietly among themselves, with more anxiety in their expressions than Chapel was comfortable witnessing in other men.

Thomas Ryland looked tired, drawn and frightened. Each of his three daughters look similarly. Matilda stood with her hands clasped in front of her, chin high but quivering. Georgiana sat next to Caroline, grasping her sister's hand. If determination alone could beat an illness, then the expression on Georgiana's face would do it. And Caroline, poor sweet Caroline, chewed at her lower lip in an effort not to cry.

They were worried. Worried and frightened.

He would have liked to offer them some comfort, but it wasn't something he was good at. He would have liked to take comfort from them, but he hadn't known Pru long enough, hadn't ingratiated himself into the family enough to expect such emotion.

Her family had no idea that he would gladly sell, trade or destroy whatever soul he had left to make Pru well. She had come to mean something to him during his short time at Rosecourt. Something important and precious.

The door to Pru's room opened and Chapel jumped to his feet. No one but Molyneux seemed to notice that he was more agile than a man his size should be. But instead of a chastising gaze, the priest offered him a hopeful smile instead.

Was his concern for Pru as evident as that of her family?

The physician, a tall, lanky man of middle age with thinning dark hair, spared him the slightest glance before turning his attention to Pru's father.

"Miss Ryland is resting," he informed them. "I gave her something for the pain and I expect she will sleep through the night."

"Is she . . . all right?" It was Matilda, the motherly one, who asked.

The doctor—Higgins or something was his name—favored her with a smile. "She's comfortable and I expect she will feel more herself come the morning."

Chapel wasn't the only one who noticed that the doctor hadn't answered her question. Matilda did not look convinced, and turned to her father.

Thomas Ryland sighed. "What about her condition, Philip? Has it worsened?"

Condition? Chapel glanced at Higgins, very anxious as to what his reply would be.

"The cancer is progressing," Higgins replied in the same calm tone, "as we knew it would. But Prudence is as stubborn as her father and I expect she will be with us for some time yet."

Cancer. Chapel leaned his shoulder into the wall for support. Christ. He knew it had to be serious, but . . . cancer.

His last priest had died from cancer of the stomach. It had been an awful thing, watching a hale and vibrant man dwindle to a shrunken husk. Chapel hadn't recognized him at the end.

The idea of Pru meeting that kind of fate made him feel as though he might vomit.

It also made him angry—angry enough that he didn't dare look anyone in the eye lest they see just how inhuman he was.

But cancer wasn't something he could beat or kill or intimidate. Cancer didn't give a whore's honor who or what he was. Cancer was one of the true monsters of the world. Oh, he could change Pru into what he was, that would destroy the cancer that was killing her.

It might also destroy Pru as well. God knows it had destroyed Marie. Chapel wasn't quite sure if it had destroyed him or not.

"May we see her?" It was Caroline who asked.

Higgins nodded. "She's asleep, but I do not see

any harm in having one or all of her sisters sit with her."

The women didn't even look at one another for encouragement. It was as if the three of them simply knew that each would want to sit by Pru's bed. They moved as one, just as he and his companions had, knowing instinctively what the others were thinking. He envied these women that closeness. He hadn't felt it for a very long time—not until he'd felt Temple's presence at the dig site.

He watched the sisters go. They would get to watch over Pru and keep her comfortable and safe, not he. There was no reason for him to sit with her, but he wanted to. He wanted to watch her breathe, just so he could know she still drew breath.

Christ, Molyneux was right. He had to get out in society more if this was how he now reacted to being confronted with death. He, who had killed plenty in his lifetime, both as man and as beast. Pru Ryland would die and go on to a better place. He would still be there long after her bones had turned to dust.

He really was going to vomit.

He excused himself and escaped down the stairs as quickly as he could without raising questions. Molyneux and Marcus were hot on his heels.

Chapel went for the drawing room, where he poured himself a liberal amount of whiskey. Molyneux abstained, but Marcus nodded that he would like one as well.

When the three of them were seated, Chapel turned his anger on Marcus. "You knew about this?"

The young man seemed surprised by his rancor. "About Pru? Yes, I knew. I've known since we first met."

This must be what Grey had hinted at before. "And you didn't tell me. Why?"

"It was none of your business."

"None of my business?" The tumbler in his hand groaned as his fingers tightened around it. "How is that?"

Marcus shrugged his broad shoulders. "She didn't want you or Father Molyneux to know. Nothing personal, she didn't like anyone knowing. She said people treated her differently once they found out. How about you, Mr. Chapel—will you treat her differently?"

Something in the young man's tone sounded very much like a taunt. *Yes.* "No."

"You like her, I can tell."

The tumbler began to crack. Chapel set it on the table. "What I think of Pru is none of *your* business."

Marcus merely shrugged once more. He looked older than he normally did—finally showing his true age. "That's shit and you know it. Pru is my friend and you're just some vampire sent here to make sure she doesn't uncover something that could save her from a painful death."

Molyneux gasped, his pale gaze whipping around to meet Chapel's. Chapel merely looked away.

Marcus was right, of course—painfully so—but that didn't stop Chapel from wanting to rip his throat out. A low growl escaped his throat and he felt his control waver for a second as the urge to pounce rose to the surface.

"Save her?" He lifted his chin, looking Marcus directly in the eye. "Is *this* what you would want for her? A demon inside that demands blood? Would you deny her the sun, deny her the embrace of heaven? Do you really want to spend the rest of your friendship with her wondering if she'll give in to temptation someday and find out if you taste as good as she imagines you would?"

Marcus swallowed, his blue eyes wide with trepidation. "No," he whispered. "I would not, but nor would I have her die."

Chapel sighed and ran a hand over his jaw. He was tired. Here it was, the night still young, and all he wanted to do was sleep. Sleep and never wake up.

"I do not want her to die either," he admitted. "But I will not damn her. You cannot ask it of me."

Marcus tossed back the remainder of his whiskey. "What if it is the Blood Grail we find? Will you stop her from making the choice on her own?"

"*Mon Dieu!*" Molyneux crossed himself. "My boy, you do not know what you are saying!"

A sharp bark of laughter tore from Chapel's throat. "He knows exactly what he is saying. Yes, Mr. Grey. I will stop her—and you, if necessary."

The young man's gaze was pure defiance. "Then I guess I had better get inside the ruins first."

Icy fingers reached through Chapel's veins. "We had an agreement."

Marcus stared him down. He was not afraid and Chapel both despised and respected him for it. "I release you from it."

"You cannot do that. You wanted information in exchange for allowing me to enter the cellar first. If Temple is there, he will kill you."

Marcus stood, his cheeks flush with color. "Then I'd better take every precaution to ascertain that he isn't. I will not allow you—a creature who knows nothing of her—to make such a decision for Pru."

Chapel rose as well. His heart banged once against his ribs. Nothing of her? He'd wager he knew her better than Grey did. "You would make her a demon?"

Blue eyes narrowed. "Is that what you are? I thought you were just a coward. Go back to your rock, Chapel. Hide under it for another hundred years or so. Let the rest of us brave enough to want to live worry about the rest."

He might have attacked had he not been too shocked to even move. Dumbfounded, Chapel could only stand there and watch as Marcus strode from the room, closing the heavy oak door behind him.

"He doesn't understand." Chapel sank into his chair. He could not allow Marcus in that cellar. Regardless of what Temple might do to him, he could not allow him to give the Blood Grail to Pru.

"Perhaps he simply sees things differently," Molyneux suggested.

Chapel faced him with incredulity. "Are you mad?"

The priest patted him on the thigh as though he were some ignorant schoolboy having a lapse in faith. "You see your situation as a curse. Marcus Grey sees it as a blessing. It is all a matter of perspective, *non*?"

"*Non.*" Perspective? What the hell? "It is a curse. I have a demon inside me. It tells me to prey on human life, what else could it be?"

Molyneux tilted his graying head. "Prey, but not kill. You have the choice to make what you will of your affliction. You have decided to make it a curse, something to be ashamed of and be punished for."

"Yes." It made perfect sense to him.

The priest shook his head and rose to his feet. "You could just as easily have made it a gift. Think of all the good you could do with your abilities."

This was ridiculous. "Kill people out of mercy?"

Another head shake. "It is no good talking to you now, not when you are so upset about Mam'selle Ryland. It is ironic, I think."

Chapel waited. He rolled his eyes as the silence dragged on. "What is ironic?"

Molyneux crossed the printed carpet to the door, where he paused—rather dramatically, in Chapel's opinion. "That the one person you have made any kind of connection with in centuries is the very one who would no doubt trade places with you in an instant."

Chapel opened his mouth to respond, but Molyneux didn't give him a chance. The soft click of the door latch punctuated the finality of his departure.

Closing his eyes, Chapel leaned back in his chair. The quiet was sweet, but his thoughts were not. Poor Pru. Sweet, fragile Pru. She probably would trade places with him. From what he already knew of her, he doubted she would even stop to consider the consequences.

But would he trade with her? No, he wouldn't. He wouldn't pass on this curse to anyone.

But to be honest, he wasn't entirely certain he'd give it up either.

When Pru awoke late the following afternoon—after waking up several times during the day only to have one of her sisters tell her to go back to sleep—she discovered that not only had her party—the one to celebrate finding the cellar—been postponed by a few days, but so had work on the ruins.

It was an announcement that terrified her, but Marcus assured her that as soon as she was recovered, he would resume work at double speed so she could be there to reap the benefits of their work. He wanted her to be there for their triumph, not in bed where she couldn't see the Grail first-hand.

Their work. It was kind of him to say so, but it

didn't feel as though she had contributed much to the effort. True, she had convinced her father to purchase the land, but for the most part she had been as useless a partner as anyone could be.

By now both Chapel and Father Molyneux knew the nature of her illness. She really didn't mind the priest knowing. He might come in handy before all this was said and done. And she didn't expect that a man who looked forward to going to heaven would pity her. No, it was Chapel's knowing that bothered her. Would he look at her with pity now?

Or would he be angry that she hadn't been totally honest with him? Did he feel betrayed, foolish? Did he regret kissing her? Or would he see her as a potentially easy seduction? No, she couldn't imagine him thinking that way. He might be hiding parts of himself as well, but he wasn't evil.

Drawing herself up in the bed, she leaned against the pillows and considered throwing back the blankets and going to the windows to open the drapes and let in what little daylight there was left. After a moment's contemplation, she decided she was simply too lazy to bother.

But she did have to get out of bed to answer the natural demands of her body, so after a visit to the toilet, she tossed back the drapes and watched the beauty of the pinkening sky.

It would soon be time for dinner. If she hurried, she might be able to join the others. While she had no desire to see their concern—or worse, their pity—she didn't want to make them worry more by spending yet another night closeted away in her room.

Plus she would be able to see Chapel.

She rang for her maid and picked a gown out of the sandalwood-scented interior of her armoire. The gown was a shade of deep rose, which would put color in her cheeks and brighten her eyes. Perhaps she'd add just a touch of rouge to her cheeks to help. If she looked too pale, Matilda was likely to march her right back to bed.

Eventually her sisters would return to their own lives, their own homes. The summer wouldn't last forever and the house would be empty once more. Pru would miss them when they left, but the privacy would be most welcome.

Her maid came quickly, grinning and chattering about how pleased she was to see her mistress "up and around." Within the half hour Pru was washed, dressed and coifed. Just going through the regular routine had her feeling better than she had upon waking. She had much of her energy back, and her corset didn't make her stomach uncomfortable.

Her legs were a little shaky as she carefully maneuvered her way downstairs, but the drugs Dr. Higgins gave her always had that effect. It would wear off once she was up for a bit and had some food in her belly.

Given the hour, she went straight to the dining room, and found everyone just sitting down at the table. They were surprised to see her, of course, but everyone seemed pleased by her appearance.

Her father, the poor thing, looked so relieved that she feared he might weep.

Everyone made a fuss, of course, shuffling themselves around so that she might have the "best" seat at the table. Her sisters knew that, for her, the best seat was the one closest to the gravy, and so that was the one she got.

It was also the one on the immediate right of Chapel. Was that planned as well? She could see no trace of conspiracy on her sisters' faces, but that didn't mean anything.

He didn't immediately say anything as she seated herself, but he watched her as carefully as a nurse watching her charge take its first steps. He passed her platters of food and held them for her as she made her selections, but he did not speak.

The only way to make this situation less uncomfortable was to make like there was nothing wrong.

She ladled gravy over the meat on her plate. "Are you having a good evening, Mr. Chapel?"

He smiled, but it didn't reach his eyes. His eyes were dark gold with concern. "I am now, Miss Ryland." He passed her the potatoes. "Would you care to have some potatoes with your gravy?"

Teasing. Not what she expected, but much more welcome. She glanced down at her plate, the contents of which were swimming in rich brown sauce, and smiled. "Of course, but I shall have to put more gravy on them. I do not believe I have quite enough."

This time the smile did reach his eyes and she puffed up for having put it there.

After dinner, the entire party retired to the drawing room for drinks and diversions. Pru had no doubt that the diversions were for her benefit—and to keep everyone's mind off her collapse the night before.

Father Molyneux regaled them with tales of his travels in the East. Pru's favorite was the one about the singing camel—which, of course, turned out not to be able to sing at all. Perhaps she was simply ignorant, but she never would have thought a priest could be quite so well traveled, or so openly tolerant of other cultures and peoples.

"Mr. Chapel," she said when the priest insisted that he could talk no more, "you must have some interesting tales of your adventures. Will you share them?"

He looked as though he would rather have his hand chewed off by mice. "I am not much of a storyteller, Mam'selle Ryland."

"Rubbish," Molyneux blurted, his teacup poised halfway to his lips. "Tell one of those stories you picked up about those knights."

Was it the lighting or her imagination—did Chapel look as though he'd like to backhand Molyneux?

And knights? Chapel didn't seem the type . . . no, wait. On closer inspection, he *did* look like someone who would know about knights and daring adventures of yore. In fact, it was very easy to imagine him as a knight atop a thundering steed, a sword at his side, chain mail glinting in the sun.

As girlishly romantic as it was, it was a vision she rather liked.

"Yes." It was Marcus who spoke, watching Chapel with an expression Pru didn't quite understand. "Tell us one of your knight tales, Mr. Chapel. Perhaps one about de Foncé."

Chapel was expressionless as he glanced at Marcus, but not when he turned to her, looking as though he hoped she'd absolve him. Whoever this de Foncé was, he was obviously a character Marcus knew of.

Since she couldn't stand to not know something, Pru smiled. "I, for one, would love to hear a story about knights."

The rest of the party concurred. Like any good man who knew when he was beat, Chapel accepted defeat with a small sigh and a resigned smile. "All right."

He began the story by telling them of the knight named Severian de Foncé. He was a young, brave man who believed that his sword and faith in God would keep anything bad from happening to him. This arrogance made him rash and often he found himself in situations that he would not have escaped were it not for his faithful friends and companions.

Severian was in love with a young woman named Marie. Marie came from a wealthy family, so Severian was constantly trying to prove himself worthy to her family. He entered contests to prove his strength and bravery. He went on quests for treasure and secret assignments for the King of France to earn the gold to keep his future bride in the manner of life to which she was accustomed.

King Philip sent Severian and his friends on a quest for a mystical object, said to grant great power to whoever claimed it. The knights fought a long battle. Their swords were bloody, their bodies battered and torn, but they finally breached their opponents' defenses. They found the object of their quest—or what they believed to be the object they sought.

"But it was an instrument of evil," Chapel told them, the entire room—Pru included—hanging on his every word. "When Severian and his friends claimed it for their king, it placed a horrible curse on each of them."

Pru's eyes widened. "What kind of curse?"

Chapel smiled gently at her. "I will explain." He went on to say that the curse was dark and powerful. It turned each of the men into a beast. They were powerful, able to take or achieve anything they wanted, but they were cursed to stay to the shadows, hideous and feared by any and all who saw them.

Severian believed that his love, Marie, would understand when she saw him. He believed that she would be impressed by his newfound powers and strength. When he came to her once he'd returned, she was disgusted by what he had become. When he tried to press his suit upon her, she fled from his embrace and threw herself from her balcony, committing the deadly sin of suicide rather than spend the rest of her life married to such a creature.

Chapel paused here, long enough that some of the party exchanged quizzical glances.

"But what of Severian?" Caroline demanded to know.

Chapel's brow furrowed, as though some unpleasant memory accompanied his tale. "He was overcome by grief and would have ended his own life if he could have, but he was a coward and he slunk away into the shadows where he belonged, leaving his home and the life he knew, never to return."

Matilda sighed. "How tragic."

Chapel nodded. "Severian learned a valuable lesson, but it was hard-learned. He taught himself to control the beast inside him and to become a better person despite his curse. His rashness and arrogance cost him the woman he loved most, and he would not have her death be in vain."

"Marie was a cow," Pru remarked.

Chapel raised his brows. "I beg your pardon?"

"No woman who truly loved a man would turn her back on him because of a curse. If she'd truly loved him she would have learned to accept Severian as he was. Who throws themselves out a window because her lover has changed? Honestly?"

He obviously doubted the conviction behind her words. "You would not reject a lover who had turned into a beast?"

"A beast whom you just said learned to change the very behavior that got him into trouble in the first place. Even the fiercest beast is capable of gentleness, Mr. Chapel. I wish I could say the same of all men."

Molyneux gave a sharp nod. "Well said."

Chapel regarded her strangely, with an expression that looked oddly hopeful. "You have obviously never encountered a true monster, Miss Ryland. I pray you never do."

She smiled at his melodramatic tone. Was she to take from that that *he* had met a true monster? "If I loved him, Mr. Chapel, he would never be a monster in my eyes. I applaud your knight for changing, but it is unfortunate that he did it for such an undeserving wench."

Chapel looked as though she had dumped cold water over his head.

Marcus burst out laughing. "On that note, if you all will excuse me, I will take my leave."

"Oh, Marcus, wait!" Pru rose to her feet. "I want to talk to you for a moment."

She turned her head to excuse herself from Chapel, and of course to apologize if her remarks had insulted him in any way, but he wasn't there. Pru raised her gaze to see him exit the room via the French doors. He was slipping out for his evening cigarette, no doubt.

Either that or he didn't agree with her that Severian's Marie was a wench.

Chapter 11

Pru did not see much of Chapel over the course of the next two nights. He was present at dinner, and though he conversed with her as though nothing were amiss, he did not come to the library at all—at least not while Pru was there.

He was avoiding her, and she could not help but wonder if he spent his evenings with the little maid. Her heart told her no, that it was not another woman who kept him from her, but her mind had a hard time accepting that.

Then again, the reason he avoided her might be entirely of her own making—except that she had absolutely no idea what she might have done to deserve his dismissal.

Well, maybe there were two things she could

think of: Number one, that she bored him and he had decided to stop trying to charm her. Or, number two, that he had taken offense at her remarks about the story he had told them all in the drawing room two nights earlier.

Of the two ideas, the former sounded the most likely, even if she did not want to believe it.

Perhaps it was her illness that put him off. She hated thinking that of him, but she could understand if that was the case. Blood could be so off-putting for some people, not to mention frightening.

Or, she thought as she slipped on her earrings, perhaps there was nothing amiss at all. Perhaps his attitude meant nothing other than the fact that he didn't have to be all over her every time they were together.

Disappointing, but not nearly as final as her other thoughts. Why waste time trying to make a villain or libertine out of him? The worst he could do was break her heart, and a broken heart didn't seem like that much of a tragedy given her circumstances.

In fact, she rather fancied the idea of having her heart broken. She didn't know what it felt like, but she'd read enough novels and poems to know that heartbreak generally followed a grand passion or romance.

Either of those was certainly worth a little pain, were they not?

Why could it not have been Marcus who caught her fancy? Why did they end up being nothing more than friends? She and Marcus could have been having an affair for months now. She knew Marcus, there would be no trying to guess at what he was thinking or feeling.

But it wasn't Marcus who made her heart beat faster. It wasn't Marcus with whom she wanted to spend the long evenings when she couldn't—wouldn't—sleep. She wanted Chapel. Part of his appeal was that he treated her like a person, not a lesser being. And he didn't treat her like a sick person. *God, please don't let him start now.*

So here it was, the night of her little evening party that had been postponed due to her illness, and she was dressed to catch Chapel's attention.

Her gown consisted of a tea-colored *peau de sole* underskirt topped by accordian-pleated chiffon in the same shade. Ivory lace in a large floral pattern topped the chiffon, allowing a bit of the delicate fabric to trim the decolleté. The tiny sleeves hugging her shoulders were chiffon as well.

The neckline was low and her breasts were pushed high against the gown's snug bodice. As her maid laced her into her corset, pulling the strings tight, Pru prayed that she would not have one of her attacks that evening. So far, she did not feel the least bit uncomfortable.

Pearls completed her ensemble—pale golden pearls that shimmered in the light and made her skin look like alabaster. They wrapped around her neck and dangled from her ears. Her hair was piled loosely on top of her head in a elaborate coiffure that looked as though it might tumble loose at any moment, but was in no danger of any such thing.

She looked good. There was no remaining bruising beneath her eyes. Her cheeks were flush, her eyes bright. She looked healthy and robust—enough that even she was content to believe it for a bit.

And come tomorrow it might be a reality. Oh, thank goodness for the party and the diversion it brought, for she didn't know what she would do if she had to spend the entire evening wondering what would be found tomorrow if—*when*—they finally breached the cellar entrance.

But that didn't stop her from uttering a little prayer as she descended the stairs from her room. Nor did it keep a frisson of disappointment from trickling down her spine. If—argh, *when*—they found the Grail, there would no longer be a reason for Chapel to stay in Tintagel. Unless, of course, he decided to stay for her.

It was a chance she wasn't prepared to take. Yes, he might stay for a bit, but realistically she knew he couldn't stay forever, nor would he be likely to want to. If they did not find the Grail, her chance to experience a grand passion would leave with him. Her chance to live what was left of her life to its fullest would slip through her fingers.

The very thought was enough to make her chest tighten to the point where she struggled to draw breath. Better not to think of it.

Tonight was her night to seize the moment. And to seize Chapel.

It wasn't simply passion she wanted. She wanted to feel loved and treasured. She knew that he would give her that. Once upon a time she had been a normal woman with all the hopes for the future that came with her station. Many of those hopes had been taken from her, or she had given them up. She had a chance to grab something that she believed would be truly special, something fleeting and all too rare.

The party was held in the music room on the ground floor. Folding doors opened the far wall into the peach drawing room, doubling the entertainment space and giving guests a place to dance if they so desired.

It wasn't a large party, perhaps fifty to seventy-five locals—gentry and families of good standing. Her father had even invited the local curate so that Father Molyneux would have a contemporary to converse with. Although, as far as Pru was concerned, Mr. Feathers was a tad too pious and judgmental to make friends with the French priest.

But Molyneux was the least of her concerns. She entered the room, smiling and greeting the guests who caught her attention or sought her out. She stopped and said good evening to her sisters and their husbands and paused long enough to give her father's arm a gentle squeeze.

She did all these things as though guided by an unseen hand. Meanwhile, her gaze was constantly scanning the room, searching for a familiar golden head.

Her heart leapt when she finally spotted him. He was exiting the room through the French doors, out into the garden. Perfect. She would have him all to herself for a moment.

It seemed to take a lifetime to weave through the crowd, even as small as it was. Everyone wanted to chat with her. It was her own fault. The excavation took so much of her time that she was rarely in the village anymore. She had shirked many of her old habits and responsibilities. She would have to remedy that.

Finally, she reached the exit. No one seemed to notice as she slipped through the doors after Chapel. Turning the handle, she stepped out into the cool night.

She stood for a moment, in a puddle of light that spilled out onto the cool stone, allowing her eyes to adjust to the lantern-lit dimness.

A flash of snowy white cravat and the glowing tip of a cigarette caught her attention and she moved toward it, leaving the safety of the doors for the darker fringe of the garden below. It was like leaving one world and traveling into another, unfamiliar and exotic. It was a trick of her mind, of course, but anticipation flared in her belly all the same.

Her skirts swished against the shallow steps. Grass tugged at her hem as she made her way toward Chapel, her heart beating a little harder with every step. Never in her life had she been so apprehensive about a meeting with another person. Never had she been so afraid of being rejected.

"Pru?" His voice was sharp, almost a reprimand. "What are you doing out here?"

"And a good evening to you as well." It came out a bit sharper than she had intended, but did he have to make her feel every inch the idiot for seeking him out?

She could see his face now, illuminated by the flare of his cigarette as he inhaled from it. He had the good grace to look abashed as he exhaled. "Forgive me. Good evening, Pru, what brings you out here?"

As if he didn't know. "Looking for you," she replied honestly. "You have been avoiding me these last few days. I thought I might ask why." There, she'd asked what she wanted to ask.

Now he looked indignant. It was an arrogant expression, one that he wore well. "I have not been avoiding you."

He offered her the cigarette, a gesture that both surprised and warmed her. It was something shared with a close companion, and a choice not normally given to a woman of her station. She took it, rolling the slender length between her fingers.

"Please." It was all she could do not to roll her eyes as she raised the cigarette to her mouth and tentatively inhaled. "Do not insult my intelligence by trying to deny it." She coughed and handed the cigarette back to him. "What I want to know is why. Is it because I'm . . . sick?" It made her stomach roll to even think it.

His handsome face creased with a scowl. "Of course not. Is that how low your opinion is of me?"

"I did not want to believe that, but I cannot think of any other reason for you to go out of your way not to see me." How brazen she was now compared to her youth. Somewhere over the last year or so she had begun losing patience with coyness and it had been increasing ever since.

"Can't you?" He took one last draw off the cigarette and flicked it into the fountain. Better that than the bushes, she supposed. "Not one?"

There was something threatening, something harsh in his tone, as though he thought her a liar or a simpleton. She didn't like either suggestion.

"No." Her arms folded across her chest. "Unless, of course, kissing me was just a game to you and you have decided to move on to a target who might live long enough to give in to your seduction."

Oh, it was cruel of her, and it showed on his face. "Kissing you was one of the biggest mistakes of my life."

That was more cruel than anything she could have thought of. The words were like a punch in the stomach. "I see."

She moved to walk away, numb and rejected, but he grabbed her by the arm. "No, you do not, you little fool." He pulled her closer until she could feel the heat and smell the tabaccoed warmth of his breath. It did not occur to Pru to fight him, not when she wanted to be closer to him.

Only when she could feel his legs against hers through the layers of her skirts did he ease the pressure on her arm. His fingers released their hold on her to move around to her back, holding her prisoner in a more gentle manner.

His expression softened, but his eyes were bright and dangerous. "Do you know why kissing you was a mistake, Pru?"

Lifting her chin to meet his gaze took almost all of her resolve. The rest was spent on trying to keep her chin from quivering. "Because you did not like it?"

"No." Pru shivered as his warm breath caressed her cheek. "Because I liked it too much. So much that I've thought of little else since."

Butterflies burst free behind her ribs. Elation made her brazen. "Would you like to do it again?"

His only answer was a low groan before lowering his head and claiming her lips with his. Pru gasped against his mouth, parting her lips for the bold intrusion of his tongue. He tasted sweet and smoky, his lips so smooth and firm her knees trembled.

His fingers were gentle but firm, the strength there obvious as one hand pressed against her spine, the other cupping the curve of her bottom. He pressed her against him so that her hips cradled him, and even through the layers of fabric between them she could feel the hardness of his body.

His hands slid up her back to her shoulders and neck. His fingers were warm against her bare flesh, so gentle as they caressed the ridge of her collarbone. Like the whisper of a sweet breeze, they drifted up her throat to her jaw and then back, cupping her head as though he were afraid she might pull away before he had his fill of her mouth.

The pressure of his mouth eased to a lazy exploration. He kissed her as though they had all the time in the world, when he knew damn well that they didn't. Pru railed against the restraint in his embrace. She wanted his body pressed full against hers once more. She wanted fierce fingers biting into her backside. She didn't want restraint. She wanted passion.

All her life had been restraint. She could not afford to spend any more time behaving as she thought she should. She wanted him to treat her as a man treated a woman he desired so much it consumed him, and she wanted to be consumed. Desperately, she caught at his shoulders, feeling the muscles there beneath his clothes. She tried to pull him closer, but he wouldn't budge. Her fingers clenched into fists as she rose up on her toes, trying to force her will upon him, but he was stronger.

Changing tactics, she pushed against him rather than pulled. She pressed herself full against him, gasping at the delicious shock of the softness of her body meeting the muscled hardness of his. The move caught him off guard and broke the contact between their lips.

"Please," she whispered, peering up into the dark pools of his eyes. "Don't treat me like something fragile. Treat me like a woman you desire more than anything in the world. Please, let me feel that just once."

They stared at each other for the span of a

heartbeat before he lowered his head once more. He hesitated.

"Please, Chapel." Her hands came up to hold his face—such a sad and beautiful face. "I want you to be the one to show me what it is to be loved."

His grip on her tightened. Then Chapel's control snapped.

Chapel didn't just kiss Pru, he devoured her. His lips plundered hers, his tongue savoring the hot, sweet taste of her mouth. He held her tightly so she could not escape—his hands once more on her back, on the delicious curve of her bottom, pressing her against his pelvis. Could she feel his erection? Did she have any idea how badly he wanted to possess her?

Could she feel the sharpness of his teeth against her sweet, hot tongue? All it would take would be a tiny bit of pressure and her essence would be on his own tongue. She would be rich and earthy and sweet in the way of chocolate rather than pure sugar. Would she accept fangs and cock with a warm rush of heat or would she reject him?

Worse yet, would the woman who called Marie a wench for rejecting him be repulsed when faced with the reality of what he was? It was one thing for her to make such claims of love and devotion when she believed it nothing more than a story, but what if she learned it was true?

God help him. He had tried to stay away from her, tried to resist her temptation, but he was simply not strong enough. He hadn't fed off a human in decades, perhaps even centuries, he had lost track, but he couldn't go two days without giving in to Pru's allure.

She matched the demanding fervor of his kiss with an intensity of her own that in anyone else he might mistake as desperation, but not with Pru. This was passion and desire, pure and simple. She wanted him as a woman wanted a man, and it damn near killed him.

Pru didn't know that he was a monster. She didn't know the terrible things he had done, and yet it felt as though she knew him better than anyone, even Molyneux.

This woman wanted him enough to risk her reputation by kissing him in the garden where anyone might find them. She wanted him badly enough to ask for his embrace, and not the embrace of the demon inside him, or the man he once was, but *his* embrace.

Her hands roamed his back and shoulders, up to his hair, where they tangled in a death grip. Did she think he planned to leave her? Even if he had such a notion, he wasn't strong enough to pull away. Not yet. He hadn't had enough of her yet. He doubted he ever would.

This woman was dangerous to him—more dangerous than any religious zealot or demon hunter. Somehow, she had managed to find a tiny thread of him that was still human, that part of him that hungered for human contact. She had found it and she fed it and it sated him more than blood ever could.

That wasn't to say he wasn't tempted to bite her.

He was, but his desire for her as a man was far stronger than his hunger for her blood.

He wanted her to love him. Sweet God, he wanted her to know what he was and have her look at him without fear or revulsion in her eyes.

She was so sweet in his arms, so supple and graceful, her spine arched beneath his palm. Her skin flushed, warming her perfumed skin and surrounding him with her scent. Like mulled wine, she was, full-bodied and rich with spices. She would burst on his tongue like the most exotic of tastes.

Pliant breasts pressed against his chest. He moved one of his hands from her back to splay her side, then up, pushing between them until he cupped one gentle mound in his hand. She was soft yet firm in his palm. He squeezed her, gently. She sighed against his mouth, pressing her hips into his groin. His cock throbbed in response. Damn the tightness of her bodice. There was no way he could get his hand inside without doing damage to her gown.

He could unfasten it. Or he could rend it from her with one tear. Or he could just bend her over a bench and . . .

The taste of blood filled his mouth. It was faint, hardly anything at all, really. He might not have noticed were it not for the fact that the blood wasn't his own. It was Pru's.

Good God, she had nicked her tongue on one of his fangs. Thank Christ—and he meant that—that she hadn't noticed.

But he had. And the demon part of him had. Oh, God, it was a faint taste, but it was every bit as heady and marvelous as he'd dreamed it would be.

The muscles in his gums contracted, pushing his fangs farther from their sheaths. She would notice soon. One wrong sweep of her tongue and he'd do more than nick her.

Hunger cramped his stomach, clawed at his insides, climbed up to his chest. His muscles stiffened, tensed for the strike. He could move so quickly she wouldn't feel it until it was too late. He could bury his fangs in the softness of her breast, or the smooth column of her throat, and be drunk on her essence before she knew what was happening.

He couldn't do it. Gathering his strength, Chapel pushed Pru away. She stumbled backward, but she didn't fall and he made no move to catch her. It wasn't safe. His breath was ragged, the night roaring in his ears.

"Chapel?" Her voice was thick and low with longing. How *he* longed to give her what they both wanted, but it was what he wanted that had him ready to run if necessary. He'd rather hurt her feelings than hurt her physically.

"I have to go," he gasped, and winced at the rough edge to his voice. Yes, he had to go. His control was so fragile right now. He could hear the tremulous pounding of her heart, smell her desire, feel her heat. The taste of her, however faint, burned on his tongue, driving him mad with hunger.

"What's wrong?" She reached for him, but he lurched just out of reach, his stomach cramping so hard it almost doubled him over.

It would be so easy to claim her. Bend her over his arm, or perhaps take her to the soft grass. He could do it where no one would notice—on the inside of her thigh, high up so he could slip his fingers inside her as he drank. Or he could bite her *there*, between the damp lips of her sex, bring her to climax as she sated his hunger.

But she wouldn't sate him. He hadn't fed enough recently. If he lost control now, he would kill her, just as Dreux had killed that poor girl the night before he killed himself.

Oh, God.

"I'm sorry." It was trite, but he wanted her to know she hadn't done anything wrong. "I'm not . . . I'm sorry." Pivoting on his heel, he fled then. He ran past the house toward the darkness beyond. His eyes saw every obstacle, every hole, every rut. When he knew it was safe and far too dark for human eyes, he took to the sky and sped toward the nearest, largest town.

In his heart he knew what he was about to do was wrong, but it had to be done. He couldn't keep putting people at risk with his hunger, not when he knew what would quench it.

Time to find out if Molyneux's theories were right. Time to risk everything he believed and clung to, because he would not risk Pru's safety for his own beliefs.

And he would admit, if only to himself, that, if and when the time came that he took Pru's blood, he could trust himself not to kill her, because right now he couldn't do that. And he would rather burn in the dawn than harm her. Not her.

He flew for a long, long time. He wasn't worried, the evening was still relatively young, and he would be back in time to investigate the cellar before Marcus made his entrance. Even if he wasn't, Molyneux was there to make certain things went as they should. Molyneux would make sure Marcus didn't go into that cellar without him. An old priest he might be, but Molyneux was still one crafty bastard.

After some of the things the young man had said to him the other night, Chapel didn't trust him not to go into the cellar earlier. Marcus wasn't stupid enough to go in while it was still dark, though. Chapel was worried he would go at dawn, when people thought vampires were at their weakest.

Wrong. Those fragile hours of waning day and fading night were when a vampire was at his most dangerous. Temple would be tired, but the survival instinct would be kicking in with a vengeance. Dawn had a way of making a vampire edgy and unpredictable.

Which was why Chapel had asked Molyneux to watch Grey's room. Chapel would be useless once the sun began to rise, but Molyneux could make certain that Marcus did not get into that cellar.

But he had to admit it, right now he really didn't care about Marcus Grey and whether or not the man was stupid enough to risk facing Temple's wrath. He was focused solely on his own hunger.

He could make all the excuses he wanted. He could justify it any way he wanted, but it boiled down to the same thing: he was about to break the vow he'd made the day Dreux committed suicide. After hundreds of years, he was giving in to his darker nature.

His true nature.

He found his destination with little effort. The house had stood in the same part of town for many years now, passed down through the generations, sometimes family to family, other times purchased or gambled away. But always, the occupants stayed the same. He had never been inside, but he knew Reign often came here for . . . relief.

The madam looked up as he entered the brothel, her eyes brightening as they lighted upon him.

"Good evening, sir. What is your pleasure?"

"I need girls." That edge was still in his voice, but not as much now.

The madam smiled. "Of course you do. Come with me."

He followed her down the narrow hall to a parlor where a dozen prostitutes lounged in flimsy, frothy lingerie like a box of expensive candies.

The woman was still smiling, evidently proud of her stable, and rightfully so. They were all healthy women, glowing with vitality. No common whorehouse, this.

"Here are the ladies who are not already engaged for the night. Go ahead and pick whomever you would like."

He shot her a lazy glance. "I want all of them."

Her eyes widened. "All of them?" Then she smiled seductively. "As you wish, sir, so long as you can afford to pay."

Chapel pulled a wad of notes from inside his jacket. He had learned over the years to always carry money, since he never knew what kind of situation he might find himself in.

He handed the madam the bills. "Is that enough?"

Her heavily shadowed eyes brightened as she counted. "Yes, sir. This will get you twelve girls, certainly. Ladies, this gentleman would like to spend some time with the lot of you."

The girls began making all the appropriate noises as the madam turned to go. Chapel stopped her with a hand upon her arm. Her questioning gaze met his. "Sir?"

A slow smile curved Chapel's lips. His gums ached as they receded, the muscles in his jaw forcing his fangs to lengthen. Saliva moistened his dry mouth as instinct began to overwhelm him.

"I do not want twelve."

She colored, something he'd wager she didn't do very often anymore. "But sir, I thought you said you wanted them all."

He met her wide and inviting gaze with the smile of a cat eyeing a particularly plump mouse. He leaned closer to the woman, breathing in her perfume and warmth. Deliberately, he exhaled near her ear. "I do."

She shuddered. He was so close he could see the gooseflesh on her skin, smell the fear and arousal coursing through her veins. He did nothing to persuade her, but she tilted her neck in invitation anyway. They always did, as though there was something so very tempting about his embrace. He should back away, but she was so close and so willing and he was so very, very hungry. . . .

"I believe, my dear madam, that *you* bring the number to thirteen."

Chapter 12

Either she was like poison to the man, or there was something seriously wrong with Chapel.

As she sat at her dressing table in her nightgown, brushing her hair, Pru reflected rather glumly upon the evening. Her beautiful gown that she had worn for nothing more than a few moments' notice was draped over the back of a chair near her armoire. Tomorrow it would be packed away, and God only knows if she'd ever wear it again.

Setting the brush on the vanity, she stood. What had happened to Chapel to send him away like that? He had doubled over as though in pain and then fled into the night. Had he returned? If he had, he hadn't bothered to make an appearance at the party. Not even Father Molyneux knew where he was.

And Pru hadn't dared tell anyone that she had seen him in the garden. That her kiss had been what had sent him screaming into the darkness.

Maybe screaming wasn't the appropriate term, given that he hadn't screamed at all, but he might as well have.

How was she supposed to experience passion when the one man she wanted to experience it with wouldn't yield to her?

A soft sound permeated her thoughts. What was that? It came again. It was a knock at her door.

Hope suffused her. Was it Chapel? Quickly, quietly, she sped across the carpet and opened the door. But it wasn't Chapel her sinking heart encountered there outside her room. It was Marcus, holding a cloth bundle in his arms.

"Marcus, what are you doing here?" It wasn't nearly chastising enough when it came out as a whisper.

He backed her into the room and followed her, closing the door behind him. Dear God, what was he about?

He thrust the bundle at her. "Put these on and come with me."

Pru accepted the offering, seeing now that it was men's clothing.

"Why are you giving me men's clothing?" Had she more vanity, she might think he was trying to seduce her into running away with him, but Marcus wasn't the kind to run—or seduce, for that matter.

· "You can't very well go into the ruins in that." He gestured to her nightclothes.

"The ruins?" The mere mention was enough to send her heart skipping. "We're going to the ruins? Now?"

He nodded. "Go dress."

This impatience was hardly like him. Pru turned toward her dressing room, but her pace was slow. "But dawn's not for at least another two hours."

"That's why we're going in now. The priest is still asleep and Chapel is gone."

"Gone?" That stopped her in her tracks. "Where is he?"

Marcus came up behind her, gently but insistently pushing her toward her dressing room. "I'm not sure. He didn't go to the site, but that's just a matter of time. That's why we need to go now."

Pru dug her heels into the carpet. "Why are we going without him or Molyneux?"

A sigh of exasperation escaped Marcus's lips. Hands on her shoulders, he turned her to face him. "Because I want you to have whatever is in that cellar, Pru. I want it to be your choice, no one else's. Do you understand?"

She thought so, but seeing Marcus so intense was a little distracting. He was worried that Molyneux and Chapel might try to make off with the Grail before she had a chance to use it.

She didn't want to think so lowly of either the priest or Chapel, but what did she know of their motives? She trusted them both, but their first allegiance was to the church, not to her.

"I'll be as quick as I can be," she assured him, dashing into the dressing room.

The only things that fit properly were the stockings. The trousers were too big in the waist and tight in the hips and several inches too long. The shirt was too big as well, but she tucked it into the trousers to fill out the waist. The coat fit better—it probably belonged to a small man or a boy. She wore her own boots and pinned her hair up into a messy bun.

Marcus was pacing her room when she stepped out of the dressing area. "How do I look?"

"Ridiculous," he replied with a smile. "Ready?"

She nodded. Oh, yes, she was ready.

They left her room and crept down the stairs. Outside, he led her behind the house toward the stables, where two horses waited. Giving her a boost up, he then climbed up on his own, spurring it in the direction of the dig.

It was dark, the moon low in the sky. There was just enough light to see a few steps ahead, but that was all they and their mounts needed. These horses knew the way every bit as well as Marcus and Pru did. Around her the night sang its song and whispered delicate chants. An owl hooted, a bat swooped by, so close she could hear the thrum of its wings.

There was so much peace in the night. The breeze was cool and refreshing under the light of the moon, as opposed to the sometimes sticky heat of the day.

It wasn't a short ride to the site, nor was it a long one. The property had bordered the original southern boundary of the estate, almost a mile from the house. It took just enough time for her to think about Chapel and the kiss they'd shared.

I've thought of little else, he had confessed, his voice as molten as his gaze.

So she couldn't be poison to him, then, could she? If he wanted to kiss her so badly, why had he run off as he had?

Why torture herself this way? Had she not larger issues with which to concern herself? No doubt the next time she saw Chapel he would not only apologize for his actions, but offer an explanation for them as well.

With that matter resolved, Pru turned her thoughts to the Grail. Would it be there when she and Marcus entered the cellar? Yes, yes. It had to be. She refused to think otherwise at this point.

What would she do with her new extension on life? There were so many places she wanted to see, so many things she wanted to experience. Choosing a place to begin was overwhelming.

But one thing she wanted to do no matter what was make love to Chapel. She wasn't ashamed to admit it, though it was brazen of her. One thing she was not going to do once she was cured was go back to living her life as society thought she should. Life was too short for regrets, and when her time finally did come, she didn't plan on regretting anything she had—or hadn't—done.

She thought about those places she wanted to visit—and she imagined having Chapel there with her. They would explore the wonders of

Greece by night, see the moonlight shimmer on the Black Sea. Sunset over the Carpathian Mountains was no doubt breathtaking.

These were the thoughts that took her the rest of the way to the dig site and put a smile on her lips. Her heart was light, quick with anticipation as she and Marcus took the first step down to the cellar entrance. The steps were rough and uneven, but they were wide, so there was little danger of her falling.

Marcus held the lamp high as they descended. As the small golden halo of light touched the cellar entrance, Pru hesitated.

The door was open.

Had it opened on its own, or was there someone else there? She looked down. There were footprints pressed into the dirt, but they could belong to the workmen, not intruders. They could be Marcus's.

Had Marcus already gone inside, despite his promise to wait for her? Or were there thieves afoot? She opened her mouth to ask, but he turned and shook his head at her, his expression a mixture of fear and anger. No, it hadn't been him.

Nervously, she glanced around, but the night offered her no sign or sound of guests, unwelcome or otherwise.

Hadn't Marcus assigned men to watch the entrance? A discovery as important as the Grail warranted protection. This was not a detail Marcus would have overlooked.

Perhaps, then, it was his men who were inside, satisfying their own curiosity. But perhaps it was

Chapel. What if he had come to investigate the cellar? What if he and Molyneux meant to steal the cup from her? What if the reason he left her was because he felt too guilty about planning to betray her?

Enough questions. The answers she sought were inside the cellar and she and Marcus were going to find them. If anyone was in there trying to steal her Grail, she was going to give them a fight. She hadn't come this far to lose.

Air filled her lungs as she took a deep, steadying breath. Her knees trembled slightly as Marcus handed her the lantern, pulled a pistol from his coat and pushed the door open enough for them to enter. Did he think whoever had been in there was still present? And did he think this person enough of a threat that he might have to shoot him?

Please don't let it be Chapel.

There was no light but their lamp inside the damp, dirt-scented room. There was no sound save for their breathing—her own seemed loud enough to wake the dead.

The lamp only lit a few feet in front of them clearly. She turned the wick up to brighten the flame. She and Marcus stood side by side, their gazes taking in every detail.

The cellar was like a monk's cell. A cot sat in the corner, with a nightstand beside it. There was a lamp there as well. The blankets on the cot were wrinkled, as though someone had rested there recently.

A rough table was against the other wall, with

but one chair pushed under it. On the wall above it was a painting of a medieval knight and his lady.

Someone had once lived here. He couldn't live here still, could he?

"There's no one here," Marcus announced, having made a sweep of the small cell. The pistol went back inside his coat.

"But there was." Pru voiced what they both knew. "Does it look as though anything is missing?"

"I'm not sure I would know if there was," he replied. "Look for disturbed dust."

Pru looked, but either the lamplight wasn't enough or nothing had been moved.

Or there had been someone living there, and that someone kept a tidy house.

A tapestry on the far wall caught her attention and she raised the lamp for a better look. It was slightly askew, and what looked like a passageway peeked from behind it.

Good God, what was this place?

Pru moved forward. The Grail could be down that passage. Heart hammering, she took another step, and then another. She was almost there, just on the other side of the cot, when she stumbled. She had tripped over something.

Lowering the lamp to light her path, she looked down. Her heart jumped into her throat.

"Oh, my Lord."

Broken glass was scattered across the dirt floor. A tankard and a shirt were ground into the rubble. But that wasn't what terrified her.

It was the dead man staring up at her with life-
less eyes that froze the scream in her throat and
tightened her chest until she thought she might
pass out.

He was dressed all in black, with long hair and
a beard, and his face had been mutilated. It was as
if a wild animal had mauled him.

Bile rose in her throat. Who would have done
such a thing? More importantly, was that person
still there, waiting to do the same to her?

"Pru?" Marcus's voice was full of concern.
"What is it?"

He was coming toward her even as she whirled
on her heel.

She stumbled backward as she tried to avoid
stepping on the poor man's corpse. Had she been
wearing heavy skirts she might not have felt the
taunt resistance of something tugging at her legs,
but felt it she did. She felt it a mere second before
she heard a soft punting sound.

A stinging pain struck her in the breast. She
gasped in the darkness, almost losing her grip on
the lamp. She looked down and saw a small dart
sticking out of her chest. What the devil?

She had apparently set off some kind of trap.
Perhaps that was what had happened to the poor
man on the floor. Was she now going to meet a
similar fate?

"Pru?" Marcus's voice sounded thick in her
ears. "Pru!"

Her knees buckled as a wave of dizziness swept
over her. Marcus caught her, but not before the

lamp rolled from her fingers onto the dirt floor, illuminating the rest of the man in black.

Her vision swam as sweat beaded along her upper lip.

Poison. She had been poisoned.

"I don't want to die!" A sob lodged in her throat as she clung to Marcus's shoulders.

"I'll get help." She'd never heard Marcus sound so frightened. "Rest easy, Pru. I'll be right back."

He lifted her and put her on the cot. "Don't move," he instructed.

Move? Where the devil was she going to go?

She was so stupid. Why hadn't she stayed in her room? Why hadn't she tried to talk Marcus into waiting, at least till daylight? Or until Chapel could have come with them?

She trusted Chapel. And a part of her thought he would have been able to keep her safe. She might not have had much time left, but now her brashness had cost her whatever she might have enjoyed.

She wouldn't even get a chance to say good-bye.

So this was what peace felt like.

Soaring through the waning night sky, Chapel felt a lightness that he hadn't known in centuries. It was as though by committing this one unpardonable sin and damning his soul, he had bought himself contentment.

The madam had known what he was as soon as he'd smiled at her. Oddly enough, the sight of his fangs had extinguished the fear from her gaze.

All he had to do was mention Reign and she and her girls knew exactly how to service him. He didn't have to worry about losing control, because the madam was there to make sure he stopped when he had taken enough of one girl and gave him another. He took a little from each—not even enough to weaken them—but it was enough to strengthen him as he hadn't been strengthened in a very long time. He didn't give his own blood, so there was no danger of passing his curse.

He could resist Pru now. He didn't have to worry about hurting her, or worse. He would not force his bite upon her as he had Marie. He could kiss her, touch her and not fear that he would lose control—not of his demon anyway. He couldn't guarantee the man inside him wouldn't go absolutely mad when he touched her.

And he would touch her. If she let him, he'd do more than just touch. It didn't matter that she was a gently bred lady and most likely a virgin. He wanted her and she was old enough to know what she was doing. Virgin, yes, but she wasn't green.

He would take his time with her. He would make it good for her. He would caress her, taste her, worship her until she was limp and sated in his arms. He would possess her with long, easy strokes, and watch her face as her pleasure built to a crescendo.

The mere thought of how Pru would look as she reached climax was enough to give him a rock-hard erection.

Of course, he'd have to apologize for running

off on her earlier. He'd have to think of a reasonable excuse—one that she would accept but that
wouldn't make him look weak or sickly.

God, he hoped the Holy Grail was in that cellar,
and not Temple and that cup of damnation. He
wanted it so badly for Pru. He didn't want to
see the desolation on her face if her hopes were
dashed. And yet, even though he didn't want to
see it, he hated the fact that he wouldn't be able to
be there for her, because the sun would fry him
to a crisp. At least if Marcus held to his word and
allowed him to investigate first, he might be able
to share Pru's disappointment and pain as they
first struck.

Veering west, Chapel propelled himself closer
to the ground. He was almost there. The shadow
of Rosecourt loomed in the distance.

He landed on the balcony outside Pru's room.
The doors opened easily—and he stepped inside.

Pru wasn't there.

He checked the library. She wasn't there either.
Where the hell was she?

A thought, small and awful, came to him. Swift
and silent, he swept through the house to Marcus
Grey's room. It was empty as well.

Damn them both for being rash and foolish!
They had gone to the site.

He was outside, about to wing his way to the
ruins, when he heard a horse approaching. He sped
toward it, instinct telling him it was Marcus who
rode as though the hounds of hell chased him.

Where was Pru?

Both horse and rider started as Chapel came

to a halt before them. The run hadn't even winded him.

Fear rolled off Marcus in waves, but not fear of Chapel. Fear of something else.

"Pru's hurt. In the cellar. She needs help."

Terror seized him, but Chapel pushed it aside. "Wake Molyneux. I'll get her."

He didn't wait for Marcus to respond before taking off once more. He raced through the night, seeing perfectly in the darkness. Soon he saw the ruins appear before him, the mound of dirt and rocks near the cellar his focal point.

He sniffed the night, and caught a familiar, heart-swelling scent. It wasn't Temple, though there were traces of his friend there.

Pru.

She was indeed there, but he also discerned something tainting her scent, something that threatened to allow his terror to break through his carefully constructed defenses. He knew that smell but couldn't place it just yet.

He didn't hesitate. He jumped over the steps and landed in front of the door. He pushed it open so hard it slammed into the wall and lodged there.

Nothing came at him. No feral vampire attacked. No friend greeted him. There was nothing.

No, not nothing. There was a dead man he didn't know on the floor, and on the cot, in the pitiful glow of a dropped lamp, was Pru.

She was on her back, limp as a discarded doll. He could hear her uneven breathing, see the glassy pallor of her skin.

He knew without touching her, without any idea of what had happened there, that she was dying.

He was beside her in a flash, gently gathering her into his arms. Her eyes didn't open. Her lips were as colorless as her cheeks. A film of perspiration clung to her skin and she was clammy to the touch.

But he could see no readily discernible mark on her flesh, no sign of a struggle. He hadn't been expecting there to be—not once had he caught the scent of her blood. Temple hadn't done this to her—not directly. The dead man beside Pru hadn't been so lucky. Temple's scent was all over him. Temple had killed him.

A shudder wracked Pru's slender frame. She drew a breath—a shaky, tremulous sound like a child's rattle.

Panic tore through him. She couldn't die. She couldn't. Not like this. He pressed his hand over her breast. Her heart struggled to beat, but it was beating nevertheless.

The sound of rending fabric punctuated the awful silence. He pulled the dart from Pru's poor flesh. An ugly purple stain spread faint tentacles outward from the puncture. Scowling, Chapel sniffed the tip of the dart. He closed his eyes as the familiar scent sickened him.

Oh, Christ.

He knew the poison. It was rare and old, and hard to combat. It would incapacitate a creature such as a vampire or werewolf, and to humans it was deadly. He knew this because it was the same poison that had nearly killed him the night they found the Blood Grail.

He knew of only one cure, and that was his blood.

No, there might be another way.

Dawn was almost upon them. He could hide inside the passageway behind the tapestry, but Pru wouldn't be so fortunate. If he waited much longer, she would die here and he would be powerless to stop it.

He could only pray that what he was about to do would be enough to save her.

"Please," he whispered, lowering his head as his fangs slid from his gums. "Please."

He prayed for strength as he sank his teeth into the delicate flesh of Pru's breast where the dart had entered. He opened her savagely, making a larger wound to draw the poison out as quickly as possible. He drew from her with great force, taking her bitterly poisoned blood into himself. He gagged with every swallow, and still he drank, until he could no longer taste the poison, only sweet, heady Pru.

She was even more pale when he raised his head. The wound he had made was ugly, but he had stopped the flow of blood with a gentle pass of his tongue. In a day there wouldn't even be a scar.

That was if he managed to get her back to the estate, back to Molyneux, who would know what to do. She would need fresh blood—he had taken too much of hers. And she would need herbs and medicine. Molyneux would save her.

Cradling Pru in his arms, Chapel rose to his feet. The poison would hit him soon and he had precious little time to waste. It wouldn't kill him, but it would hurt him.

He held Pru in one arm as he yanked a blanket from the cot and draped it over his head, tucking it between himself and Pru to hold it in place.

Then he ran. Up the steps into the brightening morning, he moved as fast as his feet would allow. The poison slowed him, made him awkward, but he managed to remain upright.

The sun peeked above the horizon, searing him with a blinding slash of agony. He stumbled, regained his footing and ran on.

Every second was excruciating as he tore through the grass, across the dew-kissed green toward safety. His body was on fire, burning from the inside out, or from the outside in. He didn't know where the blaze started, he knew only that his skin was blistering beneath the blanket and his clothes.

He wasn't going to make it. He was going to explode just as Dreux had. He would splinter and burst into the sun in a million crystallized shards.

It was only the fact that he would be taking Pru with him that kept his burning feet moving. It was only the thought of Pru that gave him the strength to go on despite the agony that threatened to destroy him.

He was going to make it.

How he managed to make the leap from the ground to the balcony outside Molyneux's room, he would never know. It was as though an invisible hand had scooped him up and set him there. It might have been the blood he had taken from the prostitutes, it might have been fear for Pru— or it might have been the work of either God or Satan—but somehow he managed to get them both inside the priest's room.

Marcus was there as well. They had prepared the bed for Pru. Molyneux crossed himself at the sight of him, while Marcus stared with horror. He must look a fright, with his burned flesh and wild eyes.

Marcus caught Pru as Chapel collapsed to the carpet.

"Help her," Chapel pleaded of Molyneux as he crawled toward the huge wardrobe against the far wall. It was the only place where he could hide from the dawn that spilled into the room and continued to sear him.

"She's been poisoned. Temple's poison. She needs blood." Summoning what was left of his strength, he hauled himself inside the wardrobe, heedless of the contents pressing around him.

"Save her."

Molyneux nodded, and Chapel knew his old friend would not fail him. "Who will save you, *mon ami*?"

Chapel didn't answer. He allowed himself one last look at Pru, so fragile and pale on the priest's bed. Marcus was already rolling up his sleeve, prepared to give Pru his own blood. When this was all over, Chapel was going to pound Grey senseless for taking Pru to that dig. Obviously the young man didn't trust him.

Or he had wanted Pru to have the choice of drinking from the Blood Grail if it had been there. Stupid, stupid boy. He'd deal with him later.

Chapel drew the wardrobe door shut, encasing himself in blessed darkness. His head swam and pounded. His entire body throbbed in pain, but the fire of dawn could no longer touch him.

The only person who could save him was himself. He had to draw on his own strength and will himself to heal. If he did not, the combination of poison and the dawn just might bring his end. He had to hang on despite the pain, despite the peace that final death offered.

And he would hang on, because after centuries of wishing for death, he had something to live for.

And Chapel wanted to see her face just one more time.

Chapter 13

❦❦❦

"**O**ur Father must have a plan, *mon ami*, for you to live another day, *comprendez vous*?"

Strangely enough, Chapel did understand, and he agreed wholeheartedly. He was not going to die. He didn't want to die. For the first time in centuries he very much wanted to live, even if it meant hurting like hell for a while.

Most of the pain had subsided. He had spent much of the day before in Molyneux's wardrobe, healing himself with sleep and darkness. As far as the household was concerned, Chapel suffered only from his "allergy" to the sun, but that didn't stop the seemingly endless knocks upon the door inquiring after his health.

Every time someone came calling, the arrival

woke Chapel, put him in an even more feral, on guarded state. It wasn't good for the healing process, so Molyneux finally left the room for a few hours. He gave the family an update on Chapel's condition and left express instructions that the servants not enter his room. He even went so far as to lock the door, for which Chapel was thankful. It would be hard enough to explain his appearance, never mind the murder of one of Mr. Ryland's servants.

Molyneux looked after him, as he had many times over the course of their partnership.

Every once in a while, the sight of Francis Molyneux was a shock to Chapel. When he looked at him, he expected to see that same fresh-faced young priest who'd been assigned to watch over him as though he were an unruly child or an exotic pet. He'd let the church believe they could contain him and his fellow vampires, all the while praying that they could.

Molyneux had been assigned to him forty-five years ago, an eager young man with the fire of God burning in his belly. Now his black hair was liberally streaked with gray, his once-youthful countenance lined and not as bright. He was heavier, a little shorter, but to Chapel he would always be that stiff-spined boy who stared down what he had been told was a demon, confident that God would protect him. Chapel had delivered him of that notion quickly enough. He bared his fangs, took the boy down to the ground and held him there, letting Molyneux stare death in the eye.

Molyneux had lain beneath him, his heart hammering like the flutter of a hummingbird's wings. He stared with wide eyes, and then Chapel felt the sharp point of the stake against his chest. The boy was as brave as he was terrified, and he was the first of a long line that Chapel actually believed could and would kill him if the need arose. That knowledge alone had earned the young priest his respect, and eventually his friendship. That friendship was why it was sometimes so painful to watch Molyneux age. He was going to die someday—they all did—and Chapel would miss him greatly when he was gone. There would be another young priest, eager to prove himself, determined to drive the demon out of Chapel, or worse, master it, but there would never be another Molyneux.

Just as there would never be another Pru.

He was in his own room now, almost completely healed from the combined torture of poison and sunlight. Molyneux returned with news of Pru's recovery—and with the assurance that the family physician would not attempt to call on Chapel.

"How is she today?" he asked as he threw back the covers of his bed. The room was dark, but he knew the sun was sinking in the sky. He could feel the peace settling over his body.

Molyneux went to the window and pulled back the curtains, letting in the fading daylight. Chapel winced at the sight, his eyes still a little sensitive, but there was no pain.

"Mam'selle Ryland is expected to make a full recovery from her experience. I understand she will be joining us for dinner later this evening."

His chest tightened. Whether or not he would be at dinner was still a mystery. "Do I look presentable enough for dinner?"

He had no idea what he looked like, only how he felt, and his high threshold for pain didn't always allow for a reliable estimation.

As for looking for himself, that was a last resort. He didn't look in mirrors much because the silver backing interacted with his curse, changing his appearance in an almost indescernible but disturbing manner. Since the incident at the cellar, he hadn't wanted to look.

The priest smiled. "Your cheeks are a little pink from the burn, but other than that you look virile and healthy."

Chapel arched a brow. "Virile, eh? Will the ladies all swoon, do you think?"

Molyneux blinked. "What is this, humor? Perhaps you are dying after all."

"It's not that unusual," Chapel said as he crossed the carpet toward the small bathroom attached to his chamber. Rosecourt was equipped with all the modern luxuries and this lovely deep tub was Chapel's favorite, especially since it was outfitted for shower bathing as well.

"I can count on one hand the number of times you have uttered a humorous remark this past half century."

Chapel paused at the bathroom door. "No. Really?" He couldn't be that somber and depressing, could he?

Molyneux nodded. "Ah, *oui*."

"How do you stand to be near me?"

"I am witty enough for the two of us."

Laughing, Chapel had to agree.

"In fact," his friend began, carefully avoiding Chapel's gaze as he brushed lint from the sleeve of his coat, "since coming to Rosecourt you have not been your usual self. The change has been most . . . pleasant."

Stripping off the soiled dressing gown, Chapel turned on the taps and stepped naked into the tub. The water filling it was warm as it swirled around his ankles. From a jar at the side of the tub he took a scoop of herbs that would help with this healing process and sprinkled them into the water. "You think Pru is responsible, don't you?"

The priest was all innocence. "Why would I think that?"

Because Chapel knew it to be the truth. Because Pru made him feel more alive than he had in . . . than he ever had.

"I'll be back to myself in no time, don't you worry." He'd meant the words to be jovial, but they weren't.

Molyneux's expression saddened. "That is what worries me."

Chapel had no reply.

After bathing, Chapel returned to his bedroom clad in a fresh dressing gown of thick quilted black silk. Today's rest had helped considerably, as had the bath. There was no reason why he couldn't go downstairs and join Pru—and the others, of course—for dinner.

He dried his hair ruthlessly with a soft, fluffy

towel. These modern times spoiled him and often made him feel as pampered as a woman. Now even men used perfumed soaps. He could remember having to bathe in cold streams with nothing but sand to clean the dirt from his skin.

Truth be told, he rather liked his perfumed soap; it smelled like sandalwood.

"Did you speak to Marcus?" he asked, seeing that Molyneux was still there, sitting in a chair by the window. There was very little daylight left. The sunset was a smear of orange against a violet sky.

The priest nodded, his expression somber. "Yes. He took care of the dead man's body."

That was good. The last thing they needed were the local authorities snooping around and asking questions. "What did he do with it?"

"I did not ask. I do not want to know. He assured me that even if the man is found, there will be nothing to link him to the Rylands."

"That's all that matters." So long as the body was off Rosecourt property, it would most likely be assumed the man was killed by robbers. "What else did he say? Did he find it?"

"The *Sang Graal*? No, he did not find it, but you and I both know that does not mean it is not there. It would be hidden, I hope."

The Blood Grail? Molyneux thought he asked about the Blood Grail? "I meant the Holy Grail. Did he find that?"

Molyneux crossed his legs. The movement looked painful, reminding Chapel of his friend's age. He suddenly looked very old, and very tired. "No, my friend. I am afraid he did not."

He clenched the towel in his fist, so tightly that water actually seeped around his fingers.

"Does she know?"

If possible, Molyneux aged five years before his eyes. "I do not believe so."

Chapel turned away. Poor Pru. What now?

"I will tell her." He made the decision in an instant, as unpleasant as it was. "Marcus won't have the heart for it." Marcus had wanted the Grail for Pru so badly he had challenged Chapel for it. He would no doubt rather die than be the one to tell her they had failed.

"That is very good of you."

A bitter laugh scratched its way up his throat. "Yes, I am very good."

"You saved her, did you not?"

Chapel glanced over his shoulder. "Yes, and for what? A lingering death?"

Molyneux smiled. "Perhaps that is not to be her fate. God allowed you to save her, sparing her just as He once spared you."

He shook his head. How naive could a grown man be? "God didn't spare me, François."

"How can you say that? You live."

"I live because I went to a brothel and glutted myself on thirteen women. I live because I was strong enough to face a few moments of sunshine." He tossed the towel across the room and turned to face his old friend. "I live because I was not going to let *Him* have Pru, not before I have to. That is why I live."

Molyneux was pale. "You did not kill any of those women?"

He growled. "Of course not."

The priest's relief was palpable. "Good. There is no need for you to torture yourself, then. If you hadn't done that, you might not have been able to help Miss Ryland."

Chapel didn't bother to tell him that those women were probably what had saved Pru from his hunger. And he didn't tell Molyneux that he'd gladly kill twenty humans—men or women—if it meant Pru could have her full life. Hell, he'd change her if it didn't mean damning her soul.

But while he'd kill for her, he didn't dare change her, because he knew he wouldn't be doing that for her.

He'd be doing it for himself.

Blood filled Marcus's mouth. He spat it onto the boot of one of the men holding him. There was one on either side, holding his arms so that he couldn't attack their leader again. He didn't strain against their grip, but he kept his muscles tense, ready to pounce if the opportunity presented itself.

He had come here looking for answers, looking for some way to fix what his involvement with these men had wrought. Instead he found more lies, more deceit.

He hadn't been able to control his temper, not when he thought about what these men had cost him—had cost Pru. He simply attacked, going straight for the man he believed responsible for all of this.

He glared at the man before him—the man who had hit him—before turning his attention to the older man farther back, dabbing at the corner of his own mouth with a snowy handkerchief.

The man—he'd only heard him addressed as Magus—raised his black gaze to Marcus's. "You are a brave and stupid man, Mr. Grey. What did you hope to achieve by coming here and attacking me?"

"You were in the cellar." Marcus's jaw hurt, it was clenched so tightly in an effort to keep himself from pulling against the hands that held him. He kicked the body at his feet—the one he had delivered himself. "He's one of yours, isn't he?"

Magus's gaze flickered briefly to the corpse, but he didn't deny it. "We did not find the Holy Grail, if that is what you think."

Marcus held the man's gaze even though it made his flesh crawl. He doubted these men would admit to finding the Grail even if they had. They were smart enough to conceal possession of such an item. "What did you find?"

A coy smile curved thin, bloodless lips. "Only vermin. Only old relics. Nothing you would find interesting."

Marcus's heart skipped a beat. There was something in the way Magus spoke. Yes, he was smart enough not to be specific, but pleased enough to brag. Vermin. Relics. *Temple. The Blood Grail.* God help them all.

"You promised me an interview with Temple."
As if that mattered now. At first he had jumped at
the chance to learn about Dreux Beauvrai, and the
creature he had become. He wanted to unlock the
deep dark secret in his family's past—and yes,
the idea of immortality intrigued him, but now . . .
now it all seemed so stupid and petty when held
up against Pru's struggle to live.

What had he done? At least the poison hadn't
killed Pru, but the Grail hadn't been there either.
They had promised him the Grail. He had promised them silence—that no one would know of
their involvement.

More importantly, he all but promised the Grail
to Pru. His belief that something in those ruins
could save her had nearly killed her.

Promises meant nothing to these men. All they
understood was power. And now they had it all.

He could only hope that Pru would forgive him.
That Chapel would help him rather than kill him.
Help him make this as right as he could.

"Do you want me to hit him again, master?"
The man who had punched him asked.

Magus came closer, the cut in his lip raw but no
longer bleeding. "No. I will take care of this one
myself."

Marcus grinned. He couldn't help it. "Are you
up for it, old man?" No sooner had the words left
his mouth than he pulled free of his jailers, seized
them both by the back of the neck and smashed
their heads together. They hadn't even hit the floor
when he struck the third man hard in the throat

and then to the back of the neck, knocking him unconscious.

Then he pulled the revolver from his pocket and leveled it at the older man.

A scholar he might be, but Marcus had learned to fight with a professional his father had hired for him as a young man. The skills he learned at the gentleman's pugilist salon had been honed on the exotic and sometimes deadly streets of the East and even closer to home. He knew how to fight and he wasn't above being dirty about it.

Magus's eyes narrowed even further—they were little more than black slits in his face.

Marcus shrugged his jacket into place. "I just wanted to give you a chance to end this."

"The end is here for you, dear boy."

The air around him seemed to grow heavy, as though a great storm were coming. Marcus wasn't certain what Magus was capable of, but the man thought himself a mage. If he was responsible for this sudden change in the air, and was able to wield that kind of magic, Marcus and his pistol would not be able to stand against him.

He stepped back toward the balcony doors, the pistol unwavering and fully loaded. "You miscalculated, Magus. I'm ending this engagement, but this isn't over. I'm not going to let you take the Grail—Holy or Unholy—and I will not let you use Temple in your quest for power."

The smile the man gave him was smug and tinted with blood. "And how will you stop me, Mr. Grey? You don't have the power."

Marcus stepped out onto the balcony. It would be a quick slide down the trellis to the ground and the car he had waiting on the street below.

"I don't need power," he replied, flashing a grin as he swung one leg over the railing. "I have Chapel."

"What I want to know, Mr. Chapel, is how you knew where my daughter would be at such an ungodly hour."

Were it not for the smile on Thomas Ryland's face, Prudence might have worried for the man being asked that question. Chapel merely grinned. "It seemed only logical given Miss Ryland's natural curiosity, sir."

Even Prudence had to laugh at that. "Are you implying that I am nosy, Chapel?" She didn't care how much he teased her, it was just so wonderful to see him again. So wonderful to know he was all right.

He was all mock innocence. "Of course not, Miss Ryland. It would be boorish of me to do so."

Their gazes locked for a moment—long enough to make Pru's insides melt—and then her father spoke again.

"Well, I, for one, am very glad you came along when you did. Thank you for risking your own safety to bring her back to us."

Her father looked close to tears and now so was she. Her sisters were decidedly emotional as well. None of them were ready to say good-bye, not yet.

His expression decidedly sober, Chapel inclined his head toward her father. "I did it gladly, sir. And I would again."

There was nothing but utter honesty in his tone. He meant what he said. He would risk personal injury to protect her. Why? He had been burned by the sun in saving her—at least that's what Georgiana had heard. His condition had made saving her dangerous for himself, and yet he had done it.

That he had risked himself for her made her chest tight in a way she didn't want to ponder. The backs of her eyes prickled with tears of gratitude and affection.

Yes, affection. She liked Chapel. She more than liked him. Her every day brightened as the sun began to set, knowing that she was about to see him. She was attracted to him, interested in him as a person, and now that he had proven himself a hero, she was very much in danger of becoming completely infatuated with him. This was not good. Liking him, even being intimate with him, was one thing, but becoming attached . . . well, that could just be painful for everyone.

Speaking of painful, Marcus hadn't joined them for dinner. In fact, Pru hadn't seen him since her "accident." Was he blaming himself for what had happened? Or was he truly as busy as Caroline said he claimed? She hoped it wasn't the former. It wasn't his fault she had been hurt. She had gone to the ruins of her own volition, well aware of the risks.

Or was he simply avoiding having to tell her

that all hope was lost? It wasn't a possibility she wanted to dwell on, but she had to accept that it might be true. She had to accept that she was going to die before ever sprouting a gray hair or lines around her eyes, all those things that had terrified her in her youth and now she'd give anything to live to experience.

It would have been so amazing to have found the Holy Grail, to have held that legend in her hands.

But she wasn't dead yet, so she wasn't going to act like it. She was tired from her ordeal, her body still somewhat achy and sore, but she sipped at her rich wine and indulged her appetite for rare roast beef and opened herself up to enjoying being with people she cared about. Father Molyneux had told her that eating was one of the best things she could do to regain her strength, and it seemed she had been doing nothing but eating ever since waking.

After dinner, the ladies retired to the drawing room, where they were joined a bit later by the gentlemen. As soon as Chapel entered the room, Prudence beckoned him to her. Matilda rose from her seat beside Pru so that Chapel could take it, and left them in privacy, gently brushing her hand against Pru's cheek before doing so.

Chapel took the vacated seat, his long, muscular frame settling beside her with grace and ease. This love seat was supposed to hold two people comfortably. There was no comfort in sitting this close to Chapel.

Good gracious, but he looked fine in his evening clothes!

She placed her hand over the one he rested on his thigh. His skin was warm and firm. She could feel the strength in his fingers. "I want to thank you personally for saving my life."

He looked uncomfortable and stared at her hand as though he weren't certain what it was. She didn't remove it, however.

"Please don't. As far as I am concerned, there was no other choice." His gaze met hers. "I did what was right, not something that I wanted recognition for."

Was he being humble, or was he trying to dismiss her? His tone wasn't cruel, but neither was it as warm as she might have hoped. "Right or no, it means something to me and so I thank you for it."

His head dipped in a sharp nod. "Then you are welcome."

Silence followed as they stared at one another. She could stare into those pale golden eyes of his forever and not grow tired of it.

She broke the silence a few seconds later. "I hope you are not suffering any long-term effects of your heroism?"

He shook his head. "I am fine."

And he certainly looked it. Other than a little high color in his cheeks and across the bridge of his nose, he didn't look any the worse for wear. Then again, she looked surprisingly well for someone who had been poisoned such a short time ago.

"How did you get the poison out of me?" The question was out before she could think of a less blunt way to phrase it.

He didn't even blink. "I sucked it out."

Oh. Dear. Fire ignited in her cheeks as her hand pressed against the silk covering her breast. It was still a little tender and bruised, but the wound was almost completely healed—which was odd. He had *sucked* it out?

She glanced away. Could he see how he affected her? They were talking about him saving her life and she was aroused by it!

And she was amazed by it. Not only had he risked sunlight for her, but he had risked ingesting some of that awful poison as well. It was more than she could ever hope to repay.

Composing herself, she faced him once more. "Again, you put yourself at risk for me."

He turned his hand over, so that her palm rested against his. His hands were so long that the ends of his fingers could curl over hers. It was an interesting—and strangely intimate—sensation. "You seem to find that strange."

"I do. In my experience, people are often reluctant to risk their own safety for someone else."

"Not just anyone." He tilted his head as though surprised that he had to explain himself. "*You.*"

There was that heat again. Was she reading too much into his words, or did he truly think of her as something special? "You are making me blush."

A whisper of a smile curved his sensual lips. "I am too bold. Forgive me."

"I would much rather you continue." There. She could be bold as well. Perhaps it was time to allow her own feelings to come out. What was the purpose in hiding her regard?

Chapel's smile grew—in breadth and seductiveness. "Very well."

More silence, this time all the more heated and electric for their reckless confessions.

"Did you look around the cellar?" The question was sure to kill this intimacy between them, but she needed to ask this question before she could go on to make her request of him.

As she suspected, his expression sobered. "Briefly."

She straightened her spine. "It wasn't there, was it?"

A second passed—an eternity. She didn't have to explain what "it" was, did she?

He shook his head. The pity—no, not pity, *sorrow*—in his eyes answered her question. "No. I'll look again, I promise."

She knew he didn't expect to find it. It shouldn't be a surprise. Shouldn't make her want to cry so hard. "You know why I wanted to find it now, don't you?"

This time he nodded. "Yes."

"It wasn't for recognition or fame or even satisfaction." Why was she saying all of this when it wasn't necessary? He knew why she wanted the Grail, she could see that from the sadness in his eyes.

Tears threatened again, but she blinked them away. "I didn't want immortality or even fame. I just want to live the span of a normal life."

His fingers fully closed around hers. He didn't seem to care that it wasn't proper or that others might see. "You deserve no less. Were it in my power to grant your wish, I would."

And she saw the truth in his eyes. "You are a lovely man, Chapel."

He removed his hand, emotionally withdrawing from her as well as physically. "I am not lovely. You do not know the things I have done."

Not content to let him go, Pru seized his fingers in her own. "I do not care what you have done in the past. All that concerns me is what you have done for me. I would ask more of you if you will allow me."

Dark gold brows knitted. "I will do all that I can."

Pru's heart hammered like the pounding hooves of a galloping stallion. He couldn't possibly know what she was going to ask of him, and yet he offered himself freely.

"Do you drive, Chapel?"

He arched a brow. "You mean drive an automobile? Yes, I can drive."

"Will you teach me?" Surely her father wouldn't deny her the Daimler if Chapel was with her. As far as her father was concerned, Chapel could do no wrong now.

And it was something she had wanted to learn to do ever since her father arrived home with the Daimler. It would be fun, something to take her mind off things. She spent too much time in her own head and not enough time out in the world.

He shrugged, relief coloring his features. Had

he thought she might ask for something more personal? "Of course."

Pru smiled. "Thank you." That hadn't been so difficult. Perhaps soon she'd work up the courage to ask him to go share secrets and dreams with her.

Perhaps by then it would be easy to ask him to make love to her.

Chapter 14

"**D**id you find anything?" Molyneux asked after thirty minutes of silence.

Chapel pulled the tapestry over the tunnel entrance and brushed the dirt and debris from his trousers. "Nothing. Temple obviously used the tunnel as a way in and out of the cellar but nothing else."

The tunnel led to the beach, to a secluded location near the base of the cliffs. It was high enough off the ground to prevent humans from climbing in and dangerous-looking enough to be uninviting. No wonder Temple had chosen this spot as a hideaway.

The little cell was surprisingly clean and free of dust, which meant that Temple had been living there recently. The vampire's scent still lingered in the air, which meant that he had been there prior to Pru's accident.

But it was no accident. The poison might not have been meant for Pru specifically, in fact Chapel doubted it was, but the trap had definitely been meant for intruders. Had Temple set it? Probably, given that the poison was the same they had encountered centuries before. Either that or whoever came for Temple was descended from those ancient Templars. Both explanations seemed somewhat improbable, but not impossible. And one of them had to be true.

Chapel squatted near the bed to get a better look at the weapon used. A small wire across the dirt floor proved to be the trigger for the dart that had hit Pru. She had obviusly tripped it when she went to investigate the dead man. It wasn't a sophisticated setup. And yet, whoever had left the body had probably done so knowing that whoever found it would be poisoned.

Perhaps it had been meant for him.

"Did you accompany Grey when he disposed of the body?"

Molyneaux paused in his search for a hidden compartment in the floor. He dropped the corner of the rug and coughed on the dust it stirred. "I will be honest: though God may judge me for it one day, I was too concerned with your recovery and that of Miss Ryland to worry about what Mr. Grey did with a man who may have played a part in nearly killing you both."

Chapel rose to his feet. "Or may have abducted Temple." The idea of anyone kidnapping the vampire was ludicrous, but not impossible, especially if they knew what they were doing and what they were up against.

That was the theory that frightened him. Had Temple been abducted, or had he made a quick getaway after killing the intruder? There were signs that could confirm either theory, such as the dead man. There had been a struggle, but it didn't look as though anything—or anyone—had been dragged through the entrance, nor had anyone used that passage recently.

But vampires, as stealthy as they could be, didn't just disappear. And unless Temple had learned some new skills, there was no way he could have flown out of such a confined space.

Realistically it made more sense that Temple had simply escaped, but evidence—and his gut— told Chapel that his friend had not left this cellar willingly, or on his own. Which meant that whoever did this had incapacitated Temple and simply removed him from the cellar like a sack of potatoes.

"I do not like this," Molyneux remarked, easing himself into a rough-hewn chair with a sigh.

"I don't either." A glimmer of gold caught Chapel's eye and he reached for it, careful to be sure there wasn't another tripwire ready to release a hidden dart. A simple gold band sat on the small stand beside the cot. He recognized it instantly.

It was the ring Temple's wife had given him.

Chapel held it up as he turned to the priest. "He would not leave willingly without this."

Molyneux rubbed his forehead with trembling

fingers. "Who would have the strength to take Temple?"

The ring slid easily onto the ring finger of Chapel's right hand. He was not going to leave the ring there for thieves. He would give it back to Temple himself once he found him. "It would have to be a group who knew what they were dealing with. The question is, how did they know?"

"I may be able to answer that."

Marcus's arrival wasn't a surprise to Chapel, as he had heard him coming, but his statement was unexpected.

As unexpected as the scent of blood and rage clinging to him. Chapel's eyes narrowed as he watched the young man enter the cellar, into the pool of lamplight that illuminated the interior. Something had happened to change Marcus Grey. The scholar was looking a little more warriorlike.

"They knew because I told them." Marcus continued, "In fact, I'm pretty much responsible for all of this."

Black rage darkened the edges of Chapel's vision. The audacity of this pup to stand before him, knowing what he was, and to take responsibility for what had happened to Pru.

He actually growled at Marcus. It made him feel like little more than an animal. "Give me a reason not to kill you."

The young man's voice didn't even tremble. "I can't make things right if I'm dead."

No, but it might make Chapel feel better. "You think you can make things right alive?"

Marcus looked him squarely in the eye. "I don't know, but I want to try."

"Try isn't good enough for Pru." He ground his teeth together. His fangs scratched the inside of his lip. All it would take was one strong rip and Marcus Grey would be no more.

And Pru would hate him for it.

"I never promised to save her. I offered to help her save herself. Try was all I offered and all she asked." He lifted his chin. "Tell me, Mr. Immortal Being, what have you offered her? Certainly not your blood?"

"*Mon Dieu,*" Molyneux whispered. Chapel heard it despite the roaring in his ears.

"What do you know of my blood?" Surely he wasn't hinting that Chapel should change her? By God, he was. He had hinted at it before, had he not?

Marcus shrugged as though it should be obvious. "I've researched your kind ever since I first heard the stories about Dreux. I know that your blood would save Prudence."

"It would stop her from dying, but it won't 'save' her." What an idiot this boy was. Was that why he had brought Pru into this cellar that night? Had he known of the trap?

Chapel moved closer to Marcus. The younger man didn't budge, but Chapel could smell his wariness. "Did you bring her here hoping to find the Blood Grail?"

"I brought her so that if either Grail were here she would be able to decide for herself whether or not to use it."

He shouldn't be as astonished as he was. "Even the Blood Grail?"

Marcus nodded. "I assumed you wouldn't change her, but if given the choice, she might decide to save herself."

"Save herself? Have you lost your mind?" How could Grey have entertained such a notion? "If anything, it will damn her soul."

Grey looked at him as though Chapel were the idiot of the two of them. "Where did you get that idea?"

"Vampires are a demonic race, my dear boy."

Grey shrugged. "I prefer to look at them as the descendants of Adam's first wife and a fallen angel, but if you want to make them demons, go ahead."

"Is there a difference? Fallen is fallen, and both Lilith and Sammael were that."

"They were also both created by God," Marcus argued. "Falling to darkness doesn't change that. Even Lucifer is still an angel."

Molyneux spoke up. "On any other day I would love to debate these issues with you, Mr. Grey, but we do not have time. Please, tell us what you know."

Chapel watched warily as the young man swung himself up onto the table where Molyneux sat. He could rip Grey's throat out for putting Pru in danger, and yet he couldn't bring himself to do it—partially because he knew Grey might still be of some use to them, and partially because he wanted to believe some of what the young man was saying. Perhaps if he heard it from enough sources, he might eventually be able to hope, to believe that salvation was possible for him.

"Some time ago I was approached by a man who had heard of my interest in Dreux Beauvrai. He was very knowledgeable about the six of you." He nodded at Chapel. "He also knew about the legend of the Blood Grail. In fact, he claimed to know where it was hidden."

"What was this man's name?"

"I knew him only as Magus. He is the leader of an order of mages called the Silver Palm."

The Silver Palm. Chapel had heard of them before in whispers and old texts. They named themselves for the silver that crossed the palm of Judas Iscariot—coin imbued with the essence of Lilith, mother of all vampires. The same silver that had been melted down to make the chalice from which he and the others had drunk.

Christ, were they related to the secret order of Templars that hid the Blood Grail in the first place? And did they have Temple and the Blood Grail?

He tried to keep his panic from showing. "Did he orchestrate you meeting Pru?"

"No. That happened quite by accident, although it was he who encouraged me to entertain her theories. At first I thought she was delusional, but then I found her enthusiasm contagious."

"I'm sure." Oh, yes, he could take this man's head clean off.

Marcus's gaze was haunted as it met Chapel's. "I began to believe as well. We became good friends and when I found out she was sick I decided I would do everything I could to help her find the Grail." He glanced around the little cell. "I actually thought we might find it, that Magus was the one who was wrong about what lay hidden in the ruins."

"He wasn't." Chapel's tone was as flat and cold as the stone floor he stood on.

"I began to figure that out as soon as I realized who you were. I assumed you were sent just in case it was the Blood Grail we found. I didn't tell Magus how close we were to entering the cellar because I wanted to have the advantage, but it seems there was a spy among my crew, because he found out anyway. The man whose body you found with Prudence was one of the order." A muscle twitched in his jaw. "Magus sent his men for Temple and the Blood Grail. They were to kill whoever got in their way."

Silence followed. Chapel eyed him carefully, once more noting the scent of blood upon him. "Where have you been?"

"I took the body of his brethren back to Magus."

He was either lying or extremely brave—or stupid. "Were you hoping he would kill you before I could?"

"No." Much to Chapel's chagrin, Marcus didn't seem concerned at all for his own life. "I thought I might be able to get some information from him."

From someone calling himself Magus? A man who was probably a member of the higer tiers of the Silver Palm? Stupid, to be sure. "But you did not."

"No. Except I know that as of yesterday they hadn't left England."

He didn't bother asking how Marcus had managed to survive the meeting. Either Magus had willingly let him go or Marcus was smarter than Chapel believed him to be. "Do you know where they plan to go?"

"No, but I expect they will send men to kill me before they leave. I'm in hopes that one of them will be persuaded to tell me the order's location."

"How do you plan to extract this information?"

A direct blue gaze bore into his. "With your help."

Chapel laughed—harshly. "Why would I help you?"

"Because if you're not going to save Pru from death, the least you can do is exact a little vengeance on her behalf."

In a blink Chapel was on his feet. "I've had just about enough of your sanctimonious tone. You know nothing—*nothing*—about what I am, or what it is like to live forever watching people you care about die. Is that what you want for Pru, to have her watch her sisters wither and die?"

Marcus met his gaze evenly. "It is not a question of what I want. The question is, what does Pru want? Have you even offered her the choice?"

Chapel raked a hand through his hair. "Of course not."

Marcus stood. Chapel was the taller of the two, but Marcus was the more muscular. Were they both human, it would be an equal match.

But they weren't both human. And Marcus

Grey didn't seem to care. "Then stop trying to intimidate me with your huffing and puffing, and help me figure out a way to save Pru and her family before dawn."

Before dawn? That was a little melodramatic, was it not? "What? You want me to change the entire Ryland family now instead of merely Pru?"

"No. I want you to help me protect them from the men who are no doubt on their way to Rosecourt even as we speak." Marcus shoved past him. "You don't think they intend to let any of the Rylands—any of *us*—live, do you?"

Chapter 15

❧

She was not alone.

It was still dark when Pru woke, and even though she was groggy with too little sleep, she knew there was someone in the room with her.

The realization had barely registered when she was grabbed by a rough pair of hands and hauled from her bed. She fought against them, kicking, thrashing and screaming, but they held fast to her. A fist struck her jaw and she fell, shocked into silence, the entire left side of her head throbbing from the blow.

She did not try to struggle again. They might knock her unconscious next time, and then she wouldn't be able to do anything to defend herself against them.

They dragged her downstairs to the drawing

room. Two other men were there, pointing guns at Matilda and Frederick, her husband. Matilda looked terrified. Pru tried to go to her, but the man behind her stopped her with a tight grip on her arm.

She shot a reassuring look at Matilda, trying to calm her sister's fears. The rest of her family, including her father, was brought in by armed men. Corralled and cornered like sheep, they all stood there in their nightclothes, trembling and confused.

"What do you want from us?" her father asked.

One of the men who had grabbed her—Pru assumed he was the leader, given his air of authority—looked at her before replying, "Your daughter has involved herself in matters which she should have left alone. We cannot allow any of you or the information you might have to exist."

Matters? Information? What were they talking about? Surely they didn't mean her quest for the Grail?

Oh, God, they did. The man in the cellar, he had been dressed like these men. He had been one of their number. They knew about the cellar. They had been there before she was. Whatever had been in there was now in their possession.

The men were going to kill them all. It wasn't enough to take what was left of her life, but they were going to let her die knowing that she was responsible for the deaths of the rest of her family as well. Were it not for her foolish ambitions to cheat death, none of this would be happening.

She met Matilda's terrified gaze. "I'm so sorry,"

she whispered, her voice choking on the same tears that filled her eyes.

The man in the front leveled his pistol at her father. Oh, God, he was going to shoot her father first.

Her father closed his eyes, so calm and strong. Pru could never be that strong, never just accept death for the end that it was.

Unbelievably, the man was stopped by one of his companions. "Not yet. They're not all here."

As though summoned by his words, the door opened, revealing more black-clad men. They shoved Molyneux and Marcus into the room. Another man they led into the room in shackles. Pru knew who it was without seeing his face. She knew from the golden silk of his hair, the strength in his posture. Molyneux and Marcus were clad in dressing gowns like her brothers-in-law, but Chapel was clad in nothing but a pair of black trousers. On his back, high on his right shoulder, was a scar in the shape of a cross.

Despite the danger they were all in, Pru couldn't help but stare at the magnificence that was Chapel's naked torso. Golden, rippled muscle lightly dusted with darker hair. His biceps were hard and smooth and the muscles in his shoulders shifted with every movement, as though he were waiting for the right moment to attack.

God, was she to watch him die as well? Were they all going to meet their Maker together?

"Why are you doing this?" The sound of her own voice surprised her.

One of the men looked at her. There was nothing but coldness in his pale gray eyes. He shoved Marcus toward her. "Ask him."

The look on Marcus's face was one she had never seen before. Where was her boyish friend? When had he been replaced by a man who looked as though he would like to spill some blood himself? And why was there blood on the sleeve of his robe? Had one of their captors wounded him?

"Marcus?"

He met her gaze. "I'm sorry, Pru. This is all my fault."

What? "How?"

Before Marcus could answer, one of their captors stepped forward. "Enough talking. Open the drapes. It will be dawn soon and we don't want any surprises from our friend here."

Prickling cold trailed down Pru's cheeks and arms to pool at her feet. He had gestured toward Chapel, whom they had placed in the darkest corner of the room, when he had said that. How could he know about Chapel's condition? More importantly, what kind of monster was he, to sentence Chapel to such a painful death?

"Bastard," she snarled.

The man turned on her, leveling a pistol at her chest. "Hmm. Since you are the only one who objects, I think you should be the one to open the drapes."

"No."

He pulled the hammer back on his pistol. "Do it."

For the first time since this whole nightmare

began, Pru actually felt as though she had some power. "Or what, you will shoot me? I'm already dying, you cretin. Nothing I can do will change that, so if you want to shoot me, go ahead. You will be sparing me a lot of pain. But if you want those drapes open, you are going to have to do it yourself."

Her gaze flickered to Chapel. Was that admiration she saw in his eyes? Or was it something more? Whatever it was, it made her feel very warm inside. For the first time in a long time, she felt strong and in control of her fate.

Elation and empowerment was short-lived as the man shifted his pistol to target Georgiana. "Then open the drapes or I'll shoot *her* instead."

Dread, sick and vile, rolled in Pru's stomach. This was what true helplessness felt like. Once more she looked at Chapel. Would he forgive her for causing him pain in exchange for an extension on her sister's life?

He nodded at her. He understood, but that did little to make her feel better as she went to the closest window and pulled open the drapes.

For a moment she simply stared at the glass. It should be getting light, but it was just as black as the deepest night outside.

It looked like paint. The windows had been painted black. Had the three of them been expecting something like this?

This time, when she looked at him, there was no mistaking the expression on Chapel's face. It was one of satisfaction, and bloodlust. It frightened her. It excited her. It gave her hope.

There was also no mistaking the flicker of dismay on the faces of the men holding them.

The rest happened so fast it was hard to make sense of it all. The men turned on Chapel, firing their pistols in rapid succession. Even as her family members dove for safety, Pru cried out for the man who had come to mean so much to her.

But Chapel didn't fall to the floor as her breaking heart had expected. He didn't fall. He charged.

Marcus knocked her to the floor, shoving her behind the sofa for protection. Pru crawled forward, peeking around the side. She had to see what had become of Chapel; her heart demanded it.

And her heart gave a mighty slam against her ribs as she saw him still standing. His chest was dotted with wounds, blood running down his tanned flesh in tiny rivulets. He moved with a speed and grace that was almost hypnotic and a lethal precision that took her breath away.

He wrapped the chain of his shackles around one man's neck. A quick twist was all it took to drop the man dead to the ground. He'd barely struck the carpet when Chapel launched himself at another man. He killed this one with the same efficiency. He moved so fast, he was almost a blur.

A part of Pru realized she should be horrified, but she wasn't. She was too giddy with relief. Good God, was it possible that they were going to be all right?

And what about Chapel? He should be dead. That many shots should have killed him instantly. Why was he still alive? How had he managed to free his legs of the shackles that had bound them when he entered the room? And what had he done to snap the chain that connected the bands around his wrists? When had he snapped it? It had been whole just a moment ago. . . .

She watched him as he mowed the men down one by one. Then a man attacked him with a dagger, driving the blade deep into his chest. Pru gasped.

This was it. This was when she would see him die. *Oh, God.*

But he didn't die. He pulled the dagger from his chest and tossed it casually to his right. It hit one of their captors in the throat. He fell to the floor twitching.

Pru's mouth dropped open.

Marcus tried to draw her back behind the sofa. "Don't watch. You shouldn't see this."

She turned to him, disbelief numbing her limbs. "What am I seeing, Marcus?"

His smile was grim as he shrugged out of his dressing gown. He was dressed in trousers and a shirt. A crimson-stained bandage adorned his left arm. Apparently the dressing gown had been used to make their attackers believe they hadn't been expected.

He pulled a pistol from the waistband of his trousers. "You are watching Severian de Foncé save all of us from certain death."

"Severian de Foncé?" But that was the knight in Chapel's story. Chapel couldn't be Severian, not if the story was as old as he claimed.

Could he?

She peeked around the sofa once more as Marcus leapt to his feet and began shooting. Around her, her family huddled beneath the protection of furniture while Marcus and Chapel—and even Father Molyneux—waged war.

Chapel's eyes seemed to glow from within, lit with a preternatural force Pru couldn't explain. He smiled at a man who threw himself at him. Were those *fangs* in his mouth?

She ducked back behind the sofa, leaning up against it for support. Was she losing her mind? Was fear driving her insane?

And then the room fell silent. There were no more shots, no more cries or crashes.

Cautiously, Pru peered out from her hiding spot.

"Ahh!" she squealed when a man suddenly appeared before her. Not just any man, but Chapel, who now looked surprisingly normal for a man whose chest had been shot full of holes. Oh, yes, and he had been stabbed as well.

"Are you all right?" he demanded.

She could only stare at the blood splatters on his face, at the wounds on his chest. "I should be asking you that question."

"I'm fine."

She swallowed hard against the lump in her throat. "Oh, Chapel, no, you're not." No one could be fine after all that. No one.

The surface of his chest changed. Pru blinked. Eyes narrow, she leaned closer, not caring that it was a man's naked chest she was examining. Either she was hallucinating or . . .

Well, she just had to be hallucinating, because there was no way the wounds in Chapel's flesh could be healing.

Yet they were. She watched as the gash where the man had plunged the dagger began to close and shrink. It was healing before her very eyes!

Her stunned gaze lifted to Chapel's. "What are you?"

He tried to smile, but it just made him look sad. "I'm a vampire."

And then Pru—who had always prided herself on being anything *but* a weak, vacuous female—fainted.

Chapel caught Pru as she went limp. His blood stained the virginal white of her wrapper, twisting his stomach as he realized it could have easily been her own blood ruining the delicate cotton. Thank God she hadn't been hurt.

He rose to his feet, cradling her against him. Slowly, he lowered her onto the sofa, reluctant to attempt to wake her. When he straightened, he found her family clustered together like a basket of kittens, watching him.

"I'm not going to hurt you," he told them. Any minute now, they'd be running for their torches and pitchforks.

"I think if that was your intention you would have done it before this," Thomas said.

Matilda looked at him as though he were

mad, but the other women—and their husbands—regarded him like children watching a tiger. They looked as though they wanted to embrace him, but were afraid to.

"Who were those men?" It was Pru who asked. Turning, Chapel saw that Molyneux had helped revive her. The priest held her hand as she spoke.

It was surprisingly easy to meet her gaze. There was no hate in her eyes, only disbelief. No doubt the fear and hate would come soon, once the shock had worn off. "They belong to a group called the Order of the Silver Palm."

It was obvious from the blankness of her expression that the name meant nothing to her. However, she seemed to grasp what they were doing there. "They were going to kill us because of my search for the Grail."

The pain and conviction in her tone tore at Chapel's heart. "Not because of you, Pru. Never because of you."

Either no one noticed that he had used a pet name for her, or no one cared. At this point it was hard to tell. They were still watching him as if he were some kind of mix between wild animal and god.

All except for Pru, of course. She was too busy looking guilty and hurt to gaze upon him as a god. It surprised him just how much he would have liked to see adoration instead. Despite his own guilt and disgust at what he was, he would like her to see him as something special.

He wanted to be special, not a monster.

"It wasn't the Holy Grail they were after," Chapel

told her. He wasn't about to make Marcus Grey's explanations for him, but he couldn't let her blame herself for this bloodshed. "They were after something much older called the Blood Grail. It had been under the protection of a friend of mine, but they used your excavation to get to it and, I fear, have captured my friend."

His gaze met Marcus's over Pru's head. The blue-eyed man nodded, understanding that Chapel was leaving other details up to him. Marcus knew this family better than Chapel, and he truly hadn't intended anyone to be hurt. Plus, he was the one who had been duped by the order. The story was his to tell, not Chapel's.

Pru's brow puckered. "What of your friend? Is he dead?"

A sharp, piercing pain lanced his chest. She thought of him, of his pain, even now. "I don't think so, no." He wasn't sure how he knew, but he was almost certain Temple was alive. He was also certain that Temple was in the custody of the Silver Palm. The one calling himself Magus had not been among this group, which meant that the leader was probably already on the move. Whatever the order was up to, they apparently wanted all vampires alive. He had heard one of the men remind another not to kill him when they were attacking.

In fact, he'd be willing to bet that the order had thought the dawn would make him weaker, that he would be sleeping when they arrived and an easy capture.

Caroline found her voice. "You're a vampire."

It wasn't quite a question, but he answered regardless. "Yes."

She came forward a little, enough to stand before her family, but not too far from safety. Or rather, what she perceived as safety. Chapel wasn't about to tell her that not even her entire family combined could save her if he wanted to attack.

"Like Count Dracula?"

Mon Dieu, was there no one who hadn't read that damnable book? "Not quite."

"Perhaps Varney?"

"No."

"Lord Ruthven?"

She certainly was well read on the topic. "To my knowledge there has never been an accurate depiction of the vampire in literature." Either that or he and his four former companions were freaks even among monsters.

Not something he wanted to consider at the moment.

Caroline's lips thinned. "One would think *someone* would write an adequate account."

Chapel tried to smile. "Most of us try to avoid prolonged contact with humans."

"Why is that?" Caroline's tone was as curious as any scholar's.

"Probably because they start to wonder what kind of wine complements us best, Caro."

Chapel scowled at Pru's sarcasm. "Red."

Now she looked at him like he was a monster. He had expected it, but it hurt all the same. When had he ever tried to harm her or her family? He wore the blood of many to protect them, blood that overwhelmed his senses and made his gums ache. Still, he controlled himself and the lust within. Had he not sated himself with the prostitutes days before and kept himself strong with Molyneux's daily offerings, he would not have such control.

"Because," he informed her in a cool tone, "humans tend to react hatefully toward those things which they do not understand. It is safer for us to avoid such situations."

She flushed and lowered her gaze, her attention going to his chest. The wounds there were still healing, the flesh around them burning and itching as his body repaired itself. Did he repulse her? Frighten her? He picked up Marcus's discarded dressing gown from the floor by the sofa and put it on, pulling it as closed as he could and belting it tightly.

"I did not mean to stare," Pru murmured, still avoiding eye contact.

Chapel shrugged. It wasn't as though he had expected her to accept what he was. "Think nothing of it."

A snort of laughter left her, as though the idea of *not* thinking about it seemed an impossibility.

He hadn't meant to show up shirtless, but the one he had been wearing had black paint on it and dirt. He had been in the midst of changing when the Silver Palm showed up. It had been difficult enough trying to fight them without actually winning, given his rage, but they needed them in one place. Needed to protect the family. Finding clothes suddenly hadn't seemed so important.

"What happened to the windows?"

She was certainly very full of questions for someone who acted like she couldn't stand him. Why not demand this information from Molyneux or Grey rather than him? "The evidence in the cellar led us to believe there might be an attack on the house. Marcus had the idea to cover the windows to keep the sun out so the attackers couldn't use my weakness against me."

"Is sunlight your only weakness?"

"I am a man. I have many weaknesses."

Pru snorted. "We know that a vulnerability to bullets and daggers isn't one of them."

She sounded almost jealous. Perhaps it wasn't disgust she felt toward him at all. "It is difficult to kill me, yes, but not impossible."

"But cancer couldn't kill you, could it?"

He wouldn't have been more surprised if she had doused him with holy water and shoved a crucifix down his throat.

"No," he replied truthfully, though he didn't want to. "I'm not vulnerable to disease or sickness at all—at least not human sickness."

There was a hardness to her expression now. "So disease can't hurt you, and neither can personal injury. Yet you claim to have weaknesses. What are they?"

She was angry with him. And she was looking for a fight. He supposed she felt betrayed, alone and confused. And helpless. He could see that in her eyes. Still, he didn't like her tone, even if he did deserve it.

"Poison can make me sick," he informed her.

"Such as the poison I took from you in the cellar. And sunlight, such as the dawn I carried you through that same morning, can kill me. In fact, had you been conscious, I imagine the sight of me then would have been bad enough to give you nightmares. Will those do for weaknesses, Pru, or shall I go on?"

"No," she whispered. "That is enough."

Too far. He had gone too far, he could see it in her eyes. He'd hurt her when he hadn't meant to. No, that wasn't quite true. A part of him had wanted to hurt her, wanted to make her realize that he wasn't to blame for her illness, that she shouldn't envy his life.

Because it wasn't a life when you didn't *live*.

And perhaps there was a small part of him that resented her for making him see something worthwhile in living. It would have been so easy for him to give up and die that morning he'd carried her from the crypt. He could have given up, begged for forgiveness for his soul and gone wherever his kind went in the afterlife. Instead, he had clung to life, clung to this world. And he had done it for no other reason than he wanted to live to see Pru one more time.

In fact, he had the rather acute thought that he would continue to want to see Pru one more time even after she was gone. Maybe once she was at rest he would be able to go as well, but he doubted it. The chance to sacrifice himself for someone else didn't come very often. This was his first in six centuries.

He had managed to save Pru and her family, at

the cost of Pru's trust. He could live with that, so long as she still breathed. But what if the order returned when they learned the Rylands were still alive? The next time they might wait until the sun was high in the sky to attack, instead of foolishly thinking he was weakest at dawn. They had been lucky this time with Marcus's cooperation. Next time . . .

He would just have to ensure there wasn't a next time. If he had to hunt and run to ground—or grave—every member of the Silver Palm, then he would do just that.

Some of his bloodlust must have shown on his face, because it was a room of pale faces that watched him.

Molyneux finally came forward. A cut on his head oozed bright red down to his eyebrow and around his left eye, but otherwise he appeared unhurt. The old priest could probably wrestle Satan himself and come out none the worse for wear.

"I know this is all very *fantastique* for all of you. I have spent more than half my life with Chapel and sometimes I expect to wake and discover it has all been a strange dream. Perhaps I can make it easier for you to understand."

Molyneux's words seemed to give a little comfort to the family, except for Pru. A pained expression came into her eyes when Molyneux admitted to having spent most of his life with him. His immortality was like a raw wound to her right now. What was worse: that she had believed him to be just another man, or that he would outlive her even if she found a miracle cure?

"Please excuse me," she murmured, rising from the sofa before Molyneux could go one. "I believe I will retire to my room."

Chapel started to follow her, but Marcus stopped him with a firm hand upon his sleeve.

The dark-haired man nodded to the hall beyond the drawing room. It was bright with light—light so bright it stung Chapel's eyes. The sun.

"She needs some time to herself," Marcus said in a low voice. "And you broiling yourself won't change that."

Chapel nodded, his movements jerky with suppressed frustration. He would hide in this darkened room like a snake under a rock until it was safe to emerge, and then little Pru would have to face him. He could wait a few hours for that.

After all, what did he have if not time?

Chapter 16

Marcus didn't look up as Pru entered the sitting room he used as a study. He sat bent over a stack of papers and a journal that was yellowed with age. His hair was mussed, and as he scribbled notes in a notebook, he drove the fingers of one hand into the dark waves.

"Did you know?"

He looked up. He seemed surprised to have company but not at all surprised that it was her.

He didn't bother with hello either. "You mean about Chapel?"

Pru nodded. "Of course."

Withdrawing his hand from his hair, Marcus leaned back in his chair. He was rumpled, his shirt creased but thankfully clean. He had at least changed clothing after the bloodshed in the drawing room earlier. He looked more like the Marcus she knew and loved, not the stranger she had seen that morning.

To think it had been but a few hours since men had come to kill her and her family. A mere few hours since she'd learned that Chapel wasn't human, and that he'd already lived close to a dozen lifetimes while she wouldn't be allowed the fullness of one. And then she had found out that Marcus had befriended her because he had been urged to by those same men.

And yet, as much as she wanted to hang on to her feelings of betrayal, she couldn't. Marcus had helped her and had proven himself a true friend by risking his own safety for her. He had done what he did because he was offered a chance to learn about his family—a quest he'd been on for years. She couldn't hold that against him.

As for Chapel, he had saved not only her life but the lives of her family as well. How could she be bitter about that?

She was not totally innocent in all of this. It was her own selfish desire to prolong her life that had made all of this possible. The order wouldn't have been able to use Marcus to get to her if she hadn't been so obsessed with finding the Grail. Back when it had been nothing more than a historical fascination, she wouldn't have been quite so quick to jump at the carrot dangled before her.

She wasn't bitter about that either. There was no point, although she would be lying if she said she didn't harbor some guilt for whatever part her actions had played in leading up to this morning's attack.

She blinked and found Marcus watching her in silence. "I've known about Chapel since I first started my research on Dreux Beauvrai, though I didn't know him as Chapel then."

"Severian de Foncé."

"Yes. His strange aversion to sunlight and penchant for nocturnal wanderings made me curious to check my notes, and there it was—a reference to the names the knights took when they first gave themselves to the church. Chapel was listed as Severian's new name."

He hadn't known for long, then, but long enough to have purposefully withheld the information from her. "Why didn't you tell me?"

A dubious smile curved his lips, making him look more his age. "Would you have believed me?"

Probably not. "Perhaps."

His smile widened. "You would have thought me mad."

Exasperation left her in a loud huff. "Fine, I would have, but that is not the point." She pulled herself together, leveling an even gaze at him. "You lied to me, Marcus."

"Yes."

At least he didn't try to deny it. She waited for him to continue. He stared at her. "Aren't you going to apologize?" She prompted.

"But I'm not sorry I lied." Only he could say something like that and still look innocent. "I'm only sorry that you found out, and that your association with me put you in danger."

He might not be totally honest, but he was certainly direct. "You are not sorry you lied?"

"No. I lied at first because I've found it more advantageous than admitting to searching for creatures of myth. Then I merely lied to protect you and your family. I had no idea it would go this way."

"And yourself." It was difficult to keep the sneer from her voice. "You lied to protect yourself."

Not even a flinch. "Of course. Did you not lie to me at first about why you wanted to find the Grail?"

Heat flooded her face. "That was different."

Marcus linked his rough hands across his belly. "If that makes you feel better, fine."

What did it say about her that she found him somewhat attractive now that he had revealed this side of his nature? A scholar he might be, but underneath his thirst for knowledge lurked a side of Marcus that liked a little danger. It was a side of him that reminded her of Chapel. Protective, dependable and yet untamable. A romantic notion, but true.

Obviously she was drawn to dangerous men, because they didn't come any more dangerous than a vampire.

But ever since Chapel had admitted what he was, she'd been thinking about what it would be like to feel his fangs in her flesh, to have him take her blood. Or had Mr. Stoker and all the other writers been wrong about that as well? It seemed that most vampires in fiction were blood-hungry fiends who took advantage of impressionable young women.

God knows she was impressionable, and here she had yet to be taken advantage of.

Had Stoker been wrong in saying that vampires could turn humans into vampires as well? And if he could, would Chapel turn her? And if he offered, would she allow it? She just wanted a normal life. Immortality wasn't normal.

But it would be immortality with Chapel, and that was an idea that appealed to her more than she would ever dare admit.

Imagine all the things she could do and see if she lived forever!

God, she shouldn't think such awful thoughts, but she couldn't help it. She was dying damn it, how could she not wonder? She'd always been a selfish creature, and death wasn't about to change that. In fact, her impending demise often made her more self-centered.

"So aren't you going to ask?"

Her attention snapped back to Marcus with an annoyed frown. "Ask what?"

He looked at her as though he thought she was playing coy. "About Chapel. That's why you really came here, isn't it?"

So maybe he wasn't so attractive after all, the bloody insolent git.

He was also right, and no doubt the color in her cheeks was proof of that to him as well. She had wanted to confront him about his involvement in the situation, of course, but even though Marcus had his own reasons for hunting the Grail, he hadn't truly betrayed her. He simply hadn't trusted her with a fantastic tale, and she supposed the fault for that had to rest on her own shoulders as well as his. Had she not been so desperate, she might not have been so eager to admit to thinking that drinking from a particular cup might cure her.

What had driven her to his room was the fact that he seemed to know more about Chapel than she did, and she couldn't stand that.

She swallowed. Her pride tasted bitter as it went down. "Will you tell me about him?"

Hands still linked across his abdomen, he spread his thumbs wide. "Of course, but he would be the more reliable source."

She colored. "I would rather hear it from you first." The truth was, she wasn't ready to face Chapel just yet. She needed to be prepared, to have something to fortify her. Knowledge was something that always gave her comfort. She preferred being well schooled where her adversaries were concerned, be they the cancer in her or the vampire who affected her like no mortal man had.

Marcus studied her, his keen blue gaze seeing far more than she was comfortable with him seeing. "Sit. I'll tell you what I can."

Pru settled on the window seat and Marcus began to speak. His tale was very similar to the one Chapel had told them that night after dinner, but Marcus's was more detailed. He told her about Chapel and his friends being sent to find Templar treasure and how they had found the

Blood Grail instead. He told her about the poison that had driven Chapel to drink from the cup and she shivered. Taking the poison from her as he had must have been a terrible reminder of that.

He told her about how the men had returned home expecting to be exalted as heroes, only to find out their families thought them dead. And he told her about Marie. How hard it was to believe that the silly woman had actually tossed herself to her death rather than embrace forever with the man she was supposed to love.

Pru had the same opinion of the woman now as she had when she'd thought her nothing but a character in a story—Marie was a twit.

Or perhaps Marie hadn't loved Chapel as she had claimed to have. Regardless, Pru knew without a doubt that she wouldn't fling herself off a balcony if Chapel told her he wanted her with him for all eternity.

All eternity. It was a frightening and exciting thought.

"When Dreux Beauvrai, my ancestor, committed suicide, the rest of the brotherhood turned to the church, offering themselves in service, in the hopes of saving their souls. Only Temple and Chapel stayed."

"Brotherhood?"

He nodded. "The Brotherhood of Blood."

Pru's eyes widened.

Marcus waved a hand. "It is melodramatic, I know, but it is the name most often applied to their group."

The Brotherhood of Blood. Very dramatic indeed. Very violent as well. Before today she never could have imagined the kind of violence Chapel was capable of, but she had witnessed firsthand the ease with which he killed. He hadn't seemed to enjoy it, however, which was a small point in his favor.

No, not a small point. He had killed to protect her family. For that she would excuse him almost anything.

"Whatever else you think of him, Pru, he is not evil. He has spent the last five centuries serving God and the forces of good. He came here not to trick or lie to you, but to protect you. To protect all of us from the potential danger Temple and the Blood Grail might have posed."

She stared at him. "How could you have endangered us that way?"

His mouth twisted in distaste. "I was stupid. I foolishly believed the order when they told me I could stand against Temple. They told me he would be weak and easily overpowered. They seemed to know so much about the brotherhood I readily believed them. I *wanted* to believe them, because doing so served my purpose."

This was more the Marcus she was familiar with—the one who could never forgive himself for being wrong or overly eager.

"Can you forgive me?" he asked after a moment's pause.

Pru nodded. Oddly enough, she found it rather easy to forgive him. Perhaps she was feeling charitable, or perhaps she simply understood that he had forsaken logic in his fervor.

Or perhaps she finally understood that life was too short to hold grudges.

"I can and I do," she replied. "You are my friend, Marcus. A mistake doesn't change that."

He seemed surprised. "It was a pretty large mistake."

"Yes, well, we've all made those, haven't we?"

His expression softened—saddened. "I'm so sorry we didn't find the Grail for you, Pru."

She could only nod, her throat suddenly tight. She wouldn't cry, not now. Not here.

"What happens now?" she asked when her voice returned.

"Molyneux is sending word to the church about what has happened and I'm waiting to hear from contacts of my own who might know of the order's plans and movements. They have vacated the nearby location I knew of, so it seems likely that they will move to another part of England, if not another country. Possibly France, especially if they have Temple with them as Chapel suspects."

France. "So Chapel and Molyneux will be leaving soon."

Again he seemed to peer right to the very heart of her. Were it anyone else, she might have squirmed. "It is possible, though I doubt they will want to leave your family unprotected should the order return."

Terror clutched at her heart. Oh, God, what if that happened? What if they hurt her family? She could see that man pointing a gun at her sister so clearly in her mind. She'd had no doubt that he would have pulled the trigger if she hadn't done what he ordered. These men would not hesitate to kill her family to protect themselves.

"I won't let any harm befall you or your family, Pru."

She dipped her chin. Marcus was true to his word, of that she had no doubt. His voice was rife with promise and determination, yet he was but one man against many.

No, there was only one man who could protect them from the order, and he wasn't a man at all—at least not a normal one. And he was a man who seemed to have spent most of his existence hiding from life rather than fighting for it.

Still, there was no denying that Chapel was a warrior. She had no doubt that he would protect her and her family with every last breath.

But when all was said and done, who was going to protect him?

She didn't have the same luck sneaking up on Chapel as she had with Marcus. The *vampire* didn't even pretend not to hear her. In fact, Pru wondered if he had sensed her long before she ever reached the library. Somehow she had known that was where she would find him.

His back was to her as he stood at the window. She saw herself reflected behind him in the glass. "Good evening, Pru."

Was it? She was alive. Her family was unharmed, but her father, Marcus and every other man in the house, with the exception of the one who couldn't face sunlight, had spent the early hours of the day disposing of the bodies of the men who had come to kill them. She didn't know if the evening itself was good, but it was certainly better than the day that had preceded it.

Then again, Chapel had set off after their leader by himself as soon as the sun had set. She would ask him about that later. She had some bitterness to relieve first.

"Six hundred years." She entered the room cautiously despite the sarcasm in her tone. "That must be some kind of record."

He glanced over his shoulder, the clean, rugged lines of his face haloed in the soft light. "A record for what?"

"Self-pity," she replied, the words bitter on her tongue. "I doubt I could manage it that long."

If she'd made a dent in the personal armor he wore, he showed no trace. "Are you angry that my existence has been too long or that yours is to be too short?"

Damn him for knowing exactly what she felt, for knowing exactly where to strike. "Both. And is that how you see it, as merely an existence?"

He finally turned to fully face her. His handsome face was a study of fatigue and resignation. She would not pity him. She would not. "What would you have me call it?"

"How about living?" She couldn't keep the disbelief from her voice. "Or a gift. Had I an eternity spread before me, I would be sure to make the most of it."

His lips twisted. "As you have with the time you've already had? It's not the time that matters, Pru. It is what we do with it."

His words stung, but she ignored the implied rebuke. "What have you done with your time? Spent it mooning over a woman who didn't want you and hiding behind a church that despises you?"

For a second—a mere blink—there flashed, in the golden depths of his eyes, a glimmer of something untamed that made her remember this was not an ordinary man before her.

"I have been chasing my salvation, *my* grail, if you will. I have been busy trying not to make attachments, as everyone I come to appreciate dies. Or will die. Eternity can all too easily be a curse."

She hadn't thought of that. It must be horrible to be so alone. But wasn't that part of life? No one knew how long they had on this earth. If anyone knew that for certain, it was her.

He regarded her with such naked pain and vulnerability that it hurt to look upon him. "Resent my immortality if you want, but I would trade places with you in an instant so I wouldn't have to know the darkness of a world without you in it."

"You—" Her voice faltered. Her stomach fluttered inside. Even her lungs seemed to react to his words by refusing to work. "Liar."

Arms loose and at his sides, he moved lazily

toward her, his gaze never leaving hers. "Are my words that difficult for you to believe?"

She swallowed. She wanted to step back but couldn't. Why wouldn't her legs move? "Yes. You would say anything to get what you want."

"If you think so lowly of me, answer this: why would I bother with words when I could take almost anything I might want?"

Another gulp. "Perhaps you want something you cannot just take."

"Such as your heart, perhaps?" He was so very close. "Your very soul?"

She nodded.

He smiled—sadly. "But then you would have to believe that you mean something to me, that I have genuine affection for you, and you don't want to believe that, do you?"

Damn him.

He was close enough to touch her now, and he did, cupping her cheek in his warm, rough palm as that beautiful gaze searched her face. "Either way you have to realize that I do care about you, Pru, regardless of what you think of me."

"You haven't known me long enough to care about me." Her voice was hoarse, her throat tight. What in God's name was he looking for?

"I cared about you the first moment I saw you, trying to be so bold in that red gown when inside you were a cage of butterflies."

His keen insight would not break her resolve or her heart. "You must have thought you'd been handed a full-course meal with the lot of us."

He tilted his head, regarding her with a mixture of remorse and amusement. "The only one I thought about nibbling on was you." The fingers slid around to the back of her neck, pulling her closer, but not forcing. She could pull away if she wanted.

She didn't.

"I bit you that night, remember?"

Her eyes widened. She hadn't imagined it! "My hand."

He nodded. "I hadn't meant for it to happen, but you were . . . overwhelming."

Pru flushed. She wanted to be angry with him, but it was so difficult. She expected lies, beseechment, even intimidation, but she hadn't expected him to play to her emotions. It could be an act, but he seemed so true. There was one way to find out if what he said about his . . . *condition* was true.

"Could you make me the same as you?"

He stiffened. "What do you mean?"

"If the loneliness of immortality is so awful, if I mean so much to you, couldn't you take my blood like in *Dracula*? Could I become a vampire, could you change me?"

He looked stricken, as though she had wounded him somehow. "You could. I could, but I won't." His hand fell away from her neck.

Good Lord, he looked as though she had asked him to kill her. He meant it. Every word.

"Chapel . . ." She should apologize, but had no idea what to say.

"It's because I care about you that I won't change you, Pru." Abruptly he left her, making for the door so fast she knew it wasn't humanly possible. "I would never forgive myself for making you the same as me. I don't want you to become a monster, or worse."

He was so wounded she could feel it. "Is that what happened to Marie?"

He nodded, remorse tightening his handsome features. Jealousy poked Pru between the ribs, sharp and unwelcome. Marie had been dead for centuries. She was no threat. But there would be other women. Long after she herself turned to dust, Chapel would still be roaming the earth and he would meet someone. Someone who would live long enough to mean more to him than she did.

"Marie was very devout in her worship of God." His fingers caressed the spine of a book that he obviously had no interest in. His eyes had the vaguely glazed look of a man lost in memory. "I thought she might be more devout in her passion for me, but I was wrong."

"I don't understand why she felt she had to make a choice."

His head jerked up as though he had forgotten she was there. Jealousy stung once more. "She thought me an abomination. I was the antithesis of everything she believed."

Yes, the woman was such a twit. "Why? Had you renounced God? Were you suddenly a disciple of Satan?"

He looked offended. "No, but my behavior was hardly that of a devout Catholic."

"You were a mercenary. I don't suppose sin was anything new to you."

He laughed at that and Pru allowed herself a small smile of satisfaction. "No, it wasn't. But as a mercenary I never preyed upon humans for sustenance."

"Mr. Darwin might argue that you have simply evolved. One more step up the food chain, so to speak."

"The church doesn't recognize Mr. Darwin's theories."

"The church might not recognize itself if it took a good look at some of the atrocities it has committed in the name of God."

He seemed to look at her in a whole new light— one that felt very flattering. "Are you a heretic now, Pru, or a philosopher?"

Was he making sport of her? "Just because you have lived longer than me doesn't mean you can patronize me, Chapel. It is almost the twentieth century, you know. You might want to join the rest of us living in it."

He stared at her, a smile curving his lips. "You're not the least bit afraid of me, are you?"

She shrugged. No, she wasn't. She probably should be, but she felt more herself with him than she did with her family. "The worst you could do is kill me."

His smile faded, replaced by a look of such horror Pru instantly regretted her words. "I would not."

"It wouldn't matter." She tried to give him a

smile, but failed. "My body is already seeing to that itself. So, no. I'm not afraid of you."

"Death is not the worst thing man is capable of, Pru."

There he went again, talking to her as though she were a child or an idiot. "You mean rape? You hardly strike me as the sort who would behave so badly."

"I raped Marie—in a way."

The way he said it—she knew then that he felt more guilt for that than anything else. He had betrayed someone he cared about, the worst sin, in his mind.

"You acted out of desperation and if Marie hadn't been such a twit you wouldn't have done what you did. Do you want to rape me, Chapel? Is that what you are insinuating?"

He looked pained. "God, no."

"Then why are we discussing it?" It happened six centuries ago. "I think we both know I'd give in easily enough if you applied yourself." Oh, sweet Lord, what had she just said?

Chapel was even more shocked than she was. "You don't mean that."

"Obviously reading minds is not one of your vampiric abilities." What was it about him that made her feel so bold?

His jaw dropped. He looked as flustered as a schoolboy. She had nothing to lose but her pride by being so open with him, and the knowledge fueled her courage.

She inched closer to him, so that she could feel the heat from his body. Mr. Stoker had been wrong about vampires being cold. If Chapel was any indication, they were very warm indeed. "If you came to me as you had Marie, I wouldn't turn you away."

Chapel's face lost all color. "Don't say that."

She opened her mouth, but he cut her off. "Earlier, you asked me what my weaknesses were."

"Poison and sunlight." Her lower lip trembled a little. She'd been such a *cow* to him them. "Yet you risked them both to save me." Lord, what could that poison have done to him? What did the sun do to him? All she saw was a bit of a sunburn on his nose and cheeks. Had it burned him badly? He'd said the sight of him would have given her nightmares.

"I would do anything to protect you, and that includes from myself, because *you* are my weakness, Pru. I will no doubt live to regret admitting that to you, but I cannot seem to help it."

Her throat tightened. "It's ironic, don't you think? You have all the time in the world and mine is running out. It appears that God has a rather twisted sense of humor."

His smile was sad. "I'm not sure He has anything to do with it."

They stared at each other for some time. What passed between them, Pru couldn't define. But it was something that calmed her, made her suddenly very glad for Chapel's appearance in her life. It was something that made her want to take advantage of what time they had left.

"There are things left I want to do. Will you help me?"

"Of course."

"You said you'd teach me to drive."

He smiled. "So I did. Are you ready to learn?"

Feeling lighter than she had in months, Pru returned the grin. "The question is, are you ready to teach me?"

Chapter 17

⟨~∘◯◯∘~⟩

"**S**o, what can you do?"

Certain that her question was just a ruse to make him take his attention off her incredibly fast driving, Chapel didn't look at her when he responded, but kept his eye on the dimly illuminated road ahead.

"What do you mean?" Was she intentionally driving this fast, or did she not know any better?

Pru glanced at him, not the least bit reluctant to take her attention off of the road. "I mean, what kind of abilities do you have as a vampire?"

"Eyes on the road, please." He might be nearly invincible, but she wasn't, and neither was any other living creature in the vicinity. "You might want to slow down, there's a rabbit up ahead."

"I don't see one." She slowed down anyway,

which answered his earlier question. She definitely had been driving fast on purpose.

"I suppose that's one of my abilities, then." He allowed himself a smile. How exotic. "The ability to see a bunny on the road in the dark."

She laughed at that. Then they drove past the rabbit and he heard her gasp. Had she not believed him?

Suddenly she was very interested. "What else?"

He told her about his sense of smell, his intuition, his hearing, his speed. In all his centuries he had never revealed to anyone the full exent of what he was capable of, but he did to Pru. He wanted to share everything with her, but they hadn't time for six hundred years of experience. Of course, being able to snap a man's neck like a twig was explained as "unnatural" strength.

"And I can fly."

The car lurched, sending his stomach flip-flopping. "What? Really?"

Why that should be so wonderful after everything else he'd told her, he didn't know. Perhaps it was the one thing she couldn't imagine.

"Yes. And please don't do that again."

She was more cautious and attentive now, her attention fixed on the road rather than on him. "Driving must seem terribly dull to you, then."

"I usually like to drive."

She laughed and risked a glance. "Usually?"

"Let's just say that it's a good thing I don't worry about dying." Damn. That was a heartless thing to say to a woman who didn't have long to live.

But Pru didn't take offense—not that he could

see, at least. She did pull the Daimler over onto the side of the road, however. He knew he was in trouble when the motor rolled to a stop. It was quiet out here. So very quiet and dark and isolated.

She turned on the seat to face him, and even though his eyesight was much keener than hers in the dark, the directness of her gaze unnerved him.

"What *do* you worry about?"

Did biting her count? Would she laugh if she knew just how nervous he was with her? "I worry about this curse I'm under spreading. I worry that my soul may never be permitted entrance to heaven."

"You cannot protect everyone from this"—she waved her hand—"curse, as you call it."

I can protect you. Wisely he didn't say it outloud. "I can protect whom I can."

She pondered that for a moment, her unflinching hazel gaze studying him. Not since he was a lad had he wanted to squirm under such scrutiny, but he wanted to now.

"Has it ever occurred to you that you were given a gift?"

He snorted. "You sound like Molyneux."

That was supposed to be a slight, no doubt, but she couldn't bring herself to take offense. "Father Molyneux is a smart man."

He smiled a bit at her brevity. "He is an eternal optimist."

"While you are a pessimist."

"Yes."

She gestured wide with her arms, as if trying to emcompass the world. "All this life you've been given, and you consider it a curse."

What was it about humans that made them long to cheat death? "What else is it?"

"Christ was granted immortality."

His jaw dropped at the blasphemous comparison. "Christ never drank anyone's blood."

"No, but he offered his own to his disciples."

"Figuratively. It is hardly the same thing."

"Why, because you say so?"

She simply refused to see reason. "No, because giving my blood will make other people into vampires."

"And that is horrible because . . . ?"

She still wasn't convinced? "Because we feed off humans."

"So you are all bloodsucking fiends? Heartless killers?"

Why was she twisting his words? "Of course not."

"Hmm."

Six hundred years and he still didn't know how a woman could say so much with that little sound. "Obviously, Pru, you have another theory."

"Maybe," she told him with a smug expression, "you were granted immortality to help people."

Good Lord, she was determined. Was this annoyance pumping through his veins or anticipation? "*Maybe* I was cursed as punishment for the life I led."

Her arms flew out as she exhaled a gusty sigh.

"Fine, you're cursed. God forbid I intrude on your self-pity. Spend the next six hundred years wallowing in it, then."

The temptation to laugh was great, but he didn't want to rile her up any more than she already was. "You are one impertinent woman."

"And you are one pigheaded man." So much for not riling her. If he wasn't mistaken, her jaw was clenched.

"I'm not stubborn." He should have kept quiet, but something drove him on. "I simply know more about this than you do."

"Oh, so you know that you won't be allowed into heaven?"

"Why do you suppose I will?"

"You're not an evil person."

Her conviction sent a pang through his chest. "You don't know what I am."

The delicate point of her chin came up defiantly. "I know God would let you into His kingdom."

"Not yet. I haven't repented enough."

"Oh, my dear Lord, deliver me!" She flounced back against the leather seat with enough force to rock the car. Who would have thought her delicate frame possessed such power? "You haven't repented enough? Most of us only get a normal measure of life to do that. You've had at least seven."

Oh, she was impertinent! The urge to laugh was stifled only by his desire to continue their debate. "Perhaps my soul is just that corrupted."

"Perhaps you are an idiot." She fixed him with a gaze that could have melted an iceberg. "Who told you that you need to repent? The church?"

She made it sound so silly. "Yes, but I know it's true."

"How?"

"The archbishop told me, centuries ago." He remembered it as though it were yesterday. The cross branded on his shoulder itched with the memory. "Once I have paid for my sins, my soul will be released."

"The archibishop told you. How did he know?"

"He was the archbishop."

"Ah, so it must be true."

He didn't care much for her sarcasm. "Look, Pru, I know you find this all hard to believe—"

"No." She cut him off with a slice of her hand and a tight expression that silenced him. "What I find hard to believe is that you believe it. I don't believe any of it, any more than I believe woman is to blame for all of man's sins."

He blinked, suddenly feeling stupid. "You have some very modern ideas."

"And you have some very archaic ones."

She was angry, very much so. "It wasn't an insult, Pru. Merely an observation." Indeed. She almost had him believing that she could accept him—not as a monster, but as a man.

No one else would be able to see the flush that darkened her cheeks, but Chapel could. "Forgive me. In my experience most men are very quick to disregard the opinions of a woman merely because of her sex, and some foolish notion that we are somehow lesser beings than men."

"I don't think I have to remind you that I am not like most men. Neither, would it appear, are your father or Marcus." Although they were nothing like him either.

"No. But neither Marcus nor Papa have squandered their lives."

"Pardon?" He couldn't have heard her correctly.

She didn't hesitate. "I still cannot believe that you have lived all these centuries and have so little to show for it."

"Little?" How had she reached that conclusion? He had much to show for his life. On the other hand, the things he had seen and experienced . . . well, any well-traveled mortal might give him significant competition.

"Molyneux told me you live in a church basement."

"It is safe for me and I can protect the church." God, it sounded lame even to his own ears.

"It's the rock you hide under so you do not have to face the world."

His own temper sparked. He did not need some cloistered little girl telling him that he hid from the world. "I don't know where you've gotten this idea that I have wasted my immortality—"

"Marcus told me about your history. If you haven't spent hundreds of years hiding, you tell me what you have been doing. What wondrous things have you experienced?"

He thought about it. He had traveled most of Europe, but that seemed trivial now when he could have seen much more of the world. Most of what he knew came from books and research, not from firsthand knowledge.

"Being with you has been wondrous."

She actually rolled her eyes! "You're just saying that because you want to shut me up."

"That's not true."

She pinned him with an unflinching gaze.

"It's not true," he insisted. "Maybe I have wasted my life according to your standards, but meeting you has been a significant experience."

She opened her mouth to argue and that's when he struck. He was so very aware of her by now that he couldn't help it. He had to taste her—one way or another.

Pru gasped against his lips as he slid his tongue inside her mouth. He pinned her body against the Daimler's bench with his own, sighing as her softness enveloped him.

He kissed her, savored her, until the tension eased from her body and she yielded against him, her arms twining around his neck. Chapel groaned. If he didn't stop soon, there would be nothing to stop him from trying to take this encounter to the next level. Pru might want him as badly as he wanted her—and he knew that she did—but he wasn't going to make love to her in her father's car.

Pulling back, he smiled at her in the indigo light. She was breathless, her eyelids as heavy as her gaze was soft.

"*That*," he informed her lightly, "was to shut you up."

Her laughter rang through the night before she pulled him to her once more.

The sun was well into its descent when Chapel woke. The days were shortening now and soon the seasons would turn to his favor with long nights.

Not that he needed more time to "squander," as Pru put it.

The thought of her brought a smile to his lips. They certainly hadn't squandered the remainder of their time together the night before. They'd spent an hour simply kissing and talking before the dawn threatened.

There was a lightness in his chest that hadn't been there before. A lightness for which the blame rested entirely on Pru. There was hope in his heart. He thought he had lost all ability to feel such lightness.

No, he hadn't lost his hope. His faith, perhaps, but not his hope. He had let the church poke and prod him, study and demean him. He even let them burn their brand into his flesh—a cross on his right shoulder. The hot silver had seared him like nothing before, and the holy symbol still burned and itched, the scar tissue pink and bright. It was the only mark he had kept since becoming a vampire. Had it done anything to save his soul? Doubtful.

Being with Pru had done more for his sense of salvation than any of the trials the church had put him through. With her he was totally open. He felt he could share anything. He'd never felt that way before, not that he could remember.

Footsteps outside in the corridor alerted him to the approach of a guest. Molyneux, if he wasn't mistaken. He crossed the carpet and opened the door to greet his friend.

The aging priest favored him with a dry smile. "You never tire of that, do you, *mon ami*?"

He didn't, no. "You are wearing your determined face. What is it?"

"The time to leave has arrived."

Chapel nodded, even as his heart froze. He knew the priest's words to be true, but the thought of leaving Pru . . . it hurt.

"When?" his voice was hoarse and unfamiliar to his own ears.

"Tomorrow."

So soon? Hardly enough time to say good-bye to Pru, but perhaps that was for the best. The sooner he left, the easier it would be for both of them. He was already much more attached to her than he had any business being. And she was attached to him as well.

"Marcus will be accompanying me to France."

Chapel shook his head. "Pardon?"

A kind smile curved his friend's lips. "I believe you should stay here."

"Why?" As welcome as this news was, he couldn't help but be offended to be so readily dismissed. And he was angry at himself for wanting to be dismissed. *He* should be the one out combing the continent for Temple. It was his duty, not Marcus's.

"Marcus is interested in helping remedy this situation. He will come with me to France and together we will use the church's connections to find Bishop. Perhaps he has crossed paths with the order before."

"If he hasn't," Chapel replied absently, "Saint has." Bishop was a hunter, seeking out demons and evildoers and dispensing his own brand of judgment. Saint, on the other hand, did everything possible to make a mockery of his name. He reveled in what he was, and woe to anyone who got in his way.

Obviously his disbelief at the situation was not concealed from the other man. "I know this must be a bit of a shock, but I think this is the best course of action."

"How? What protection will Grey be against the order, or Saint, for that matter?"

Was that pity in the old man's eyes? "He will be fine. We have nothing to fear from Saint, not that I plan to get close enough to test that theory. You would serve us much better if you remained behind."

"You said yourself the order is no doubt long gone from these parts." And Chapel hadn't forgotten that his friend hadn't given him an explanation as to why he was asking him to stay.

Molyneux's expression was somewhat sad—and sage. "Are you certain enough that you would leave Miss Ryland and her family here unguarded?"

The thought was like a punch to the stomach. Molyneux knew him too well. He knew Chapel would not be able to leave Pru while the chance of danger remained.

"No. But we both know the chances of the order returning are slim."

"True." Molyneux's gaze never left his. "But the Rylands are not the only ones I am concerned for."

Chapel stared at him with a sense of wonder. "You are worried about me?"

The priest nodded. "I see how much she has come to mean to you, *mon ami*. I know what you would do to the man who poisoned her and attacked her family."

He would kill him. Painfully and slowly. The church obviously didn't want him dead. They wanted to uncover the man's plan, discover how deep the roots of his order burrowed. Chapel understood it, but he didn't like it.

"Without your blood . . ." It was a feeble grasp to hold on to the familiar.

"I think we both know you can take care of that on your own." Molyneux's tone wasn't accusatory, merely matter-of-fact.

Chapel's brow pinched. He had nothing more to argue. "You will keep me informed of your progress?"

There was only kindness and understanding in the priest's expression. "*Oui*. And when you are needed, I will send for you."

"I will be ready."

"I hope not, *mon ami*."

Sickening dread curled inside Chapel's stomach as the meaning of his friend's words sank in. Molyneux knew the truth just as he did.

The only thing that could make him ready to leave Rosecourt was Pru's death.

"When is Father Molyneux leaving?"

Chapel and Pru were strolling through the abandoned stillness of the garden. Crickets sang a gentle song and in the distance an owl hooted. Farther still was the beach, where waves sloshed gently against the shore, scenting the air with a breath of salty richness.

"Tomorrow." He paused as she opened the door to the hothouse, and then followed her inside.

"Will you miss him?"

Warm, humid air welcomed them, thick with fragrance. There were easily a dozen tables piled with potted plants and flowers. Larger flora lined the floor and walls.

"Of course," he replied. A trellis of roses caught his attention. "But it isn't as though we will never meet again."

"Do you think you and I will ever meet again?"

He turned toward her. She wasn't looking at him, but staring through the dark at some indiscernible point. It was unlikely, and they both knew it. Damn it. "How do you mean?"

Now she turned to him. He could see her sad smile. "Someday in heaven."

He swallowed. Hard. The lump refused to budge. "I'd like that."

A small sound escaped her. It sounded like laughter, but it was too mocking and self-deprecating to be true. "I do not want to die a virgin."

Like a boy, he jumped at her shocking confession. A sharp, tearing sensation scored the pad of his thumb as he jerked his hand free of the roses.

It was light enough that she saw him jump. And no doubt she heard his soft hiss.

She came to him, closing the scant feet between them, a frown creasing her fair brow. "What happened?"

"It's nothing. A thorn."

She took his hand in her smaller, more slender one. Her touch was as light and delicate as the fall of night. She handled him as though he were something to be treasured, something special, not a creature who could snuff out her life like the flame of a candle.

She lifted his hand to her mouth. He knew her intent and it both frightened and disappointed him. Had she planned this? And what exactly did she want from him? Did she want him, or what she thought he could give her?

"It won't change you, not this way."

She smiled, the tip of his thumb resting against her full lower lip. "Poor Chapel, so suspicious. Did you ever stop to think that maybe I'm trying to seduce you, not use you?"

Before Chapel could stop her, Pru opened her sweet mouth and took the ball of his thumb inside. Her warm tongue swept across his flesh and his heart stopped.

Seduce him? She was killing him.

It was a death he would gladly embrace.

Chapter 18

Chapel's skin was warm and salty against Pru's tongue, his blood faintly coppery and sweet. There was nothing distasteful about it. In fact, there was something highly arousing knowing that she was taking some part of him inside her, a part that could never be taken away. Knowing what he was, knowing that blood was so integral to his survival—it was like joining with him in a way that was more profound than even lovemaking.

She opened her mouth and let him go. Only a few seconds had passed, but it had felt like an eternity.

His hand slowly moved away from her. Chapel watched its progress as though he thought it might burst into flames at any moment. His gaze raised to hers, wide and pained in the moonlight. He looked so vulnerable, so touched yet horrified. How was she going to make him understand that she would be with him even if she did have something to lose?

"Why?" His voice was a ragged whisper.

Tilting her head, Pru raised her hand to his cheek. Poor, poor Chapel. "Because I want to take a little of you with me when I go."

He knew what she meant by "go." Were it possible, his gaze became even more raw. "I wouldn't take anymore—not if you want to get into h-heaven." He frowned and swallowed hard.

Pru's heart twitched. How bittersweet it was, discovering that the thought of her death affected him so. She moved toward him, closing the scant distance between them until there was nothing but a sliver of night and the reach of a breath between them.

"I would like to give you something to take with you," she murmured, reaching out so that her palm pressed flat against his chest. She held his gaze. What if he rejected her?

His frown faded into shock. He shook his head, golden hair mussing in the breeze. "No, Pru. I won't take your blood."

Her fingers against his mouth shushed him. "That's not what I want."

He blinked, eyes going from bright to dark as he realized what she meant.

"You said you'd help me do the things I want," she reminded him, not giving him a chance to deny her just yet. Her legs brushed against his, his torso pressed against her chest as she closed what little distance there was between them. "I want to experience passion, Chapel. I want to know what it is to make love. With you."

He was so pale in the darkness. Lips parted, but nothing came out as he pressed a hand over hers, holding it tight against the place where his heart seemed to struggle to beat. He looked at her as though she had just shoved a dagger between his ribs.

"Don't do this to me. Please. I don't want to hurt you."

He was hurting her now, just by allowing her to see his pain. "I don't want you to hurt me either. I want you to make love to me."

"Pru—"

She cut him off. "I want to make love to you. When was the last time someone loved you, Chapel?"

Were those tears in his eyes, or just the moon playing tricks on her? "Never." His voice was barely audible.

No, the tears were in her eyes. "Then let me, please."

His free hand came up to cup her cheek. The other still held her palm to his chest. "I'm sure I've done nothing to deserve you, *mon ange*, but I'm not strong enough to deny you, even though I'll no doubt be damned for it."

Pru parted her lips to argue, but never got the chance to speak before his lips came down on hers.

One thought made its way through her mind. His angel. He had called her his angel.

His mouth was hot—insistent yet surprisingly gentle as it claimed hers for his own. Joy overwhelmed her as she clung to his shoulders. Her knees trembled and her heart slammed against her chest. She was nervous and afraid and so terribly impatient now that she knew where this night was headed. Their tongues stroked and teased, a pale substitute for the dance their bodies would soon perform.

One by one, he plucked the pins from her hair. They fell to the floor with soft pings. She would never find them again—not that she cared. At least it was late enough that no one would be up to see her as they sneaked in later. Soon he had her hair free and tumbling down her back, his fingers combing through the heavy strands. Pru moaned, her head falling back into his hands, offering him her throat as she rubbed herself against his fingers like an affectionate cat.

The fingers in her hair slid down her back to her waist and then farther still to cup her bottom. His mouth slid down her jaw as her spine bowed. Her hips pressed against his, welcoming his hardness. Through her skirts he was a delicious pressure that sent little spirals of pleasure radiating throughout her. She arched against him, retreated and then arched again, the ache within her growing as his lips traced a heated trail along the sensitive skin of her neck.

He lifted his head. In the gray light, she could see the chiseled beauty of his face. His golden eyes glowed with a heat that melted her insides, and this time she knew it was no illusion.

"Are you certain?" he asked.

Pru's heart clenched at the tenderness in his tone. And he thought himself a monster. How could anyone so wounded and gentle be anything but good and pure? Her hands pulled his shirt from the waist of his trousers. Thank God he dressed so improperly with her. Her fingers slid underneath the fine lawn, itching to feel the warm velvet of his skin.

"Yes," she told him.

He kissed her again, almost reverently, but with a hunger that hadn't been there before. This was it. Elation and anticipation flooded her blood. For a time, even if it was just this night, she was going to hold this man in her arms. She would know what it was to be treasured and wanted. She would know what it was like to be one with another person.

She wanted to be one with Chapel.

His tongue teased hers with sweet, forbidden promise as his fingers made short work of the fastenings on the back of her gown. The soft blue silk sagged about her shoulders, but only for a moment, and then he was sliding it down her arms.

When the gown pooled at her feet, he lifted her out of it, sitting her atop the one bare spot on a nearby table. The wood was rough against the back of her thighs through her delicate chemise. Wantonly, she hadn't worn any drawers, in the hopes that the evening would culminate in precisely this.

She had chosen her prettiest corset—pink satin with lace trim. The top was low, just covering her nipples and pushing her breasts upward. She shivered as Chapel's rough but gentle fingers brushed the sensitive swells above the pink lace. His fingers crept lower, inside the corset, cupping her breast to lift and release it from the satin cage.

Cool air tightened her nipple, and when his thumb brushed that same hard peak, Pru sighed into his mouth.

His mouth left hers, trailing along her jaw and throat and down her chest, building the knot of anticipation in her stomach with every soft kiss. Finally, the wet heat of his mouth closed over her nipple, replacing his fingers. Pru moaned in pleasure, arching toward him.

Chapel's hand slid down the smooth front of her corset to grasp the gauzy fabric of her chemise. Slowly, he drew the garment up her thighs until it bunched about her hips. The flat of his palm caressed the inside of her leg, sending tingles of pleasure snaking across her sensitive flesh. The ache within her grew as his fingers drew ever so slowly toward the heated part of her that craved his touch.

All her life she had been taught that "good" unmarried ladies did not indulge in this kind of behavior, that it was wrong to do so if one wasn't married—and sometimes even if one was! Somehow, she couldn't bring herself to think that what she and Chapel were doing was wrong.

His hand slid farther, nudging her legs apart. Her body jumped as his fingers stroked the curls there, teasing the cleft between. Pru gasped, her hands clutching at his hair as his mouth drew insistently on her breast.

One of his fingers parted her, moving with tortuous slowness between the slick folds of her flesh. Jolts of pleasure flared deep within her, rolling into one tight, pulsating ache that demanded release even as she wished it would go on forever.

His teeth nipped at her breast, drawing a cry from her. Lifting his head from her swollen, glistening flesh, he gazed down at her, his ruthless fingers still stroking the wetness between her legs. The bright gold of his eyes made her heart thump with excitement.

God, the way he made her feel.

"Do you want more?" His voice was low and thick. Pru nodded, unable to speak.

Chapel held her gaze as he unfastened the buttons of his waistcoat. He tossed it behind him without a glance. The white linen of his shirt followed. Dry-mouthed, Pru watched with greedy eyes as the tautly muscled flesh of his stomach and chest was revealed.

He was beautiful and golden as a Grecian god. His shoulders were wide, the bones there sharp. Tawny hair dusted his chest, drifting downward to the waist of his trousers.

There was no trace of the wounds he had endured during the attack on the house, nothing to mar the perfection of his body, save for a satiny scar high on the back of one shoulder in the shape of a cross.

"Did you have that when you were mortal?"

"The church branded each of us when we turned ourselves over."

Branded them? Like animals? Wide-eyed, she stared at him, tears threatening. "I'm so sorry."

The depth of his gaze shifted, softened. It was as though her words affected him greatly. "I am not a man, Pru. As far as the church and world is concerned, I am an abomination. Is that what you want as your lover?"

Reaching up, she smoothed the silky strands of dark blond hair back from his face. "I want *you* as my lover. I don't care what anyone else thinks of you, I think you are wonderful."

He stood between her splayed thighs, so close that she could feel his heat. "I don't want to hurt you."

She smiled. How sweet he was, this man she had seen kill with his bare hands. "So don't."

He kissed her again, his lips achingly tender as they claimed hers. Too soon he pulled away, staring at her for one long puzzling moment before sinking to his knees. The movement put him at a most embarrassing level.

"What are you doing?" Her heartbeat sped up as he seized her by the hips, pulling her closer to the edge of the table.

"I want to taste you," he told her, his golden eyes holding hers. "I want to give you pleasure."

And how was he going to do that from down . . . oh! Pru fell back on her elbows as his tongue stroked her, exploring the dampness of her sex in the same manner as his fingers had before. Hot, wet and firm, his tongue was like rough silk against her sensitive flesh. His jaw was rough against her inner thighs, and his hands came up to press her legs apart, as though he realized he was scratching her. Held as she was, Pru was wide open to him, totally vulnerable to the sensual assault of his mouth as he licked her into an aching, wanton state of submission.

Pru's fingers clutched at his hair, tangling in the thick strands as her hips undulated against the onslaught of his mouth and tongue. She cried out as he found the tightest, most sensitive part of her and ruthlessly stroked it. The ache grew, building and building as her hips rose and fell. Her knees came up to give him deeper access and she dug her heels into the tabletop, bracing herself as she pushed her hips upward.

One more stroke sent her over the edge, reducing her to moaning mindlessness as pleasure swept over her.

His mouth left her, but she scarcely noticed, so acute were the aftershocks racing through her.

He stood between her spread knees. She watched as he unfastened his trousers. They fell down his legs with a soft whisper.

The lower half of his body was as tanned as the upper, and dusted with the same fine golden hair. Between his legs, nestled in a thick downy thatch, was his penis. Long and broad, the sight of it both frightened and excited her. He was going to put that inside her, fill her.

She watched as he guided himself to the entrance of her body. He stroked the thick head of his sex through the slick cleft of hers, igniting that familiar inner fire once more.

"Do you want me, Pru?"

Raising her gaze to his, she met the burning of his eyes without flinching, without shame. "Yes. I want you. All of you."

Slowly, he fitted himself against her. He pushed—not hard, but insistently all the same. Pru gasped as he slowly filled her, stretching her. He held her ankles with his hands, keeping her heels on the table, her legs spread wide. There was a slight pinching sensation, and then he was fully inside her.

He felt alien and too big. This wasn't what she'd hoped for. It wasn't as bad as she'd heard the first time could be either, but it hardly compared to the feelings he'd aroused in her earlier.

"Just be still a moment," he told her, as if reading her thoughts. "It will get better."

Forcing her muscles to relax, Pru trusted him. He was right. After a few moments her body seemed to adjust to having him inside. One of his hands left her foot and glided up her leg to where their bodies were joined. Gently, his thumb parted her, finding that tiny nub that his tongue had tormented earlier. He stroked her, sending sparks to the tinder within her, until her hips began to move, seeking the burning where his body joined hers.

He moved inside her with deep, gentle thrusts, churning his hips more than pushing. There was very little discomfort now, and whatever was left was nothing compared to the sheer pleasure of being joined with him.

But it wasn't enough. She wanted more of him, wanted to give more of herself. Slowly, she pushed herself upward, wrapping her legs around his waist as she rose into a sitting position.

His arms went around her back as hers went around his shoulders. He pulled her closer for a kiss, but she tilted her head back, offering him her throat. She didn't know much about vampires, but the neck featured in everything she had read and heard.

"Will it change me if you bite me?"

His movements stilled and for a brief second she saw pain in his eyes. "No."

"So there is nothing to stop you from taking my blood?"

His eyes widened. Obviously he was only now realizing that she didn't want anything from him, but that she was offering herself, trusting him with her very life.

"Pru . . ."

She pressed her fingers against his mouth. "I want you to."

She took her fingers away and pressed closer to him, wrapping her arms about him once more as she tilted her head back.

The hands on her back stroked gently, one coming up to cup her shoulder. His breath was warm against her throat, the brush of his lips as soft as a butterfly's wing.

"Ah!" A brief sting as his fangs penetrated her,

and then a rush of pleasure as she felt him draw her into himself. Liquid heat flowed through her veins, flooding her with the most intense of sensations. His mouth worked at her throat as his hips pushed against her, his rhythm increasing.

Pru clung to him, her body writhing into his embrace, pliant and so terribly aware in his arms. The tension between her legs grew, bringing her closer and closer to a second climax.

Gripping him with her thighs, she arched upward, pushing her pelvis against the sweet pressure of his hand and the delicious thrust of his body. The suction at her throat deepened and she knew he was as close to release as she.

Suddenly she was no longer simply close. Suddenly she was lost in the maelstrom of ecstasy his mouth and body wrought. She clutched at his head, holding him tight against her throat as orgasm tore through her, convulsing with mind-numbing pleasure.

Dimly, she was aware of Chapel stiffening as his own climax struck. She felt him groan against her throat, felt the hot swipe of his tongue against her punctured flesh, and then a tingling, and she knew that come morning there would be no evidence of his bite.

He held her for some time, his face buried in the crook of her shoulder.

"Look at me," she said finally when it became apparent that he had no intention of doing so.

"I don't want you to see my demon face."

Demon face? She was so sated and so giddy with satisfaction from his lovemaking that the notion made her want to laugh. "Chapel, you could never frighten me. Look at me."

Slowly, he lifted his head. When she looked at his face, all she saw was her beautiful vampire. His eyes were bright, but not as much as they had been earlier, not quite glowing in the darkness. His mouth looked a little darker, and when she kissed him, she could taste herself—body and blood—on his lips. But there was nothing that frightened her.

She smiled at him, smoothing back his hair from his tormented face. "Thank you."

He frowned. "For?"

"For giving me this experience."

"Is that why you think I made love to you, out of pity?"

He would have left her had she not held on. No, that wasn't true. He could leave her and she couldn't stop him, she knew that. He didn't leave because she didn't want him to, not because her strength was great enough to restrain him.

"That's not what I meant." She stroked his arm. "I just wanted you to know how much this means to me. How much you mean to me."

He stared at her for the longest time, until she began to worry that she had said too much. Then he raised the back of his knuckles to her cheek and stroked the skin there.

"I think I am the one who should be thankful," he murmured. "You are the first woman to accept what I am, and for that I will always be grateful. I will never forget you, Pru Ryland."

She let him take her into his arms and hold her.

Tears came to her eyes, but she fought them away. Now was not the time for tears. Now she simply wanted to savor this moment.

No, he might not forget her, but someday—whether it be two years from now or two hundred—he would find someone to take her place, someone who would live longer and share more of his life with him. He would find someone truly special. And then she would be nothing more than a pleasant memory.

At least she wouldn't be around to witness it.

Chapel knew that of all the things he had done, he should regret making love to Pru the most, for it was undoubtedly the worst of all his sins, taking her innocence and her blood at the same time. He knew that it was wrong of him, but he could not bring himself to be sorry for having done it.

In fact, he could remember little else in the course of his existence that had felt as right as being with Pru.

Molyneux and Marcus left, and with them seemed to go Chapel's inhibitions. Without Molyneux there was no ever-present reminder of what he was, of his duty or his curse. With Pru he could be himself, just a man, and sometimes he forgot that he wasn't simply that. Little else mattered but the time they had together. Even Temple's disappearance was but a shadow in his mind. That in itself should have been enough to fill him with guilt. When he thought of it, it did.

As for Pru, he thought of her all the time when they weren't together, and it wasn't very often that they weren't. From the moment he woke till the moment he could no longer fight sleep, they were together. Sometimes members of her family would stay up and they would indulge in normal pastimes. They welcomed him despite what he was, and it seemed as though most of the family was starting to accept him. Matilda was still a little fearful, but even she showed improvement.

He did not want to leave this little corner of heaven, though he knew one day he would have to. And as much as he loathed leaving Pru, he did not want to be there when she died.

He tried very hard not to think about her death, preferring instead to concentrate on making the most of the time they had left, living in the present.

"Are you certain you want to do this?" Chapel looked down at Pru as he asked the question.

She lifted her gaze to his. Her eyes were black in the darkness, pupils so wide they almost obliterated the irises. "I'm certain. I'm just terrified."

He laughed. They were on the balcony outside her room, both of them dressed in evening clothes. "I won't let anything happen to you."

Pru nodded, adjusting the scarf secured around her hair. "I know. I just wonder who is going to keep anything from happening to you."

That she trusted him to keep any harm from befalling her warmed him in places he'd thought long frozen to the point of desolation.

"Nothing is going to happen to anyone. Now put your arms around me."

She grinned at him as she did as he bade. "I should have known this was just a pretext. You can't truly fly, can you?"

Securing his arms around her as well, Chapel's only answer was to propel both of them into the sky like a pistol shot. Pru's squeal was lost in the night as they flew up toward the clouds.

Laughing at the expression on her face and the way she clung to him, Chapel turned onto his side so that while they were face to face, they both had a good view of the earth below and the sky above. Pru, however, couldn't seem to pry her gaze from his face.

"We're flying!" she cried.

Wind whipped through his hair and threatened to pull Pru's carefully tied scarf from her head. Where they were going no one would care how her hair looked, but she wanted to look nice anyway. It would take a stronger man than he to deny Pru something she wanted.

Tonight's destination was a burlesque show at a London establishment discreetly known for such things. It had been a long time since Chapel had witnessed such a raunchy display, but it was one of the things Pru said she wanted to experience and he was not about to deny her. Of course she was curious. This modern world was just as obsessed with pretending sex didn't happen as they were with perfecting every kind of vice they could associate with it.

They were given masks as they entered the house, in case they wanted to protect their identity.

Chapel wasn't going to take one but then changed his mind. There was a slim chance that someone who knew Pru might be there—and might see them together in more socially acceptable surroundings later. He didn't want anyone to know that he had taken Pru to this show. Her reputation would be sullied forever.

She held his hand during the entire show—and asked a thousand questions that never failed to amuse or arouse him. That she enjoyed the show was apparent by the way she stroked her thumb against his hand the entire time.

Chapel enjoyed the show as well—it was difficult not to. After all, that was the point of these displays—to titillate and persuade those watching to start their own endeavors.

It wasn't long before Pru's attention was pulled from the stage and began wandering around them. Just a few feet away, a masked lady knelt before a gentleman, his member in her mouth. Another couple engaged in intercourse on a sofa while others stroked and encouraged them. And farther along, two women kissed and fondled each other as a group of leering men cheered them on.

"It's time to go," Chapel told her, taking her by the elbow.

"Why?" She allowed him to steer her away, but her gaze was fixed over her shoulder.

"Because an orgy is about to erupt in there and I've never been one for groups."

She tossed a glance in his direction. "Have you ever been part of such a group?"

"Yes," he answered truthfully as he pulled off his mask and tossed it on a table. "I don't remember much about it. I was fairly drunk at the time."

And then there were the prostitutes the night Pru had been poisoned, but that wasn't the same. He hadn't had sex with them. He had only fed—and one at a time. Anything else and he would have felt as though he were being unfaithful. Anything else and he would have been using another woman to replace Pru, and neither of those things was something he wanted to do.

Pru removed her mask as well as he pulled her along. Taking the flimsy paper-and-feather confection from her, he tossed it on a chair before flinging open the front door.

Pru was silent until they were outside and a bit of distance from the house. For a moment he thought she might be upset that he had taken part in an orgy in the past. He should have known that she was simply regrouping.

"Have you ever made love in a place where you risked being caught?"

He stared at her, unable to hide his surprise. "Yes, but again it was a long time ago." At least a century, if not more.

Her lips curved. "Were you sober?"

He couldn't fight a grin. "Yes."

"Would you like to make love in public with me?"

His grin turned to a stunned expression. "Sweet God, woman, you never cease to amaze me."

She laughed, the sweet sound music to his ears. She turned to him, pressing her delicious self against him, making him hard and willing with ease.

"Take me." Her voice was a low, seductive taunt. "Take me now."

That was all the prompting Chapel needed. Grasping her by the arm, he steered her toward the darkened alley behind the theater. He wasn't going to make love to her in a dirty alley, but he'd take her someplace that would fulfill her fantasy, all right.

She came willingly into his arms, her body pliant and ready. He held her tight as he took to the sky, pressing his hips into hers so she could feel how hard he was for her.

She kissed him, her soft, ripe mouth hungry against his. She was still kissing him when they touched earth a few moments later.

Pru glanced around at their surroundings. Chapel waited for her to realize exactly where they were. They were in a lit courtyard, but on the fringe in the shadows. Guards were stationed beyond them, not close enough to readily detect them, but close enough to be a danger.

The moment their location became apparent to Pru would be forever branded in Chapel's memory. Her eyes were huge as she looked up at him.

"Buckingham Palace!" It came out as a squeak.

He chuckled. "Is this dangerous enough for you?"

"Chapel . . ."

But he was already edging her up against one of the palace walls, into a dark corner. When he had her exactly where he wanted her, his hands went to her skirts, pulling them up around her waist. Bending slightly, he wrapped his other arm around her bottom and lifted her until she was able to wrap her legs around his waist. She did so without hesitation and he grinned. So much for her protests.

He slid his fingers between her thighs, finding the slit in the delicate fabric of her drawers. The fine lawn was damp, the flesh inside even more so.

"You're ready for me," he murmured against her lips as he slid a finger into that tight, hot passage. His other hand busied itself with freeing his erection from the confines of his trousers. His cock sprang free, rigid and eager.

She smiled around a sigh as she moved against his hand. "I've been ready for you for a long time."

Reaching down between their bodies, she wrapped her fingers around his cock, stroking the hard length with firm, determined strokes. The pad of her thumb rubbed over the head, distributing the lubrication there as she moved her hand downward. Chapel shivered. God, she was going to make him come just like that.

He withdrew his finger, allowing her to guide him to the entrance of her body. She was slick and wet against him and so incredibly hot. He wanted to take his time with her, but that was impossible.

With one quick thrust, he was buried to the hilt inside her and both of them gasped at the sensation. Chapel glanced over his shoulder to see if a guard had noticed. One of them looked in their direction, but promptly looked away again.

"Are you all right?" he asked, turning his

attention back to the beautiful woman wrapped around him, holding him in the silken vise of her sex.

"I'm fine." Her hips moved against his. "Stop talking. They'll hear."

It was on the tip of his tongue to tell her it wasn't their talking they needed to worry about, it was the sounds she made when he thrust into her, shoving her farther into the darkened corner, against the smooth stone. Finally he crushed her mouth with his, swallowing her little cries and moans.

His hands cupped her buttocks, his fingers biting into the soft flesh as she undulated against him. Her thighs tightened around him as she lifted herself up and down on him, drenching him with her juices.

He allowed her to control their movements, content to let her ride him until they both exploded in pleasure.

God, she was an amazing woman! He had lived centuries and had never known anyone so fearless yet vulnerable, so strong yet feminine. She accepted him and yet seemed to delight in the things that made him more than human. She was almost always with him and yet he didn't feel like she was making demands of him. She didn't want to change him.

She just wanted him to change her.

No, he wouldn't think of that. Not now. He wanted to. God knows the idea of spending eternity with Pru was something crossing his mind more and more as of late, but he would not bestow this curse upon his beautiful Pru.

Of course, she hadn't mentioned it again, but he knew she thought about it. He could see it in her big hazel eyes. He also knew that her thoughts now had less to do with immortality and more to do with him.

If they weren't careful, one or both of them were going to end up in love, and then it would be all the more painful to part.

Even though he knew this, Chapel had no intention of leaving her until he had to. Was it selfish of him? Hell, yes. Did he care? Not a bit.

Pru drove him to the brink of ecstasy time and time again, until sweat beaded on his brow and his entire body was tight with tension. He forgot all about the palace and the guards and the cool night air. Nothing mattered but Pru and her taste in his mouth, her tight body around his.

She was close as well, he could feel it in the tension of her thighs, the quickening of her thrusts. It was too much. He'd waited long enough. Holding her hips, he took over, thrusting deep within her as sweet, aching pressure built between his legs. His sac tightened as climax neared and he thrust harder. Pru wrapped her arms tight around his neck and moaned her approval.

Arching his hips, Chapel practically came up on his toes as he pumped into her. Her thighs stiffened and her back arched as she cried out her climax into his mouth.

Her orgasm sent Chapel over the edge. One fierce thrust sent him spiraling into the abyss after her, ripple after ripple of intense pleasure shuddering through his body. Thank God their lips were still locked together, or else it would be him alerting the guards to their presence—if they hadn't done so already.

Moments passed as they stood, still locked together, their breath warm against each other's cheeks. Slowly, Chapel withdrew from the embrace of her flesh and lowered her to her feet. She was a little unsteady as he tucked himself back into his trousers.

She laughed—a throaty, sated sound. "I can't believe we did that."

"Who's there?"

Now it was Chapel who chuckled as one of the palace guards started toward their corner. The man squinted at the darkness. Another few steps and he would see them for sure. Pru quickly stepped forward, snuggling against him, wrapping her arms tight around him once more.

When the guard reached the corner, they were already flying toward home.

Chapter 19

She was dying.

The certainty of her death was something Pru had long ago faced. From the time she was old enough to grasp the concept of death, she knew that she, along with every other human being in the world, would someday die.

The doctors simply told her it would be earlier than she had expected. The tumor in her womb told her it would be soon indeed.

Her time on this earth was waning, just like the present century. She doubted she would live to see the twentieth century dawn. In fact, she doubted she would be there to decorate the Christmas tree this year.

These thoughts occurred to her in a surprisingly rather matter-of-fact manner. They were truth and there was no denying them. That didn't stop her from wishing she could. It didn't stop her from fantasizing about a miracle cure that would make it possible for her to spend a normal lifetime with her family—and with Chapel. Since she was being honest with herself about her mortality, she might as well be honest about everything else.

She wanted to live more for Chapel than she wanted to live for her family. Was that wrong of her? Was it sinful to imagine him coming to her and giving her his blood as she had given him hers, thus turning her into an immortal being like himself?

Surely there was nothing wrong with wanting to spend eternity with the man who had taken her virginity? The man she loved.

That realization was perhaps harder to face than her own demise.

She had fallen in love with a man who would continue to exist long after she stopped. A man who had been born centuries before herself. Even if she were able to have children, he was not the man who could give them to her. She knew all of this and none of it mattered. When she thought of Chapel, she didn't think of a vampire. She thought of the man who seemed to delight in making her smile, who didn't treat her like she was made of glass. He made her feel special, like the only woman in the world.

She would love him no matter what he was.

A week had passed since they had made love at Buckingham Palace. Pru still smiled when she thought of it. That was a memory Chapel would carry with him for a long time, if not forever. They had made a lot of memories during their time together.

He was so good about indulging her whims. Anything she wanted, whatever she cared to do, he gave it to her. Some nights they flew—flew!— off to another part of the country to experience some part of English culture she had never experienced before. Some nights they stayed close to the estate and drove her father's Daimler. She was actually quite good at driving now—even Chapel thought so. He no longer told her to slow down or to keep her gaze on the road.

Her family was proving amazing where Chapel was concerned. They treated him like anyone else, even though they knew him to be as far from ordinary as possible. Her sisters, who should have returned to their own lives by now, still lingered. It might be because they were afraid to leave in case she died while they were absent, or they simply didn't want her to think they were all right with her spending so much time alone with Chapel. Regardless, it was nice having them there. She wanted all the time she could have with them as well, so the daylight hours while she was awake she spent with her sisters and father. Nights she saved for Chapel.

It was a tiring schedule, but one she wasn't prepared to change.

Today it was a chore to get out of bed. She wanted nothing more than to lie about and drift in and out of sleep. In fact, a little sip of the tonic she took for pain and she could probably do just that. It might do her good to get a little extra rest. But then she would miss spending the day with her sisters, and she just might miss spending the night with Chapel, and she couldn't allow either to happen. There would be time enough to spend in bed when the cancer conquered her.

It hadn't conquered her yet.

Yes, she was going to die. There wasn't a Holy Grail for her and perhaps there never had been. She and Marcus had been pawns of the Silver Palm, and the order had used them accordingly.

She was through with chasing miracles. Even miracles had a price. Look at Chapel. He had been given the gift of immortality, extraordinary abilities and youth, and yet he saw it all as a curse because the price was that he was forced to feed on humans. A part of her recognized the habit as repugnant, but another remembered how blissful his mouth had felt at her throat.

He obviously had enjoyed taking her blood just as much as she had enjoyed giving it. Where was the sin in that? She could imagine drinking blood herself if it always felt so good.

She could imagine being like Chapel, being able to do all the things he could. The only downfall would be watching her family die.

And that was a tremendous price to pay.

Still, a little voice inside her whispered ever so softly that anything was worth spending eternity with Chapel. As long as they were together she could face anything.

That wasn't true, of course. It couldn't be. She

wasn't *that* much of a romantic, but it sounded nice and it was true that she could imagine spending the next four hundred years or more exploring the ever-changing world with him. No doubt there would be times when she'd miss the sun, or want to kill him, but nevertheless, the idea still appealed.

Yet the idea was useless, and she put it at the back of her mind as she rang for her maid. It was almost time for luncheon and she was supposed to dine with her sisters.

Her maid arrived and helped her dress and pinned her hair. Scrubbed clean and clothed in a gown of soft rose, Pru felt instantly better. She went downstairs just in time to join her sisters in the dining room.

"I was just thinking we were going to have to go fetch you," Matilda chastised lightly as Pru seated herself. "That's what happens when you do not go to bed until dawn."

She didn't go to bed until dawn because she was often in some other part of the country or making love—if not both—with Chapel, but she wasn't going to tell her sisters that. They'd only worry about her gallivanting around England and they'd most likely accuse Chapel of taking advantage of her.

"Then I deserve to be tardy, I suppose." Pru smiled at her sisters. "My apologies for keeping you waiting."

"Bah," Caroline said. "You didn't. We were just coming in ourselves when you arrived. Pay no attention to Mattie. She's always snippy when she's hungry."

They all laughed and seated themselves around the table, where a meal of meats and salads, bread and cheese waited for them.

"You do look tired, Pru." Georgiana selected a large slice of cold ham for her plate. "Are you feeling unwell?"

Three sets of varying shades of green eyes watched and waited for her reply, wide with concern.

Pru shook her head. "Just staying up too late, as Mattie guessed." She wasn't going to tell them she could feel her health shifting. It was almost as though she could feel the thing inside her draining her life.

Out of spite she took a huge piece of ham for herself. She was going to eat, blast it. If the cancer wanted her strength, she was going to make sure she had plenty to spare.

They talked about mundane things, day-to-day happenings, their father and the local gossip. There was much speculating, laughter and the occasional raised voice as they ate and talked.

Then, just as they were enjoying a cup of tea, Caroline fixed Pru with an uncertain gaze.

"Dearest, might I ask you a question at the risk of being impertinent?"

Pru chuckled. "I've never known you to do otherwise."

Caroline didn't quite return the smile, even though both Georgiana and Matilda giggled at her expense.

"You know, I'm fairly well read on the subject of vampires."

"Morbid!" Georgiana exclaimed around an overly loud cough. The others chuckled. Caroline's penchant for gothic novels was hardly a secret.

Sweet Caroline shot her younger sister a look that could have frozen an entire pond. Georgiana had hit a sore spot. "At least I read."

The sisters laughed at that as well. Georgiana rolled her eyes. Shaking her head, Pru called Caroline's attention back to her. "What about vampires, Caro?"

Caroline's pale brow pinched as she fidgeted with her teacup. "According to what I've read, they can change humans into vampires by taking the person's blood and replacing it with their own."

There was no use in lying. "It seems that way, yes."

Caroline cleared her throat, her gaze hesitant. "Is Chapel doing that to you?"

Matilda gasped. "Caroline!"

Pru ignored her oldest sister. Matilda acted as though it were none of their business—or that it was horrible to even think such a thing—when in fact they had every right to ask such questions. "No, Caro. He's not."

Caroline wasn't done. She leaned forward, as though afraid someone might walk into the room and overhear her. Her voice lowered. "Is he going to?"

No point in lying about this either. Pru lifted her teacup to her lips. "No. He says he doesn't want to curse me."

"By curse, you mean turn you into a creature like him." Matilda's eyes were wide as she affected a little shiver. "A creature who drinks the blood of humans."

"He is not a *creature*." Pru scowled as she met her oldest sister's gaze. "He's not so different from the rest of us."

Matilda raised a dark ginger brow. "He's a vampire, Prudence. Like it or not, that is different."

Matilda had a point. "He's not different in the ways that matter. Let's not forget he saved our lives."

"I'm not about to forget that," Matilda replied. "I will be grateful for the rest of my life. Dearest, I'm not attacking Mr. Chapel, I simply don't want you to think that becoming like him will fix everything."

"I don't think becoming like him would 'fix' everything." Not everything, but most of it.

Now it was Georgiana who spoke. "Would you want to become like him?"

Oh, dear. This was going to turn into a full-fledged conversation. Pru sighed and set her cup back in its saucer. "I don't know. My selfish nature wants nothing more than to live, but I cannot imagine going on forever while my family . . ." She couldn't finish. The thought of going on while her sisters aged and died was too painful. She didn't want to lose them. Didn't want to see that.

Caroline rubbed her rounded belly, her gaze fixed on the little mound as though she could actually see inside. "But you would always be there if my child needed you—or if her children did, or her children's children." She glanced up, her eyes bright with wetness. "I like the thought of that."

Georgiana's eyes were wide with wonder. "You would always have a part of us with you as the generations continued."

Matilda's brow knitted even as her eyes grew moist. "Our great-great grandchildren could know us through Pru. She could tell them about us. Dear Lord, I had not thought of that."

"And protect them," Caroline added. "Truly protect them."

Her sisters were coming up with scenarios Pru hadn't even thought to entertain. It was a little awe-inspiring. And touching.

And frightening.

"It's impossible," she informed them bluntly, not wanting them to get their hopes up any further. "Chapel won't do it. I'm going to die. We have to accept that."

"Perhaps," Caroline told her with a surprisingly hard glint in her eyes. "But that does *not* mean we have to like it."

Pru chuckled—it was a bitter, harsh sound. "Trust me, Caro. No one likes it less than I do."

Chapel was fresh from the bath, wide awake and filled with anticipation as he strode into the library that night to meet Pru. He had received a letter from Molyneux that assured him the priest and Marcus were closer to finding the Order of the Silver Palm thanks to several contacts. Molyneux also had hopes of enlisting Bishop in their quest. Bishop had been hunting monsters both human and non for centuries. If anyone could track the order, he could.

With that news giving him some satisfaction and taking a hefty load of worry from his shoulders, he approached the woman waiting for him on the sofa.

"What would you like to do tonight?" For the first time in a very long time, Chapel actually looked forward to an evening spent among humans. With Pru beside him, he didn't fear the crowds. With Pru's blood in him, he didn't feel as though he were being suffocated by the scents of life and hope and fear.

Patting a spot on the cushion beside her, Pru raised her gaze to his. She looked tired, the delicate flesh beneath her eyes appearing dark and bruised. "I thought perhaps we could just stay in tonight."

Even had she not appeared tired and frail, he would have known the state of her health from those softly spoken words alone. Pru never wanted to "just stay in." Pru wanted to go out and do things, see things. Pru wanted to live life to its fullest and she made him want to be there beside her while she did it.

His lungs and heart did not function as a human's and yet they reacted much the same. The realization that she was not well—that her life might very well be nearing its conclusion—tightened his chest and froze his heart until he thought he too might not be long for this earth. If he thought there was any chance of them ending up in the same place in the after life, he'd die with her.

Seating himself beside her, he took one of her long slender hands in his own. Her fingers were cold and it scared him. "Did you have an attack today?" He hated that there were hours when he couldn't watch over her.

She shook her head, little auburn tendrils curling around her cheeks. "No. I'm just tired. I think I've had too much excitement these past few weeks. I'm not used to it."

Was that it, or was there more? He didn't sense a lie in her voice, but for some reason her words didn't quite ring true either. Her scent betrayed nothing, but having taken her blood, he was more attuned to the essence of her rather than her illness.

"Are you certain that is all it is?"

Her fingers tightened around his. "I'm fine, Chapel. Truly."

He chose to believe her—more because he wanted her words to be true than because he truly thought she was telling him the truth.

Looking around, he searched the shelves for a book she might like, his keen eyes easily reading the titles from where they sat. "Would you like me to read to you?"

Pru shifted on the sofa so that she could lie down with her head on his thigh. She kept a hold on his hand as though afraid he might leave.

He wasn't going anywhere. Not tonight, not for a long time. He'd stay with her for the rest of her life if she wanted him to.

"Tell me about your life," she commanded, closing her eyes. "That's of more interest to me than some book."

With his free hand, Chapel started plucking

pins from the thick coil of her auburn hair. He loved her hair, loved how it looked flowing free around her face and shoulders. The color was so rich, so vibrant. It caught the light like glowing embers and rich silk.

He plucked another pin from the thick bun. "I've told you much of it already."

She didn't open her eyes as she smiled. "Not six hundred years' worth."

He smiled as well, even though she couldn't see it. "I suppose not. Would you believe there's not much to tell?"

"Yes."

Laughter broke free at her impertinence. She made him laugh, made him feel joy. "Minx. What would you like to know?"

"Were you close to your family?"

"Very much so." In fact, he still remembered their faces, their voices and mannerisms, even after all this time.

Her eyes opened and he saw the darkness of her gaze. "It must have hurt to have to watch them grow old and die."

"Yes." He wasn't going to lie to her. "But it has also been amazing to watch the generations following them grow and live."

"Does that make it easier?"

"At the time, no, but time lessens the pain. When I think of them now, it's with nothing but fondness."

"But you told me that watching the people you loved die was one of the hardest things you've ever done."

"It is. The pain is for ourselves, Pru, not for those who have gone on. It has to lessen or we'd go mad with it."

That seemed to appease her for the moment. She fell silent as she thought it over. Perhaps he shouldn't have been so truthful with her; it might make the idea of becoming a vampire even more appealing to her. She didn't see it for what it was. All she saw was a way to avoid dying.

It was what he had seen when he first laid eyes on the Blood Grail—a way to postpone something he had been afraid of.

"Are you afraid to die?"

Either she was a mind reader or their ways of thinking were very similar.

"Sometimes," he admitted. "The morning I brought you in from the cellar I was afraid I'd die before I got a chance to see you again."

That brought a little smile to her soft lips. "I was afraid that I'd die before I saw you again. I'm not afraid of dying, I just don't want to do it this soon."

He couldn't think of anything to say to make it easier for her, so he simply pulled the last pin from her hair and began combing his fingers through the thick strands, untwisting them until her hair spread across his thighs and spilled onto the sofa.

She closed her eyes. "Mmm. That feels nice."

She liked it, so he kept doing it. He massaged her scalp as well. She sighed as he began rubbing little circles on her forehead.

"What were you like when you were younger?"

Younger didn't have the same meaning to him that it once did. "When I was human, you mean?"

Her eyes were still closed as she shrugged. "Whichever you prefer."

Chapel thought for a moment, conjuring a picture of his younger self in his mind. "Impulsive. Headstrong. Arrogant."

"Really?"

"Why so surprised?"

She shrugged, her shoulder nudging his thigh. "Merely that you are neither of those now."

Was he not? "I can be still, just in different ways."

Her lips curved into a gentle smile. "I don't see it."

"It's the brooding. It hides everything else."

"You make me laugh." He grinned at her reaction.

She had a knack for telling him things no one else ever had. No one had ever thought of him as particularly amusing, never. "You'd never stop, if I had my way."

Her eyes twinkled as they opened. "But if I never stopped laughing, we'd never get anything else done."

His blood warmed as he caught the meaning in her tone. "We would find a way."

Her gaze softened as she watched him. He'd do anything to take those dark circles away.

"Do you ever miss Marie?"

Why did she persist in asking about Marie? She was a painful memory, something he still felt terrible guilt over, but miss her?

"I'm not sure."

She arched a fine brow. "I would think it would be an easy yes or no."

"Would you? Sometimes, then." It wasn't much of an answer, but it was an honest one.

"Regrets?"

He massaged between her eyebrows with the pad of his thumb. "About Marie or my life in general?"

"Take your pick."

"Yes." More than he could count.

The other brow went up. "Yes to which?"

He smiled. She was so nosy. "Both. I have many regrets about Marie. I have even more about my life, but that's the point, is it not?"

The corner of her mouth quirked. "I've never witnessed Gallic indifference until now."

He chuckled. "I'm not sure what it is you want from me."

"Just the truth."

He was giving her that. "When I give it, you seem to want more."

All humor vanished from her expression. "I suppose I want to know if it was worth it."

"If what was?"

"Drinking from the cup. Becoming a vampire." She frowned a little and he tried to smooth the lines away with his finger. "Would you do it again if given the choice?"

Instinct told him to say no, but he couldn't. If he hadn't drunk from the Blood Grail, if he hadn't become what he was, he wouldn't be here now. He wouldn't be sitting in this library, warm and cozy, with this remarkable woman. He would have been dust centuries ago, killed by the poison on that blade, or by old age if he hadn't gone on that mission for Philip.

He would have married Marie, but would they have been happy? Six centuries of wisdom told him that he hadn't been the right man to give Marie what she needed, nor could she have given him what he wanted.

"Yes," he told her. "I would do it again."

A hint of a smile. "That's all I wanted to know."

He searched her gaze, looking for something, some reason for that hint of satisfaction he heard in her voice, but there was nothing. If he lived another hundred years he didn't think he'd figure out how her mind worked.

Unfortunately, Pru didn't have another hundred years.

"How do your fangs work?"

Many times he thought she was like a child with her questions and this was no exception. "They are retractable, like a snake's."

"Can you make them come out?"

"Yes."

"Show me."

He did, and hoped that it didn't frighten her to see it. Pru watched with a wondrous expression as she observed his canines lengthening. She reached a finger upward—and pushed on the fang closest to her.

"So that's what you bite me with."

He willed his fangs to recede. "They are."

"I wish I had fangs."

"Why?" Another remark he'd never heard anyone else make. It wasn't something he would have her wish for, and yet he couldn't bring himself to tell her that.

"So then I could be a part of you the way you've been a part of me."

His heart broke. "You are a part of me, Pru." It was damn near impossible to speak with his heart in his throat. "You always will be."

She stroked his jaw with her cool fingers. She was so fragile, so goddamn frail. "Chapel?"

"Yes, love?"

"Forgive me, but I hope it takes a long time for the pain of my loss to lessen for you."

She was killing him. She had to know that, didn't she?

"I think that's a safe wager."

He couldn't bring himself to admit that he didn't think the pain would ever lessen, because then he'd have to admit just how much she'd come to mean to him. She'd brought him out of hiding, and once she was gone, he had no idea how he'd ever bring himself to return to that darkness.

Chapter 20

By the next afternoon, Pru was feeling more like herself, although still somewhat tired. She dined as usual with her sisters and then her father, who suggested the two of them go for a drive since it was such a lovely day.

Surprised, Pru readily accepted. She was even more shocked when her father suggested she do the driving!

"Why?" she demanded, suddenly suspicious. "Is something wrong? Are you ill?"

He chuckled at her scowl. "No. I simply thought you might want to show me what Chapel has taught you."

She paled. "You know?"

Amusement lingered in his loving expression. "I'm your father. It is my automobile. Of course I know. Besides, Chapel asked permission before he began giving you lessons. He was raised properly, you know. No sneaking around for that young man."

Pru rolled her eyes. "First of all, he's not young. He's older than you and I and the girls all together. Second, do not make him into some kind of saint just because he asked to drive your precious Daimler."

Her father's amusement faded. "He saved all of our lives—yours twice. He can do whatever he bloody well pleases as far as I'm concerned."

Pru's eyebrows rose at her father's colorful language, but she was more surprised by his meaning than his words. *Whatever* Chapel pleased?

She took his arm. "You do not care that he isn't human, Papa?"

Slowly, they strolled through the house. "Oddly enough, I do not," her father replied. "Perhaps it hasn't truly sunk in yet, even though I saw the feats he is capable of with my own eyes, but no. I cannot bring myself to be the least concerned with what Chapel is when he has done so much for us. For you."

Her head snapped up. "For me?"

There was that smile again. Her father looked so youthful and handsome when he smiled, much like the portrait of Devlin Ryland that hung in the great hall.

"He saved you."

"Twice, yes. You mentioned that already." She didn't mean to sound short, but she didn't quite understand what her father was getting at.

"Not just physically. He saved you emotionally, I think."

She wanted to roll her eyes, even though a part of her knew him to be right. She smiled instead. "A philospher now, Papa?"

"Before he came along, all you thought of was finding the Grail."

"Yes, well, we know that was fruitless, don't we?" She still would like to find it, though. A hopeless dream, perhaps, but a dream nonetheless.

"Now you spend time with your family. Your sisters very much enjoy the luncheon ritual the four of you have."

Did they? They hadn't said anything to her. Of course, they didn't really need to. "I enjoy it as well."

He wasn't done with his list. "You smile more now. You seem more at ease."

"Perhaps I have simply accepted my fate and am determined to make the most of the time I have left." It was an honest confession if ever she'd made one. She didn't like her fate, but yes, she had accepted it.

He looked striken by her words and Pru instantly wished she could take them back. "Perhaps. Or perhaps you are in love."

That her father could see through her so easily astounded Pru. It also needled her that she was so transparent. If her father could see it, who else could? Her sisters most certainly would have figured it out by now as well. Had Chapel?

Oh, God, please no. Don't let him know. The last thing she needed was for Chapel to realize how she felt about him. She knew him well enough to know that he'd start feeling guilty. The last thing she wanted was for him to be carrying around regret for her for the next six hundred years like he had for Marie.

She didn't want some woman in Chapel's future thinking of her as "the cow" as she did Marie.

She didn't want another woman in Chapel's future at all.

"Does he love you?" Her father asked when the silence stretched between them.

"You tell me. You seem to know my own feelings better than I; perhaps you know Chapel's as well." It was a poor attempt at sarcasm. Her tone wasn't even sharp.

"I would hazard a guess that he feels the same for you, but then I'm biased. I cannot imagine anyone not loving you, even if you are a saucy baggage."

Leaning in, she gave her father's arm a squeeze and briefly rested her head on his shoulder. A good cry would feel good right now.

"I lied, Papa. I said I had accepted my fate, but I haven't, not quite. I'm still not ready to die."

"My dear girl, I am not ready to lose you. I would trade places with you in an instant if only God would let me."

He broke her heart. "He won't. And neither would I."

The Daimler sat waiting in the drive as they exited the house. Her father stopped a few feet short of the automobile, where a footman waited to assist them, and turned to her.

"I know nothing about these things, but Caroline . . . your sister seems to think that Chapel might be able to cure you. Is that true?"

How hopeful he sounded. How wistful. Tears burned her eyes, blurring her vision. "He could, but it would make me a vampire, Papa. I wouldn't be human anymore. I'd be like Chapel."

This didn't seem to bother him. "I know that. I believe the benefits outweigh the negative aspects."

Pru sighed. She detested explaining this situation to her family. She hated letting them down. "Chapel thinks of himself as a monster. He would rather die than make me into the same."

"Monster?" He was clearly incensed. "But he's a hero!"

That was one way of looking at it. "Not in his own eyes."

Her father frowned. "Rubbish."

Pru shrugged, trying to toss off the hurt. A little piece of her heart wanted to think that she meant so much to Chapel he would toss his convictions to the wind and turn her so they could be together—because he was unable to go on without her.

Obviously, that little piece was an idiot. She didn't mean enough to him that he'd throw his beliefs aside, nor would he realize how stupid they were. He was a stubborn man who was willing to give up a future with her because he thought himself less that human.

"I'm going to have a talk with that boy," her father announced, his jaw tight.

"Papa, no." She didn't care how whiny she sounded, she would add a pout and a foot stomp if she thought it would work. "You cannot change his mind."

Her father's expression was resolute. "I can try."

Before Pru could argue with him further, he guided her to the driver's side of the Daimler so the footman could open the door for her. She couldn't very well continue this conversation in front of the footman and so she was forced to be quiet until they rolled down the drive.

Even then her father refused to discuss it any further, telling her to concentrate on her driving. She did—or rather, she tried to. Truth be told, it wasn't long before all thoughts of their conversation drifted to the back of her mind. Driving made her feel so free, and her father actually praised her! Why would she want to think of anything else?

Their conversation came back to her when they returned to the house an hour later. It hardly mattered, however, as her father had visitors who arrived immediately upon their return. Pru would have to wait to make him promise not to talk to Chapel. She could only hope that in the meantime her father didn't decide to take matters into his own hands.

The least she could do was warn Chapel that her father might attack him on the subject. He might not appreciate Thomas Ryland sticking his face into matters he didn't understand. Pru didn't understand, and she was in love with the man. It was difficult for her to conceive that the man she thought so wonderful, so caring and brave, could think of himself as less than human.

In fact, that in itself was a very human trait. He hadn't stopped being human, he was simply more. Why did he have to make himself evil? Was it because of the time period in which he'd been born? The church had been such a huge part of his life—it still was—and the church had told him he was a monster.

Perhaps there were monsters in this world, but she could never believe that Chapel was one of them.

Lifting the skirts of her pale green morning gown so as not to fall, Pru hurried up the stairs. She had to see Chapel, had to see his face, feel his touch. She had to try to find some way before she died to prove to him that he was better than he thought. Suddenly the thought of dying while he thought himself evil was simply too much to bear.

The corridor outside was empty and dim. He was now the only person residing in this wing, and so it was kept dark for him on purpose during the day—just in case. If the servants thought anything was strange about their guest, they kept quiet about it. Perhaps they, like her father, were prepared to overlook a great deal due to the fact that Chapel had almost singlehandedly saved them all from certain death.

Slowly, she opened his door, cringing as it groaned ever so slightly. She would have to get one of the footmen to oil the hinges. They couldn't have this door creaking when one of them was sneaking about in the night.

The room was dark—very dark. Pru ducked in quickly, so as not to be seen. When she saw the figure in the bed, she thought perhaps her precautions were for naught. He was burrowed beneath the blankets—his entire body curled into itself, his back to the windows, facing the door.

Like a rabbit in a burrow, she thought, smiling at the absurdity. An awfully big, handsome, brave rabbit.

She tiptoed across the carpet. Why she was being so quiet when she had come to wake him, she had no idea.

She was reaching for him when he jerked upright on the bed, snarling, wild and deadly.

"Chapel!" She flung herself backward, her heart pounding in terror. She landed hard on her rump on the floor. She should have known better. Should have known not to wake him. Hadn't he warned them all after Father Molyneux left that they shouldn't wake him?

Why had she thought she could make an exception?

But he hadn't killed her. In fact, he seemed calmer now. He was sitting on the bed, a rumpled, naked delight, staring at her as though she were insane, which, of course, she was.

He ran a hand through his mussed hair. "Pru, are you all right?"

Was she? Her chest felt as though her heart had tried to bust right out of it, but otherwise she seemed fine. "Yes."

She should have said no. Perhaps then he wouldn't have frowned at her like that. At least she thought he was frowning. She couldn't see him that well. "What the hell were you thinking?"

As quickly as her trembling extremities would allow, Pru righted her skirts and rose to her feet. "Obviously, I wasn't."

"I could have killed you!"

"But you didn't."

Her reassurance did nothing to take the distress from his features. "No. I realized it was you. Somehow. Thank God."

There were those threatening tears again. Good Lord, she was turning into a watering pot! "I just wanted to be with you."

He held his arms out to her—his naked, muscular arms. "Come here."

She went eagerly, readily. He held the covers for her to slip beneath and she did so without hesitation, snuggling her fully clothed self against his deliciously naked one.

His hands stroked her back. "Has something happened?"

"No." Her reply was muffled against his chest. He was warm and hairy against her cheek. She could stay here forever just to feel his comforting warmth.

"You really risked harm just to be with me?"

She wrapped her arms tighter around him. He sounded so surprised, so totally shocked. Why should that be such a surprise to him?

"Yes." She would warn him about her father later. Right now all she wanted was to feel him next to her. She just needed to be with him—where she felt alive and daring, yet safe and secure at the same time.

"Chapel?"

He kissed her forehead. "Yes, *ma petite*?" He sounded sleepy. He was drifting off again, she could sense it.

"Nothing. Go to sleep."

She wasn't going to tell him that she loved him. At least, not yet.

"Prudence took me driving today."

Chapel turned an astonished gaze to Thomas Ryland. "Really?"

Ryland chuckled. "You sound as astounded by the concept as I was, and I am the one who thought of it." His brow pinched. "She had been after me for so long and I do hate to deny her."

Astonishment gave way to an understanding smile. "I know exactly how you feel."

"Do you?" Ryland turned to face him, sharply, purposefully.

Chapel cast a glance around the room. No one in the drawing room gave them the slightest bit of attention. Even Pru, who normally would be so curious, was wrapped up in some tale Caroline's husband was telling the rest of the party.

"Is there something on your mind, sir?" He was hundreds of years Thomas Ryland's senior and yet he felt the need to show him the respect of age.

Ryland took him by the arm. "May we speak candidly, Chapel? Privately?"

"Of course."

Pru's father released him, and led the way to the terrace doors. Outside, the night was cool and inviting, the scents of flowers and the sea on the breeze. They stood just outside the doors, blocking the way so no one could surprise them. Light from the drawing room spilled outside, allowing Thomas Ryland's direct gaze to find him easily.

It was a stare that made Chapel uncomfortable.

"I will come directly to the point," Ryland began, his gaze locked on Chapel's. "I am told that you could cure Prudence of her . . . affliction."

"With all due respect, sir, cancer is a little more serious than an 'affliction.' "

His words were dismissed with a frustrated shake of Ryland's head. "Can you cure it?"

Chapel folded his arms over his chest. The movement made his coat pull uncomfortably across his back. "I could, but I won't."

"Why not?"

Wasn't it obvious? "It would mean turning your daughter into a vampire."

"Yes, I understand that." The terse words also told him that Ryland didn't appreciate his tone.

"She would no longer be human." Again, he spoke like he thought all of this should mean more to her father.

"But she would look it."

What the hell? "Yes, but—"

"She would live." Spoken like a man focusing on one thing, and one thing alone.

"Forever, possibly, but she would have to take the blood of others to do so."

Ryland's jaw came up defiantly. It was a posture he had seen Pru take herself. "I would offer mine willingly."

"And when you are gone?" He wanted Thomas Ryland to see the whole of the situation, not just what he wanted to see. "Would you condone her taking the blood of innocents?"

"Pru is not mindless." Ryland looked offended that Chapel might suggest otherwise. "She would not kill."

"No, I don't think she would." Not on purpose, but the bloodlust could be very powerful when someone was first turned. It was so very difficult to resist. Of course, Pru would have him to help her if she wanted him. . . . No, he would not think of that. He would not use turning her merely to keep her with him.

"I don't want to bury my daughter, Chapel."

Oh, God. Were those tears in Ryland's eyes? "You shouldn't have to, sir. You shouldn't have to watch her become something that under any other circumstances would terrify you either."

"I do not know what you believe we are, Chapel, but ignorant peasants we are not. I would not chase a person with a pitchfork just because that person was something outside of my normal understanding. In fact, in this case I believe you are the one who is being ignorant."

"I beg your pardon?" He was becoming more than a little annoyed with Ryland and this conversation. Did no one in this bloody family understand that there was more to making Pru a vampire than simply ending her battle with cancer? Did they not realize what it meant?

"You have within you the power to save a life, and yet you refuse because you think you know better. You believe Pru will become some kind of monster. My daughter could never become a monster, it's not in her."

"I didn't think it was in me either, but it is." For the first century of his new life he had been a careless killer at times. He took who he wanted, when he wanted—in more ways than he wanted to admit. Oh, he never forced anyone to his will. He never had to.

"Yes, what a monster you are, risking yourself to save a family you barely know, a girl you barely know. That is the kind of monster I could condone my daughter being."

"Sir . . ." This was so useless.

Ryland held up his hand. "You disappoint me, Chapel. I thought you a great man, a hero. I was wrong. You are willing to risk yourself only when you believe you have nothing to lose. You are not willing to help my daughter because you are afraid."

Now it was he who was defiant. "I'm not afraid."

"I think you are. You care for my daughter, do you not?"

"I do." He kept his hands tucked between his arms and his body lest he use them to pummel some sense into Pru's father. She would not be impressed with him if he did. "That is why I cannot turn her into something she will regret becoming."

"Then why would you not do everything in your power to hold on to her?"

There was nothing he could say that he hadn't already said. Many reasons came to mind, but at the forefront was a little voice asking him that same question. Why wouldn't he do everything in his power to hold on to Pru? Because Marie hadn't wanted him? Marie had been dead six hundred years.

As he turned to the door, Thomas Ryland's shoulders sagged. The gaze that met Chapel's from over his shoulder was sad and resigned—the gaze of a man realizing he was about to lose a child and was powerless against it.

"You being here makes Prudence very happy. Regardless of my opinion, I hope you will at least remain here a while longer. For her."

Chapel nodded. "I will."

"Thank you." Ryland let himself inside the house. Chapel stayed where he was.

He made Pru happy. The statement filled him with such giddiness he wanted to scoff at it. When had he ever made someone happy? It had been too long. Even more astounding was that she made him happy. Happiness was something he never thought to experience for more than seconds at a time since Dreux's suicide—since realizing what he had become.

And yet, since meeting Pru, he had known the emotion many times. He felt it whenever he was with her, whenever he thought of the things they'd shared. The thought of her leaving him was the exact opposite of that happiness. The thought of there being no more Pru in this world filled him with an emptiness that made meeting the dawn seem a good idea.

Was he wrong? Everyone seemed to think so. Maybe he was, but he couldn't see it. Every reason he could think of for turning Pru into a vampire was for his own benefit. Every reason he had for *not* turning her was for her own. How, then, could he be wrong?

As if in answer to his question, the terrace door opened once more, but instead of Thomas Ryland, Pru stepped out into the night.

"Are you all right?" she asked.

He would have laughed were he capable. Dear Pru, he was immortal and she was worried about him. "I am fine."

"What were you and Papa talking about?"

He wasn't about to lie. "You."

"Oh."

He wasn't going to give her the details. The last thing she needed was to know that he and her father were at odds. He didn't want to have to explain to her why he refused to "save" her as her father wanted.

Instead, he offered her his hand. "Walk with me?"

She wrapped her fingers within his, offering him a smile as she did so. Her hand was bare in his. Had she eschewed gloves on purpose hoping to touch him? It seemed too much to hope, and yet he knew it to be true. It was there in her face.

All he had to do was look at her—his Pru was like an open book.

His Pru.

They left the light and openness of the terrace and walked toward the garden, down the lantern-lit path that was more shadow than light. He led the way, seeing every potential hazard there might be on the grassy walk. He steered Pru around a small divot that might have sprained her ankle and a bit of the hedge that could have snagged her gown.

In the center, he stopped. There was a circle of stone benches around a fountain. Two lanterns stood on opposite sides of the circle, making the water from the fountain dance like droplets of cut crystal in a riot of translucent color.

The lanterns were little more than lamps. Lifting their shades, Chapel extinguished first one, then the other, so that the only light around them was the glow of lanterns farther away and the slight glimmer from a moon on its way to becoming full once more.

"What are you doing?" There was nothing but curiosity in her low voice. He could snap her like a twig and she had no fear of him whatsoever.

Marie had been terrified.

Marie, as Pru so eloquently put it, had been a cow.

"Giving us some privacy," he replied.

A coy smile curved her lips. "Do we need privacy?"

He pulled her close. "I want you."

Her smile faltered at the intensity in his tone.

"Something happened. What happened?"

He silenced her with a kiss. His mouth ravaged hers until he felt the tension ease out of her. She melted against him, her body soft and supple.

"I need you," he whispered against her mouth. "Now. Here."

Her lashes fluttered, opened. Eyes, big and dark, stared at him from beneath heavy lids. "Yes."

He lowered them onto the grass, her on top of him so her gown wouldn't be soiled. He freed her breasts from her gown and suckled each until she ground her pelvis against him. Too many layers of clothing prevented the kind of contact he craved. He pulled her skirts up to her waist, cupping the warm curve of her bottom through the fine silk of her drawers.

She sat up, helping him arrange her gown so that it pooled around them. She straddled his hips, moving herself against him in a maddeningly seductive rhythm.

Beneath the tent of her skirts, Chapel unfastened his trousers, freeing the demanding length of his cock from its prison.

"I'm yours," he told her, his voice like gravel in his ears. "Take me."

He watched, his gaze fastened on her beautiful face as she reached down beneath her gown, her fingers closing around him in a velvet vise. Slowly, she guided him to the slit in her drawers, to the place where she was warm, wet and so inviting. She rose up, placing him at the entrance of her body, and then down, engulfing him within her slickness.

Chapel sighed. He raised his hands to her breasts, pulling and stroking her nipples as she rode him, but he didn't try to control their movements. He wanted her to do it. Wanted her to take from him, to bring herself to climax so he could watch.

She untied his cravat and pulled open the neck of his shirt as she eased herself up and down upon him. Then, as her movements quickened, bringing them both surprisingly close to climax, she lowered her head to his chest.

She bit him just below the collarbone, where the muscle of his chest was firm and heavy. Her teeth were sharp, the pressure blunt. Not hard enough to break the skin, but hard enough that there would be a mark. A mark that, of course, would be gone by morning. He couldn't even enjoy her claim for long.

He knew what she was doing and it killed him. The pain/pleasure of her teeth brought tears to his eyes—not because she hurt him, but because she was trying to be with him as he had been with her and she couldn't.

Because he wouldn't let her.

Chapter 21

"How long?"

Dr. Higgins fastened the buckle on his leather satchel, paused for a moment, as if collecting himself, and then raised his faded gaze to Pru's.

She sat on the edge of her bed, her wrapper pulled around her. Dr. Higgins hadn't liked being asked to examine her without her father's knowledge, but Pru didn't want her father to know. Not yet.

"All I can give you is an estimate, Miss Ryland. The cancer has progressed quite rapidly."

"You've known me all my life, sir. Surely you can give me more than that."

He sighed. "Prudence . . ."

"I am not a child, nor am I some weak woman

who will go into hysterics at your prognosis." She clenched her jaw against her frustration. "How long?"

Higgins's expression softened. "A month, perhaps."

Perhaps. "Or less, you mean." Odd how she felt nothing at his words.

He nodded, his gaze leaving hers. "Or less, yes."

There it was, then. Apparently she had thirty days at the most before she died.

This was one of those times when she wished she was truly, truly certain of what happened to a person after death. She really hoped there was a heaven, but she didn't want to be able to watch over her family—at least not until they'd stopped mourning.

Lord, how vain was that? She wasn't even dead yet and already she was planning out how long it would take people to recover from her death!

"I'm so sorry, Prudence."

He had to be, for him to use her first name. "Thank you, Dr. Higgins."

He looked so old, so sad. "I brought you into this world. It pains me to no end to have to watch you leave it as well."

Tears stung her eyes. "Thank you."

He handed her a bottle. "For pain, if you need it."

Pru took it. It was laudanum or something similar. She'd only take it if she absolutely had to. She didn't want to spend the last days of her life in a stupor.

She wanted to spend them with Chapel. Not

her family, not what few friends she had—if she had any left; it had been so long since she saw them—but Chapel.

She had her maid see Dr. Higgins out. She didn't bother to wait for the girl's return before leaving her room. It was afternoon and she had no business walking around in her gown and wrapper, but there was no one about but the servants, the rest of the family having gone into town for a brief outing. The idea of putting on a regular corset made her feel sick—the pressure on her abdomen would be too much.

She just wanted time to stop. Her future was too short and too frightening. Death: the Great Unknown. It wasn't dying that scared her, it was what came after. She'd always thought of herself as a good Christian, but she was so uncertain now. What if there wasn't a heaven? What if there was and she didn't go there? What if there was nothing?

And what good was heaven when she had to leave Chapel behind? Heaven was what she felt when she was in his arms, in his very presence.

She went to Chapel's room and walked in without knocking. He barely woke as she snuggled against him. He was used to her now, so he didn't startle awake when she joined him. He was no more wild or feral than a kitten. Even in the deepest of slumbers, in the darkest of darks, he would know her by scent and by sound.

A tear leaked from the corner of her eye as she wrapped her arms around his comforting warmth. His *enduring* warmth. Long after she was gone he would continue. She would be cold and gone and he would still be warm and here in the world.

She wanted to be angry with him—angry that he didn't love her enough to want to spend forever with her—but she couldn't muster the emotion. She understood that it had nothing to do with how much he cared for her. He hadn't confessed to any deeper regard, but she suspected that he might be falling in love with her. Her death would be very painful for him. It wasn't lack of feeling that made him not change her. It was rather the opposite. He cared too much about her to turn her into what he thought was an abomination.

The realization warmed her, even though she believed him a fool for thinking it. Still, he'd thought himself a monster for so long now, she held little hope of changing his mind. And she didn't have the time.

He had done so much for her, she wished she could do something for him in return. If she could just make him see how wonderful he was. If just once he could see himself the way she saw him.

"Is something wrong?" His voice was groggy and low in her ear. Just the sound of it was enough to take the chill from her blood.

Yes, everything was wrong. She wasn't supposed to die this young. She wasn't supposed to fall in love with the man who helped her experience life and taught her about passion. Or if she was supposed to fall in love, they were supposed to live happily ever after. It wasn't supposed to end like this.

"Promise me, that when I'm gone you won't go back into hiding." Another tear dribbled from her eye as she held him. "Promise me that you will live—live for the both of us."

He rose up on his elbow, now fully awake. His hair was tousled and his eyelids were heavy, but there was no denying the alert tension in his body.

"Pru, what is it?" There was a trace of fear in his voice.

"Promise me." Right now that meant more to her than anything. If he could go out into the world and savor all it had to offer—for her—then she could die with a sense of peace.

He stroked her cheek with the backs of his fingers. Surely he felt the wetness there. "I promise."

The tightness in her muscles eased. "Good." She rested her head on his shoulder and closed her eyes. The discomfort in her abdomen had eased a bit. Perhaps she could sleep now.

"Tell me what happened."

Ahh, but now Chapel was wide awake and wondering what in the name of God was wrong with her.

She could lie to him, could tell him that everything was all right, that she was just feeling melancholy, but to what end? He deserved to know that their time together was running out.

"Dr. Higgins came by to see me today."

"Did you father send for him?"

"No, I did."

He stilled. Beneath her cheek there wasn't even a heartbeat, not a rise of breath. Were it not for his warmth, it would have frightened her.

"I haven't been feeling well these last few days, as you know." Of course he knew. She hadn't felt like going out for days, and for the past two she couldn't even let him make love to her. She couldn't let him inside her without discomfort.

When the bleeding started, when the other symptoms came and wouldn't go away, she knew it was time to send for the doctor.

"So you waited until I was asleep, until a day when you knew your family would be otherwise engaged, to send for the doctor?" He phrased it as a question, but there was a degree of understanding in his voice, as if he knew exactly why she had waited.

She didn't want anyone to know. She wanted to tell them—*if* she told them—on her own.

"Yes." There were no more tears now. "I sent for Dr. Higgins. He just left."

Gentle hands rubbed her back. "What did he say?"

"The cancer . . . it's worse."

His hands paused for a split second—his only reaction to her news. "What else did Dr. Higgins say?"

Pru closed her eyes. "He said that I do not have much time left."

Beneath her cheek, she felt his heart thump against his ribs. Her throat tightened.

"Did he . . . did he say how much?"

"A month at best."

He didn't speak. He simply tightened his arms

around her, holding her close, but not so tight that it hurt.

Reaching up, she touched his cheek with the full length of her fingers. She needed to feel his warmth, feel his flesh against hers.

"I want you to go."

"What?" He was as surprised by her words as she was.

She stroked his cheek, feeling the rasp of stubble beneath her fingertips. "You should leave Rosecourt."

"And leave you? No." He sounded offended—and angry—that she could even suggest it.

"The order isn't coming back, you know that. They have what they want."

"Fuck the order." She jumped at his harshness. "I don't care about them. I'm not leaving you."

"I don't want you to be here when I . . . go." She had an aunt who had died of cancer years before. She remembered what it did to her. "I don't want you to see what it does to me."

"I've already seen."

"It may get worse."

"I don't care." Damn him and his stubborn hide. "I'm not leaving you, Pru."

Tears spilled down her cheeks. "But I don't want that to be how you remember me."

One of his hands left her back to come around and cup her cheek. "I will remember you as my beautiful, curious, wonderful Pru. Always."

She cried in earnest then, his words, his sweet touch releasing the floodgate of tears that she tried so hard to repress. They came out of her in great, wracking sobs that she was powerless to stop once they started. He didn't try to shush her, he just let her go, let her soak him with her salt grief.

A drop of warm wetness fell near her ear, pulling her out of her own sorrow for a second. It was followed by another and then another. Chapel didn't make a sound, but she knew without looking that he was crying as well.

Matilda—clothes.
Caroline—all books except those concerning Arthurian legend.
Georgiana—jewelry and figurines.
Chapel— Pru paused, pen hovering just above the paper. Why was writing this entry to her list so much harder than the others? She already knew what she wanted to give him. Perhaps because she knew her sisters would cherish what she left them, but with Chapel it simply felt as though she had nothing else to give, so she had grasped for something she thought he might like.

It wasn't as though she could actually leave him her heart.

Chapel—books on King Arthur. Arthur was one of the first topics they'd discussed upon Chapel's arrival at Rosecourt. At the time she had thought of it, her books seemed a fitting gift to leave him, but now she wasn't so sure. Would books let him know just how much he had come to mean to her? When he looked at them, read them, would he know she had loved him?

He'd been by her side his every waking moment these last few days. Three weeks had passed since Dr. Higgins's visit. Some nights had been better than others and she actually managed to go out for a bit. They never went far—no farther than Chapel could fly in twenty or thirty minutes. Mostly they spent their time talking. He told her many stories of the places he had been and seen, of what life had been like when he was young.

She told him stories as well, recounting happy—and not so happy—moments of her life, such as her first kiss, and when her mother died. He listened to all of it with an attentiveness she found strangely heartbreaking, like he was trying to memorize every word.

He had shared his letters from Molyneux with her. She knew that the priest and Marcus would find the Silver Palm. She wondered if she would see the two men again before she died. Dear Marcus was apparently still looking for the Holy Grail for her. God bless him.

Her days—or rather, her afternoons—were spent with her family. A few friends from around the local district came to call when word got out that she was "failing." How word got out, Pru didn't know. The servants, perhaps, or one of her sisters. It hardly mattered. It didn't matter that people knew she was dying. What she couldn't stand was the pity in their eyes.

It was becoming increasingly difficult to visit with her sisters as well. Each one of them looked so down in the mouth every time she saw them that it inevitably brought her own spirits down as well. Only Chapel managed to look at her without seeming too sad. He seemed to want to enjoy the remainder of their time together.

She enjoyed the time she spent with him. It meant so much to her. A strange sense of calm had settled over her just the day before. Suddenly the thought of death didn't seem so very awful. Yes, the idea of leaving behind everyone she loved was sad, but she was no longer afraid to do it.

She still wasn't ready, but at least she wasn't afraid.

She looked down at the hand holding her pen. It was pale, the bones sharp through the skin. In fact, her entire body was looking gaunt. She'd lost a lot of weight recently. She didn't feel like eating much more than tea and toast. Her belly was the only part of her that looked like it belonged on a larger person, and she knew that was only because of the cancer.

So tired. She was just so tired. She wanted to go to sleep and never wake up. That would happen soon enough. For now she had to put her affairs in order. Fortunately, her affairs were few.

It was growing dark outside. Soon the maid would be there to bring her supper. Her family would join her as she ate. Chapel might join her as well, if he was up. He often went off to feed upon waking. She didn't ask where he went or off whom he fed, mostly because she didn't want to know. He refused to take her blood anymore, he was so afraid of making her weaker. He didn't seem to understand that him feeding off someone else felt almost like infidelity to her. She knew it was a foolish way of thinking, but she couldn't help it.

How useless she was. She couldn't even give her lover what he needed to sustain himself.

A knock on her door interrupted her self-pitying thoughts. It was Chapel—looking fresh and handsome in his shirtsleeves. He carried a cravat in his hand and had a dinner jacket slung over his arm.

"What is this?" she asked.

He smiled as he closed the door behind him. "We thought you might like to dine downstairs this evening."

She struggled to sit up against the pillows. "We?"

"Your family and I."

"Well, 'we' is right." She ran a hand over the tangled mess of her hair. "I'd love to go downstairs, but I look a fright."

His smile grew. "That's why I'm here. I'm going to take care of your bath."

Her eyebrows rose. "Does my father know that?"

"Of course not." He looked horrified by the suggestion, as if her father posed any threat to him whatsoever. "He thinks I was going to fetch you later. I'll run the water."

"Chapel . . ." She stopped, a wave of embarrassment washing over her.

His good humor vanished. "What is it?"

"I don't . . . I don't think it's a good idea for you to help me bathe."

"Why not? I'll have you know I'm very good at bathing people—I bathe myself on a regular basis."

He was being silly for her benefit; she knew because he still wasn't all that good at it. "I don't want you to see me naked."

Exaggerated confusion colored his expression. "But I've seen you naked already—quite a few times."

"Not like this."

Sighing, he tossed his coat and cravat over the chair of her dressing table. He rolled up his sleeves as he turned to her. "You don't have to be bashful with me, Pru."

"I'm not being bashful." It was more annoyance than self-pity that colored her tone. "I just don't want you to see how ugly I am."

"Ugly?" He finished rolling up his sleeves as he crossed the carpet to sit on the side of her bed. "My darling Pru, you will never be anything but beautiful to me."

"But—"

"We've already discussed this." His tone told her that was the end of the discussion. Standing up, he tossed back her blankets and lifted her into his strong arms—ignoring her protests as he did so.

He carried her into her bathing chamber—a modern convenience her father had insisted upon her having. Chapel set her in a padded wicker chair as he filled the bath. A turn of the taps soon had the tub filling with hot water. He pulled the stoppers from several bottles, sniffing each before settling on the perfect scent to pour into the water. Soon the air was lightly scented with the smell of jasmine.

When the tub was almost full, he helped her to her feet and slipped the wrapper and gown from her. Mortified, Pru noticed there was blood on her gown. Chapel either didn't notice or just pretended not to. Either way, Pru loved him even more for it.

She also loved him for the way he looked at her as though she were the most beautiful thing he had ever seen. It was enough to bring the sting of tears to her eyes. How could he look at her like that when she knew how awful she must appear?

He removed his own shirt, revealing the masculine beauty of his upper body to her appreciative gaze. She hadn't felt like making love in days, but the sight of him sent a little thrill through her all the same.

"I can get into the tub on my own," she told him as he lifted her once more.

"Why do that when I can do it for you?" A small smile curved his lips as he lowered her into the fragrant water.

She sighed as the water washed over her. How could she not? It felt so good, she broke out in gooseflesh. She stretched out in the tub, leaned her head back against the polished enamel and closed her eyes.

Chapel, however, apparently decided his job was not done. Barely a minute passed before she felt the soft brush of a soapy cloth against her upper chest. She opened her eyes.

He was crouched beside the tub, still shirtless, a warm glint in his golden eyes.

"You are going to wash me as well? I'm not an invalid, you know." It came out sharper than she intended.

His left brow twitched, but other than that there was no reaction in his expression. "I know you are not an invalid. I'm doing this for myself."

"What do you mean?"

"I am a selfish creature. I want you all to myself for a while. Now I have you completely at my mercy."

A tired smile tugged at her lips. "You and your nefarious plans."

He spent the next half hour gently scrubbing every inch of her clean. If the sight of her body bothered him, he didn't show it at all. Then he washed her hair as well, making the heavy mass feel light and bouncy again.

After the bath he toweled her dry and helped her change into another demi-corset and night-gown, and a heavier wrapper. There was no way she could wear her normal corset and squeeze herself into an evening gown. Even if her abdomen wasn't as it was, she was too thin for most of her clothes now.

Besides, it wasn't as though her family would care what she wore.

Chapel amazed her further by winding her hair into a simple bun on the top of her head and pinning it into place.

"I'm going to fire my maid and hire you in her

stead," she announced, admiring his handiwork.

He planted a small, hot kiss on the side of her neck as he finished buttoning his jacket. "I accept."

She was still smiling when he carried her into the dining room, where the others waited.

Everyone looked so happy to see her that Pru didn't care how she looked or that she was so weak Chapel had to carry her. At that moment, she felt better than she had in days. At that moment, she felt that life was very good indeed.

Dinner was delicous. She ate as much as she could, which wasn't a lot. She filled up on conversation and laughter instead. Perhaps some of the conversation was a little too silly, the joviality a little too forced, but it was still there. They were trying for her, and Pru appreciated it and loved them all for it. Even her brothers-in-law got into the foolishness, telling stories and making jokes— often at Pru's expense.

Chapel joined in, and though the air was a little tense between him and her father, they made the best of the situation. He wasn't safe from the teasing either. It was nice knowing the family had accepted him. Perhaps he'd look over them from time to time for her. Maybe, if she asked, he'd watch over Caroline's baby—make sure it grew up safe.

What a maudlin, yet romantic thought—him looking after her family for the next five generations or so because his heart was still so full of her. She'd laugh if the thought belonged to anyone other than herself.

Instead, she laughed at something her brother-in-law James said in relation to Georgiana's short stature. She laughed harder than she had in such a long time.

She was still laughing when pain—sharp and intense—lanced through her. It robbed her of all laughter and breath as it ripped her apart inside. In fact, it was so bad, it knocked her from her chair onto the floor. She couldn't even put out a hand to save herself, she just fell.

Chapel was the first one to reach her, even though he had been seated across the table. No doubt he simply leapt to her side. Did her family even notice, or were they too busy watching her lie panting and convulsed on the dining room floor?

Chapel gathered her into his arms. She cried out despite his tenderness. "Pru?"

God, she hated hearing that vulnerability in his voice! He was her warrior, her vampire. He was supposed to be so much stronger than this. So much stronger than her.

She gazed up at him, seeing more than one of his lovely face. "Take me to my room."

Chapter 22

Three days.

Three days of waiting, of watching Pru drift in and out of consciousness. She was slipping away and he didn't know if he'd hear her voice again, if he'd get a chance to say good-bye.

He should be slapped for thinking of himself. Angrily, he remembered that all that mattered was Pru wasn't in pain. As long as she wasn't suffering, nothing else mattered.

Of course, her family was suffering a great deal. He couldn't stand to look at them. They all tried to be so supportive and caring toward him, but he knew they had to blame him. In their hearts they couldn't be as good as they pretended. Did they hate him for not turning Pru into a vampire, for not "saving" her?

Did they hate him as much as he was beginning to hate himself?

A telegram arrived from Molyneux, telling him how sorry he was to hear about Pru. Both he and Marcus sent their regards and prayers. They would return to England as soon as possible. And no, they hadn't found Bishop yet. As if Chapel cared about Bishop, Saint, Reign or even Temple. He didn't care about any of them—not at the moment. How could he, when the woman he loved lay dying?

The woman he *loved*.

He sat on the floor outside her room, waiting for his turn to watch over her. Her family shared the days, but the nights were his and his alone. He woke as early as he could, and when he did there was always a small bottle of blood waiting for him. He didn't ask where it came from and no one volunteered. Contrary to Mr. Stoker's novel, vampires didn't need to glut themselves to survive. As long as they had human blood in their system they were fine. One pint could often last a couple of days if the vampire didn't expend a lot of energy. And sitting beside Pru's bed didn't expend energy at all.

He suspected the blood was from Caroline, as she was the most open to what he was, but he hated the idea of her risking weakening herself and her baby by giving him her blood. She didn't look weak, however. Just sad.

The door to Pru's room opened and Chapel was on his feet in a second. Matilda stared at him with wide hazel eyes.

"Please don't do that," she said, her hand pressed to her heart.

"Forgive me."

She nodded. He could hear her heartbeat start to return to normal. "Of course. Pru is asking for you."

Joy burst within him. "She's awake?"

Another nod. "She's tired, but she says she won't sleep until she's seen you." Tears filled her eyes. "I think she's . . . Don't tire her, please."

She whirled away from him, but not before he saw her wipe at her eyes. Her fear resonated deep in his soul. Was this the end? Was Pru's time at hand?

Slowly, he opened the door to her room and stepped inside. It was dark in the room, save for a lamp on the vanity—close enough so Pru could see, but not close enough to keep her from sleeping.

"Chapel?" Her voice was thin and soft. "Is that you?"

"Yes." His own voice was a ragged whisper. "It's me."

A ghostly arm raised from the bed. "Come sit with me."

She looked so little and fragile in that great big bed. Her rich hair spread around her, fanning out across the stark white pillow. Her face was almost as white, dark circles beneath her eyes, hollows beneath her cheeks. Where had his Pru gone?

She had told him she didn't want him to see this happen to her. He had told her he didn't care, that he wasn't leaving. He had meant it, but by

God he wished he could stop it, not for himself but for her and for her family.

He took her hand in his. Her fingers were cold and skeletal as they clung to his. He wrapped his other hand around hers to warm it. "You should be resting, *mon coeur.*"

A smile touched her lips. "Did you just call me 'my heart'?"

He nodded. "I did."

"I like that."

He gazed into her hazel eyes, and that's where he saw his Pru. She was still there, deep inside this shell of her former self.

"It will always be yours, Pru. My heart."

Her fingers squeezed his. "Not always. Someday you'll find someone else to give it to."

There was no censure in her tone, but he reacted against it all the same. "No. That won't happen."

She gazed upon him like a mother upon a difficult child. "You cannot die, Chapel. It isn't reasonable to say you will never give your heart again."

He leaned down, taking one hand from hers and cupping her cheek with it. "It does not matter how long I live, Pru. I will love you until the day God finally takes me home."

"Home. That's a nice way to think of it. I'm going home, Chapel."

His throat tightened. His eyes burned. "I know, love."

A tear slipped from her eye. "I wish we could have had more time. I would have liked for you to hold my heart a little while longer."

He nodded. He couldn't speak.

She licked her lips. Speaking seemed to take so much out of her. "I want you to know how much these weeks with you have meant to me."

"Don't talk." He didn't want to lose her any sooner than he had to.

"I need to tell you these things," she insisted hotly. "I want you to know how much *you* mean to me. I want you to know how happy you've made me."

"I've been happy too," he confessed. "Happier than I ever remember."

Another smile. "I'm glad. You deserve to be happy, Chapel. You deserve so much more than you believe. God has chosen you for a special task."

A shiver spiked down his spine. "What do you mean?"

Her free hand came up to the one on her cheek, holding it against her soft flesh with cool fingers. "You're a warrior, Chapel. A warrior for goodness and light, don't forget that."

"Pru . . ." He could argue, but what good would that do? Let her believe it. *He* wanted to believe it. Wanted to.

"You were sent to me for a reason," she told him. "I'm not sure what I did to deserve you, but I'm glad I did it."

"What *you* did to deserve me?" His disbelief was obvious. "Pru, *I'm* the one who was blessed by you."

A glint entered her eyes and he knew he was caught. "Now, why would a God who is trying to punish you bless you?"

Her words hit like a sword, cleaving him to his very soul.

"I don't know," he whispered. It was true. Why would God send him Pru? He refused to think of her as anything but a gift. What had he done to deserve such bounty?

"I think He knew we needed each other." Her voice was so soft now he could barely hear her. "I think He wanted you to know love and He knew I'd love you. I do love you, Chapel. With all my heart."

Tears streamed down Chapel's cheeks. "I love you too, my beautiful Pru."

Her fingers tightened, the only indication that she had heard him, and then a rattle of breath poured from her chest.

No! Wild, Chapel clenched her fingers, put his ear to her mouth. She was leaving him. The last of her breath leaving her body. She was dying.

"Pru?" She didn't respond.

No. Not like this. She was his, damn it. She loved him. No woman had ever given him what Pru had. No woman had ever accepted him for what he was. She asked nothing of him—nothing except that he live. Was he just going to let that go because he believed he was some kind of monster?

"So what if I am?" he asked aloud. What if he was a monster? He had free will, he chose his own actions. For centuries he'd made himself miserable, punishing himself for a stupid mistake that he had more than paid for. For the first time he felt like he could finally forgive himself and accept his fate. He could accept anything, face anything knowing that Pru loved him. Loved *him*.

What if Molyneux and Pru were right? What if he was looking at his life the wrong way? What if this was a gift?

Curse or not, he wasn't going to let Pru go. Over five hundred years he had spent working for the church, doing what they wanted, listening as they talked him into the dirt as a demon.

He wasn't a demon. He was a descendant of the first wife of Adam and a fallen angel. He was a powerful being who could choose his own destiny. He fought for the forces of good. He wasn't evil, and he made his own fate.

He lowered his head to Pru's chest. Her heart still beat, but it was unsteady and weak. There was still hope.

No more thinking. He simply acted. His fangs tore from his gums with the force of his emotion. Gently, he pulled the neckline of Pru's nightgown aside, baring the tops of her breasts to his gaze. Beneath the pale, fragile skin was a trace of blue. His mouth covered it, fangs pierced it.

He drank.

Pru's warmth and sweetness flowed through him, filling him with a sense of peace and belonging. She was his and he was hers. They belonged together as surely as the moon and stars. She flooded his mouth, took over his senses and still he did not stop. He took her into him until he felt her heart sputter. Only then did he lift his head.

He closed the wound with a gentle lick before biting into his own wrist. He didn't even wince, he was so far removed from the pain. He placed it over her mouth, willing her to drink. There was a soft pressure as she tried. Her throat worked with the effort.

Then there was nothing. Her lips were still against his flesh.

Too late. He was too late.

Chapel prayed.

Chapter 23

Her funeral was two days later.

The day was bright and sunny, the kind of day between late summer and early autumn that was clear and crisp but still retained the sun's warmth. It was the kind of day Pru had loved. The sun shone down upon the family crypt not far from the estate. The service had been held at the estate chapel, where every family funeral had been held since Rosecourt came into Thomas's family.

There was a large crowd of mourners, as befitting a family such as the Rylands. People who hadn't seen Prudence in months, or even years, came to pay their respects and partake of the refreshments served later at Rosecourt.

There were those who were sincere in their

sympathy and Thomas Ryland appreciated their kind words, even though he merely wanted to be left alone with his family. There were others—and there always were—who viewed the funeral as a social occasion, a time to catch up on gossip and comment on the fortunes, or misfortunes, of others. Those people wisely avoided Thomas and his family unless speaking was necessary.

Prudence had been sick so long, some of the more sincere of them said, it was a blessing that she was finally at rest. Yes, Thomas agreed. At least she didn't leave a husband or children behind. Yes, Thomas agreed with that as well. In time the pain of his loss would lessen and he would embrace life again. After all, Pru was in a better place.

In that, Thomas heartily agreed.

It was late when the last of the mourners left. When the family was finally alone, Thomas dismissed the servants, giving them the rest of the day off to mourn. He left word that the family was not to be disturbed. The servants, many of whom had known Prudence since she was a child, offered their condolences, and received his in return.

Thomas joined the rest of the family in the library. It was almost dark now. He motioned for James to pull the drapes.

Caroline poured her father a drink and handed it to him as he sank into his favorite chair. "Thank God that is over. When I die, I don't want a funeral. Just stick me in the ground and be done with it."

Soft laughter came from the door. "Wouldn't the village matrons love that."

All heads turned as Chapel and Pru entered the room. Her family's smiles were like beacons, drawing her closer.

"Finally awake, eh? Must be nice to sleep through your own funeral." It was Marcus who teased them. He and Father Molyneux had made a special trip back to England especially for this day.

Pru merely dismissed him with a good-natured wave of her hand. "You'll sleep through yours as well, Marcus." Now that she wasn't dying, it was easy to joke about death.

Caroline brought them both a drink. Her pregnancy would soon prevent her from going out in public, but for now her belly was a welcome sight. "I knew your funeral would be difficult, dearest, but it was all the more so for you not being truly dead."

Pru cast a sideways glance at Chapel. "Yes, funny about that, isn't it?"

Was that a blush that colored his cheeks? And was it possible that he was even more gorgeous to her now than he had been the first night they'd met? Maybe it was her improved vampire vision that made him look so fine, or perhaps it was that she loved him so much she wanted to shout it from the cliffs.

"I never thought this day would come," Father Molyneux said from his seat near the fire. "I am glad to see it has."

"Are you ready, then, my friend?" Chapel asked him.

The priest nodded. "I am."

Butterflies danced in Pru's stomach as Father

Molyneux positioned himself before them. They stood facing each other, their profiles presented to the occupants of the room. Chapel was smiling as he took both her hands in his. He wasn't even nervous, the cad! She was shaking like a leaf. Even dying hadn't affected her like this.

Of course, it wasn't every day that a girl pledged to love someone forever with the expectation that it really would be forever!

Chapel didn't seem to be the least bit concerned about making the same vow. The realization warmed her and calmed her nerves.

What he had done for her was a miracle. He didn't tell her what in particular made him change his mind, only that he had decided that there was no way he could go on another six centuries without her by his side. Jokingly she had told him that if that was his intention, then he'd better get down on one knee and ask properly.

He had. And she said yes.

Then he told her she'd have to falsify her death because the entire parish was expecting her to die. Dr. Higgins might find it strange that she made such a complete recovery, especially since he knew the full degree of her condition. She had been little more than skin and bones when she "died" and now she was as fit and curvy as she had been before getting sick. There was no way she could explain that—not even with a miracle.

So they'd let everyone—even the servants— think she was dead and arranged her funeral—no viewing, of course. During that time she and

Chapel were sequestered in his room, where they spent their waking hours indulging in the pleasures their bodies offered. It was so wonderful that Pru couldn't bring herself to feel the least bit guilty for it.

She also learned that they could feed from one another. It wouldn't sustain them for long, but it cut back on how much human blood they needed to survive. Chapel took her to London, to a brothel where the madam knew of their kind, and taught her how to properly feed.

The prostitutes seemed pleased to see him, a fact that both amused and annoyed her. It was then that he told her about visiting this place the night he saved her from the poison. Without the blood of these women, they never would have made it out of the cellar alive, either of them.

That alone made everything all right in Pru's mind. Besides, she had no need of jealousy. She knew how much she meant to this man and she knew that no other woman could compare. The thought could have made her arrogant, but it humbled her instead.

Feeding was easier than she had thought it would be. Instinct took care of most of it. Once she managed not to think about it, it came quite naturally to her.

"Do you, Severian de Foncé, take this woman to be your wife?" Molyneux went through the vows. "Until death do you part?"

"Death already tried," Chapel quipped, grinning at Pru. "It failed."

Pru laughed as Molyneux actually rolled his eyes. "I think I preferred when you did not try to make jests, *mon ami.* Answer the question."

Chapel gazed at Pru with a look so rich and warm it hurt to look at him. "I do."

Good Lord, she'd actually been holding her breath! What had she been thinking, that he'd say no?

Father Molyneux asked her the same question. She didn't make any jokes, just said yes.

And then Chapel kissed her and nothing else mattered.

"Do I have to call you Madame de Foncé now?" Georgiana asked later as they dined on a supper of cold meats, salads, bread and cheese. Of course, there was cake to follow.

Pru wrinkled her nose. "No. I don't think so."

"You don't like my name?" Her husband laughed before taking a sip of his wine.

"*You* don't even use your name. Why should I?" She plucked a tiny tomato off his plate and popped it into her mouth. It was delicious. Food tasted so much better to her now—as though her sense of taste had been heightened along with everything else.

After dining they said their good-byes—most of which were tearful—and left for London, where they would spend the remainder of the night and the next day before setting off to Paris. It would be safer for them there—no one to recognize Pru as someone who was supposed to be dead.

She promised Caroline they would return when the baby came and told the rest of the family that she would come home whenever she could. They were all welcome in Paris as well, she reminded them. Matilda seemed to like that idea. They apparently had good shopping in Paris.

"Take care of my little girl," her father told Chapel as he shook his hand. The rift between the two of them had been easily repaired. And although her father had a bit of trouble accepting that she was now immortal, his joy at seeing her alive and healthy overshadowed whatever else he might feel. She knew he was happy for her.

Someday she would have to face the mortality of her family, but not today, and not for a very long time. It was something everyone had to face in the course of a lifetime. She would be fortunate enough to have reminders of them as they continued on in children and grandchildren. Somehow, she would know them all, even if she had to reveal the truth of what she was.

"I will," Chapel promised her father. "Although I think most of my time will be spent keeping her curiosity under control."

"I am not curious," she insisted.

He grinned at her. "I have a present for you."

She practically clapped her hands. "What is it?"

Her entire family laughed as she proved him right. "You are right," Pru commented dryly to Father Molyneux. "I too liked him better when he didn't try to make jokes."

They were in Paris before Pru got her "present" from Chapel. It was a pretty little townhouse in a fashionable neighborhood not far from the Eiffel Tower—a structure that amazed her.

She loved their house, their home. It was already decorated, but she would add some personal touches of her own. That was going to be the difficult part—trying to shop at night. She had yet to get used to not being able to go out during the day. It was the only downfall to her new life.

Certainly finding out that Chapel had made himself a massive fortune over the past six centuries made the transition easier. She wasn't an overly material person, but there was something comforting in knowing that they could do whatever they wanted. Also in knowing that Chapel was smart with finances so that they could continue doing whatever they wanted for the decades to come.

"With enough money you can make people adapt to your lifestyle," Chapel informed her as they unpacked the belongings that had been sent on before them. "You'll be surprised how many shopkeepers will be more than happy to accommodate the eccentric de Foncés."

"The eccentric de Foncés, how lovely."

He swept her into his arms and kissed her as she squealed and laughed. He was so much happier than he had been before. Happier because of her.

"I love you," she told him.

He squeezed her, his eyes as bright as newly minted gold. "I love you."

She spotted something out of the corner of her eye. It was a small package on the table. "What is that?"

Releasing her, Chapel went to the parcel and picked it up. "I don't know. It came while I was gone."

"Don't you think you should open it?"

He slid her a seductive gaze. "I thought I might open you first."

With a delighted giggle, Pru grabbed the package from his hands and raced for the stairs. She almost careened into the wall, as she had yet to get used to just how fast she could move. She ran up to their bedroom and turned to face him with a grin.

He caught her in his arms and kissed her. His mouth and tongue teased and excited her, drawing her deeper into a sensual spell so sweet and joyful she thought her heart might burst.

God, how she loved this man. How alive she felt with him—more alive than she ever dreamed possible.

Chapel trembled with the force of his desire for Pru. His fingers refused to work properly as he fumbled with the buttons on the front of her gown. Finally he tore the offending garment in half, sending buttons flying in every direction. Pru merely laughed and tore his shirt in a similar fashion.

The rest of their clothes followed suit—some garments survived better than others. Chapel didn't care. There would always be new clothes.

There would always be Pru.

She was his, forever. *Forever.* Would she want him for that long? She damn well better, because she was stuck with him. He was going to spend the rest of eternity worshiping, cherishing and loving her until she couldn't imagine life without him.

She talked as though he were the one who had given her something, but it was she who gave so much to him. She had given him life where before he had only an existence. She had put light where before there had been only darkness.

Naked, he lifted her onto the bed. Her skin was so pale and pearlescent against the dark blue of the quilt. There was so much color in their new home, not like his cell at the church. There were windows as well—with heavy drapes, of course, but at night the drapes would be open, letting the beauty of the night inside.

Pru stretched on the bed, reaching her arms up for him to join her. She was so damn beautiful to look at. He had always thought her lovely, but her rebirth into vampire had changed her. Where sickness had made her thin and frail, her new vitality made her soft and strong. The scars on her abdomen were gone, and her skin seemed to glow and her body was curved in all the right places, lush and sweet against his when he held her in his arms. He hadn't thought it possible for her to be more beautiful than she had been the first night he met her, but she was. She was so beautiful that he was in awe of her.

He could deny her no longer—and why would he want to? He climbed onto the bed beside her. A wave of pleasure washed over him as he watched her gaze travel the length of his nude body. In her eyes he saw the same hunger and wonder that he felt when he looked at her.

Bracing his knees outside her thighs, his palms on either side of her head, he kissed her neck, the warm hollow of her throat where her pulse fluttered against his tongue. He tasted her there, where she smelled faintly of roses and clean skin, and lower—down her chest to the baby-fine skin between her breasts. Soon he would sink his fangs into the sweetness of her. He would bite her as her orgasm approached.

And she would bite him. They would be joined as one—body, blood and breath. It was a union no mortal being—or no immortal one, for that matter—could ever put asunder. Only death, and even then he'd find her.

He cupped the weight of her breasts in his hands, lightly dragging his thumbs across the tight peaks. A shudder raced through him as Pru gasped in pleasure. Her nipples were so sensitive, so incredibly receptive to his slightest touch. Chapel lowered his mouth to one, sucking it between his lips, pinching it gently with his teeth. She writhed beneath him, lifting her hips toward him. He lowered his pelvis to hers so she could push the heated dampness of her flesh against the eager hardness of his cock, and shivered.

God, he loved the feel of her in his mouth. Loved her taste, the texture, the way she moaned when he nipped lightly with his teeth. He loved the way she smelled, all heat and moist female, sweet and delicious.

He suckled her flesh until her fingers tangled in his hair, then he turned his attentions to the other breast. When he had her grinding herself against him, little keening noises issuing from her throat, he knew it was time to move on.

Downward he traveled, planting kisses along the soft flesh of her rib cage, dipping into her navel with his tongue, nuzzling her belly and rubbing his freshly shaven jaw over the pale curve there. She had a belly and he loved it.

Kneeling between her legs, his hands caressing the soft, generous flare of her hips, Chapel stared at the thatch of auburn curls at the juncture of Pru's thighs with heart-pounding anticipation.

He could smell the warm musk of her arousal. The scent fanned the flames of his own desire, made his gums itch with the need to make her his in every way he could.

Gently, he parted the lips of her sex, reveling in the dampness there. He wanted to hear her pants of pleasure, wanted to feel her shudder around him as her climax rocked her. He wanted to know he was the only man to ever make her feel such joy.

The only man who ever *would* make her feel such joy.

The first pass of his tongue was a quick lick just to torment. The second was firmer, had more purpose. She moaned, her heels digging into the mattress as she lifted herself to his mouth. Deftly, he licked again, savoring the salty musk of her sex. Giving her pleasure, knowing that he had the power to make her shatter into a million pieces aroused him as nothing else. He was hard and ready for her, but would not give in to that yet.

He worked her into a frenzy with his tongue,

concentrating on the firm, hooded nub that would eventually lead to her climax. Every cry and moan that tore from her throat made him more intent, more ruthless in his attack. He paused long enough to nip at her leg—a little scratch that made her jump and gasp in delight.

He could bring her to orgasm right now if he bit her there, sank his fangs into the warm flesh of her inner thigh, but he didn't. He wanted to drag out her pleasure as long as he could.

One more ruthless lick and she shuddered with a cry. Her entire body arched as her fingers clutched at his hair, holding him to her.

He waited until she was still before rising up above her once more. She gazed up at him, eyes glazed with satisfaction and continued arousal.

"Roll over," he told her, his voice low and rough in his own ears.

Her expression was uncertain, but his Pru was curious—always willing to try something new. She rolled onto her stomach, revealing the long, delicate slope of her back and the swell of her round buttocks. Chapel ran his hands down the smooth ivory of her spine, cupped the blushing cheeks of her bottom. He kneaded the flesh there, slowly drifting downward.

His. She was his. His life, his love. His salvation.

Nudging her legs apart with his knee, he slipped between her thighs.

He reached down, sliding his hands beneath her pelvis. She was so soft against his hands—like velvet. Gently, he pulled upward, guiding her hips toward his. He slipped a pillow beneath her for support.

When he had her exactly where he wanted her, Chapel grasped himself in one hand and guided the head of his cock to the opening of her body. Pru gasped as he found it, as ready for him as he was for her.

He slid the head inside her. His eyelids closed on a sigh of ecstasy. Slowly, he moved, molding his body to hers—his pelvis to her buttocks, his chest to her back. Even if he never got there, he knew this was what heaven felt like.

The sweet grip of her body around his and the soft coos of encouragement slipping breathlessly from between her lips heightened the urgency in his blood. Pru rocked her hips against him. He could feel her body tensing, could feel the tremble of her arms and thighs as she pushed herself toward climax. She was getting close. So very close.

Pushing her hair aside, he lowered his head to the warm hollow between her neck and shoulder. His fangs lengthened as he offered her his wrist. Her lips were warm and damp on his flesh and he could feel the sweet, undeniable pressure of her fangs as he sank his own into her shoulder.

She came.

Her release triggered his own. His body tightened and then seemed to explode inside. Their bodies moved a few seconds more and then stilled, allowing the residual shocks of pleasure to fade.

Chapel rolled to his side, taking Pru with him. Like spoons in a drawer, they curved together. He pulled the quilt over them and wrapped his arms around her, allowing the satiated slumber of fulfillment to take hold of him.

It was a few hours later when he woke. Dawn was approaching, he could feel it. They would be safe and fine in this room. The heavy drapes on the windows and the bed hangings would protect them from the sun's burning rays, wrapping them in a dark cocoon.

"Are you going to open that package now?" Pru's voice was husky with sleep.

Chuckling, Chapel rolled away from her. "Nosy." He leaned over the side of the bed and retrieved the package from where Pru had dropped it earlier when he kissed her.

She sat up as he straightened, pushing the mass of her hair from her face. Even half asleep she amazed him.

He offered the package to her. "Would you like to open it?"

He didn't have to ask twice. Like a child, she snatched the package from him and tore into the wrapping with a gusto that made him make a mental note to double- or triple-wrap everything he gave her just to make it a bit of a challenge.

It was a small box, much like the kind jewelers used for their wares. That in itself wasn't terribly odd, but what was inside it was.

Lying on the bed of black velvet was a silver medallion approximately three inches in diameter.

It wasn't perfectly round, nor was it perfectly cast, but there was no denying the engraving upon its surface. It was a cross—the same cross burned into his shoulder. And on one side of it was a sword, on the other a chalice.

"What is it?" Pru asked. "Something from Molyneux?"

"No," Chapel replied, knowing even as he reached for it what it was. "Molyneux didn't send this."

Warmth met his fingers as he lifted the heavy silver. It was like lightning dancing upon his skin.

It was the Blood Grail.

He didn't know how or when Temple had done it, but somehow the other vampire had had the Grail melted down and made into this medallion—no doubt part of a matched set. Temple had known someone was after the Blood Grail, after him, and so he had taken precautions to ensure it didn't fall into the wrong hands.

How had Temple known? And why hadn't he sent word?

"Is that what I think it is?" Pru asked.

Chapel nodded. "Can you feel it?"

Her eyes were huge. "It's like all the hairs on my body are standing on end."

"It's from Temple."

"There's something else." She pulled a small slip of paper from the box. "It looks like an address in Rome."

Rome. Temple loved it there. If Temple had escaped his captors, that was where he would go.

Regardless, it was where he wanted Chapel to go, and there he would find more pieces to this puzzle.

"Have you ever been to Rome?" he asked Pru with a smile.

She grinned. "Are we going?"

He nodded, stretching out on the bed once more. "If you want. I don't expect you to follow me around Europe as I search for Temple—"

She cut him off. "Of course I'm coming with you. Just try to go without me. I'm as much a part of this now as you are. If it weren't for me, the order never would have gotten to Temple so easily."

"You're wrong," he told her, "but I'm not going to argue with you. We'll leave tonight."

There was nothing they could do now. Later, when darkness came again, they would set out on the journey Temple had laid out for them. When night came, they would begin this new adventure.

But not now. Chapel was content to be here, in bed with Pru as the sky lightened outside. This feeling of joy was still so new to him, and he intended to take full advantage of it while he could.

It wasn't that he didn't care about his friend. He did. But he knew Temple well enough to know that if he had sent this medallion to him, then he had sent one to the other three as well, which meant that at least Bishop and possibly Reign might already be searching for him. Whether Saint would join them was a question only Saint could answer.

Temple was out there somewhere and Chapel would find him, no matter how long it took—one of the advantages to being immortal.

For now, however, Chapel was just going to fall asleep with his wife in his arms, his amazing Pru. He was going to need to be rested for all the living they had to do.

PROWL THE NIGHT WITH
RACHEL MORGAN AND

KIM HARRISON

DEAD WITCH WALKING

0-06-057296-5 • $7.99 US/$10.99 Can

When the creatures of the night gather, whether to hide, to hunt, or to feed, it's Rachel Morgan's job to keep things civilized. A bounty hunter and witch with serious sex appeal and attitude, she'll bring them back alive, dead . . . or undead.

THE GOOD, THE BAD, AND THE UNDEAD

0-06-057297-3 • $7.99 US/$10.99 Can

Rachel Morgan can handle the leather-clad vamps and even tangle with a cunning demon or two. But a serial killer who feeds on the experts in the most dangerous kind of black magic is definitely pressing the limits.

EVERY WHICH WAY BUT DEAD

0-06-057299-X • $7.99 US/$10.99 Can

Rachel must take a stand in the raging war to control Cincinnati's underworld because the demon who helped her put away its former vampire kingpin is coming to collect his due.

A FISTFUL OF CHARMS

0-06-078819-4 • $7.99 US/$10.99 Can

A mortal lover who abandoned Rachel has returned, haunted by his secret past. And there are those willing to destroy the Hollows to get what Nick possesses.

www.kimharrison.net

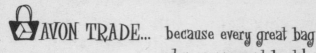